BLOOD
REACTION

BLOOD
REACTION

D.L. ATHA

foxboro press

Address inquiries to: editor@foxboropress.com

ISBN 13 – 978-0-9793356-0-0

Manufactured in the United States

10   9   8   7   6   5   4   3   2   1

For my husband and the many nights that you unselfishly shared with my laptop.

With special thanks to Debbie H. who read this book more times than I can remember. Thanks for your patience, sound advice, and encouragement.

ONE

Watching the car drive away, I let my breath out not just in a sigh of relief, but also the sigh of any worried parent watching their only child being driven away. No longer able to make out any part of my daughter in the passenger seat because of the distance, I continued to stare at the car until it was completely out of sight. I sighed again although there was no one else to listen.

Samuel, my beloved German shepherd, whined quietly beside me probably recognizing more than I did just how anxious I was as my only daughter disappeared down the drive. Although I could use some alone time and my daughter would enjoy a visit with my mother, I would worry, at least a little, the entire time she was gone.

Samuel, getting antsy, butted my leg with his nose as if to tell me we had things to do and standing here looking for a car that was already gone was a waste of time. He was right. I had a lot of chores to get done during my two-week hiatus from work so giving one last sigh and a backwards glance down the drive, I walked towards the barn to get some tools.

With both arms full of supplies, I slammed the barn door shut with my foot and made the short trek to the garden. Dropping my armload where the dark brown earth met the dead grass, I picked up the hoe and buried it deeply into the recently plowed cold earth. Dragging it hard behind me, I made several rows, more or less straight, so I could start planting an early spring garden.

Ellie and I were trying to live green, so every year since we moved here we had been planting a garden with varying degrees of productivity. We also had a few chickens and Ellie had quite a bit of fun gathering the eggs and giving the extras to the neighbors.

With spring right around the corner, there was no end to the amount of work this farm could create. I had already broken the garden up with the old tractor that the former owners had included in the sale of the house, but there was still a myriad of chores left from cutting back the roses that grew everywhere to cleaning out the barn.

Working in the dirt, I managed to get three rows of onions and a row of cabbages planted before my hands began to object to the cold. Although we were having some warmer days than usual in late February, the nights were still cool so the ground was cold and my leather gloves couldn't quite keep the damp out.

Leaning the hoe up against an outside corner of the barn, I decided to go riding for a couple of hours. Looking up at the sun, I was pretty sure it was between three and four o'clock. That would give me a couple of hours. If I hurried. Mentally, I chided myself for not putting the hoe up, but I soon forgot my laziness at the thought of the ride.

Spotting my horse at the far end of the pasture, I grabbed a bucket of oats from the nearest feed bin and shook them.

Watching her lift her head, ears pointed towards the sound, I could almost see her suspicion of what I had planned, but she simply couldn't resist the oats. Breaking into a trot, she was at the barn in no time.

Holding out a handful of oats towards her, she walked up, snorting slightly at my outstretched hand to confirm she really wanted to eat this enough to take the risk of being caught. Deciding it was worth it, she lipped at my hand, knocking some of the oats onto the ground while I reached for her halter, happy that I had caught her.

Quickly getting her bridled and saddled, I swung up and headed through the pasture to the gate at the back of my property that joined the National Forest. The cooler air of the coming evening gave her more spunk than normal and I gave in and let her gallop.

Whipping through the large pines lining the trails of the forest, her long coarse mane flew up and stung my face. By the time we stopped, tears were streaming down my cheeks from her mane and the cold. Laughing, I patted her hard on the neck. We were both winded and we spent the next hour just winding through the endless trails that crisscrossed through the woods.

It got dark fast in the forest as the thick pine trees filtered out most of the sunlight and I realized that I had lost track of time as I often did. Dusk had not quite set in but I could only see the remnants of the quickly disappearing sun. It would be a tricky ride home in the dark as the trails were nearly indistinguishable.

Luckily for me, my mare knew her way back to the barn

better than I did so I gave her a free reign and she turned towards home. Traveling at a quick trot, she weaved through the maze of trails by some internal map heading for the comfort of the barn.

Having ridden farther than I had intended, I was unable to make it out of the forest before the last of the sunlight had completely disappeared. I found myself riding in darkness except for the slight glow reaching me from the partial moon above.

Alone and in the dark, the tall pine trees closed in on me and my mare was more spooked than ever. She was probably picking up on my nerves. I'd ridden in the dark many times but this time it felt different. I felt unnaturally lonely. Not sure what was causing this feeling, I tried to analyze it and finally decided it was because I was riding home to an empty house. Usually, Ellie would be with the sitter waiting for me to get home or over at a friend's house.

Lost in thought and not paying attention, I was unprepared when my horse reared suddenly under me. Rolling off backwards, I landed hard on my back.

Certain that it was a bear that had startled the horse, I rolled over, struggling to get to my feet, but I was knocked back down by a compact body. I pulled my arms up defensively in front of my face, but the animal forced its snout through and I realized it was only Samuel.

Laughing out loud now that I knew I wasn't about to be eaten, I let him give me several wet licks to the face as I wrapped my arms around his shaggy neck. Like any truly good dog, he had taken off after my horse and tracked us in the woods. At least I wouldn't be completely alone since my mare was long gone. Getting to my feet, I dusted off my butt as best I could and started towards home. My horse had thankfully gotten me close enough to my property that I knew where I was even in the dark.

More of the moonlight was beginning to reach the ground as I approached the edge of the forest, making strange shadows and shapes from the trees around us. It was a difficult walk in the dark and I strained my eyes to catch a glimpse of the dark tree roots weaving their way across the trails before I stumbled on them and fell.

Samuel padded along quietly beside me. With his much keener senses, he never missed a step and I could just make out his ears swiveling back and forth in the dark, catching every sound the forest made in the night. Suddenly stopping in mid-stride, one paw lifted in the air and his hackles up, he growled deep in his throat.

Automatically, I stopped too and turned in every direction, studying the shadows intently for something that might be hidden. I could see nothing out of the ordinary but gooseflesh popped up on my arms and legs and a feeling of pure terror suddenly raced through my body.

The feeling came out of nowhere. I could feel eyes on the back of my head, like when you're being watched from across a room, but this was accompanied by a feeling of sheer panic. As if the person across the room was a serial killer.

I kept turning in circles trying to pinpoint where the creepy sensation was coming from, but it seemed to move quicker than I was capable of. The trees and bushes rustled around me despite the lack of wind and the feeling of terror continued to grow until I felt I would suffocate. Finally finding the courage to move, I sprinted towards home.

With Samuel at my side, I ran as fast as I could but I didn't make it more than a few strides before something knocked me down hard. I rolled twice before coming to a stop, several feet from the path, on my right side. Rocks and old branches poked painfully through my clothes, scratching my skin and bringing tears to my eyes. My eyes closed, I struck out defensively with both arms, my hands meeting nothing but cold air.

Forcing my eyes open, I could see only the interwoven branches of the tall trees above me. Pushing off of the ground, I didn't bother to look for what had hit me but focused instead on running towards home as quickly as I could while watching my every step.

Sprinting out of the thick woods at the edge of my pasture, I felt a deep sense of relief at the sight of my brightly lit house at the northern end of my property. The dark outline of my horse could be seen standing next to the barn. At least she had made it home. I couldn't be angry with her, I was as terrified as she obviously had been.

The overwhelming sense that I was being watched was now gone and besides, I couldn't have run any further as I was totally out of breath. My legs were burning and my heart was pumping so hard that my chest ached with exertion. Feeling like jelly all at once, I leaned over, bracing my hands on my knees as I tried to catch my breath.

Samuel, having never left my side, jogged little happy circles around me, his wagging tail beating reassuringly against my knees while I rested. Feeling a little stupid now, I laughed uneasily to myself. In the glow that reached me from the glaring security lights in my yard, it was easy to reason I had imagined the entire scenario. My imagination had gotten ahead of itself.

Walking the rest of the way towards the house, I dreaded having to catch my mare and unsaddle her. I just wanted to go and collapse on the couch. Making it to the barn with my lungs still burning, I quickly scooped up a bucket of oats. No longer concerned it was a trick, my horse eagerly followed me into the barn.

I poured the oats into her feed bowl and she was eating before I finished. Patting her on the neck, I quickly unlashed the saddle, pulled it off her back and set it in the corner of the tack room, thinking I would put it up later. Procrastination is one of my many character flaws.

Reaching over to switch off the barn lights, I paused in mid-air as I remembered the hoe leaning up against the outside wall. All I needed was to knock myself in the head with it if I stumbled across it. Reaching around the doorway, my hand met only the cold wooden wall of the barn.

Looking around the doorway, I scanned the entire length of the barn wall. Glancing back around behind me, I looked up automatically to where the hoe would normally be hanging on the wall. It was exactly where it belonged.

Rubbing one hand across my forehead, I took a deep

breath, releasing it slowly into the cool air, fog forming in front of me as I questioned my sanity. Convincing myself I had simply forgotten that I had put the hoe up, I slapped the lights off and headed for the house.

The walk across the yard seemed interminably long and I couldn't help but glance back at the dark border of trees marking the edge of the forest. Swaying gently in the light February breeze, the darkness of their branches contrasted against the lighter hues of the sky lit up by the partial moon.

As I stood there in the dark studying the tree line, a familiar shudder worked its way down my spine. Feeling like a mouse in a trap, I sprinted across the yard and up onto the deck, yanking the back door open with trembling arms. As usual, I had locked the door out of habit. Taking a deep breath, I slowly typed in the code to the electric lock, my fingers shaking the entire time. But it lit up green and with a quick twist of the knob, I was in the house.

Turning the bolt lock behind me, I leaned back against the kitchen wall, letting my chin rest on my chest momentarily. Shaking from head to toe, I took a few deep breaths to calm my trembling limbs.

In the house, the illogical fear I felt in the yard melted away again and I tore my jacket off, angry at myself for being such a sissy. To add insult to injury, I jumped nervously when my cell phone vibrated in my pocket.

Pulling it roughly out of my jeans pocket, I didn't bother to check the caller ID. I knew it would be my mom. "Hey Mom," I greeted. My voice still held a slight tremble and Mom picked up on it immediately.

"What's wrong?" I could hear the anxiety in her voice. Knowing where this conversation was going, I groaned as I walked into the kitchen.

Getting inpatient because I didn't answer immediately, she asked again, "What happened?"

Grabbing a jar of spaghetti sauce out of the cabinet next to the fridge, I held the phone between my shoulder and ear while I opened it. "I had a little scare in the woods tonight while I was out riding. It was nothing. I'm fine," I told her, trying to downplay it but knowing it wouldn't work.

"Exactly what kind of scare?" Mom's voice had gone up about half an octave.

"Nothing bad. I lost track of time and had to ride home in the dark. The dog spooked the horse and I fell off."

Intentionally leaving out the part where I thought I had been knocked down, I waited to see if my explanation pacified her. I wasn't really trying to keep anything from her, I was just sure that my nerves had gotten the better of me and I had created a spook out of thin air.

Pouring the sauce in a pan, I placed it on the burner over a medium flame and then put the water on to boil for the noodles.

"What were you thinking riding at night? You've got to be more careful. You have a daughter to think about." Mom had that tone in her voice that said, "I'm glad you're OK but I'm mad at you at the same time." The one that always made me feel guilty because she was usually right.

"You have got to be more careful." She repeated it again. "Besides the fact that you live in the middle of nowhere,

15

completely alone except for Ellie, you risk your life by going horseback riding in the dark." She emphasized the last four words, her voice now at least an octave higher.

"Mom, please don't turn this into an argument about the house. But you're right. It was irresponsible of me to ride in the dark, but that has nothing to do with the house."

Hoping to avoid the never-ending argument about my home, I tried to end it before it got started. My back was hurting from where I had fallen from my horse and I was dirty from rolling around on the ground. I just wanted to take a shower and eat my dinner, but from past experience I knew she was not going to let this drop.

The house was a contention point between us at every turn and to say she hated the place was an understatement. The house, actually its location, terrified her. She wouldn't even spend the night with me when she came for a visit now that my dad had died. She stayed in town at the Day's Inn. She preferred to not even drive out the dirt road except in the daylight. I could understand why. After leaving the paved road, it was an eight-mile drive to my house on a very lonely one-lane dirt road.

I had bought an older home built in the antebellum style so far out in the country as to even be called remote. It was large, much more room than I would ever need. The realtor had showed it to me on a whim.

Falling immediately in love with it despite it not being what I was looking for or needed, I had made an offer within the hour. Imagine my surprise when it was accepted just as quickly.

When my parents drove in from one state away to look at the house, Dad had taken one look at the place and announced, "Well, I see you met a salesman." And he had been right. It was too big, too old, and way too far from civilization to be right for me. Probably the exact same reasons the former owners had sold it. They had even thrown in most of the furniture, they were so desperate to sell. Of course, I was too blinded by the beauty of the house to have thought about that at the time.

Grabbing a long wood-handled spoon to stir the sauce, I tried to multi-task while we talked.

"Annalice, you have absolutely no business living that far out by yourself. You could've been killed out in the woods and no one would have ever known. You should have come and spent the week with Ellie and me. Not stayed out there in the boondocks all by yourself." Boondocks, she was really laying it on thick tonight.

"Mother, I do not live in the boondocks. You're being ridiculous. Besides, I like it out here." Now I was laying it on thick. Of course it was the boondocks.

A quiet thump from upstairs made me jump and I splashed spaghetti sauce out of the pan onto the stove where it sizzled on the burner. Laying the spoon down on the stove, I walked into the entryway and looked up the stairs onto the landing above me. I could see nothing out of the ordinary.

Mom was still lecturing me. I had pulled the phone away from my ear but could still make out the buzz of her voice in the background as I listened intently for any more noises upstairs. Hearing no more, I brought the phone back up to my ear.

"Annalice, are you there? Did you hear anything I said?" Her voice was going back up again.

I lied and told her yes. "Mom, look. You and Ellie will be back in a week. Just enjoy yourselves. Have a good time together. I'll keep the doors locked. You know, I'm actually looking forward to being by myself for a while. Everything will be fine. And I won't go riding in the dark any more, I promise." She wouldn't drop this until I had made at least a few concessions.

"Promise me you'll keep your cell phone with you." She expected an easy victory here, but I was not giving in to that one.

"NO! Absolutely not! I want no contact with the hospital while I'm off. They always call and I am not carrying my cell. I promised I would be careful and not ride at dark. That's as good as it gets, Mom. Now, listen. Have fun and call me when you head back this way in a few days with Ellie. Enjoy your time with her, Mom. She's growing up fast."

She was angry. I could tell by the flavor of the silence on the other end of the phone. I could almost see her setting her lips in a thin line, wanting to say more but afraid she would say too much.

Another thump from upstairs caught my attention again. I was scared, but I didn't want to alarm my mom so I told another lie so I could get off of the phone.

"Hey, Mom. Ms. McElhaney's at the door. She's probably

brought me some homemade bread I'd better go." I continued to stare up the stairway, listening intently and trying to get a better angle, but still seeing nothing while Mom talked.

"Oh, you remember her. She's the little old lady that lives in the first house when you turn off the highway. She doesn't have much family at all and she spends all of her time writing down the license plates of the cars that use this road. She knows I'm going to be here by myself. She'll probably endanger everyone who lives out here by driving down to check on me every day."

Now pacified that someone besides herself knew that I was here alone, Mom warned me to be careful again and said her goodbyes.

"Tell Ellie I love her," I ended, clicking the phone off gently. I hadn't told a complete lie. Ms. McElhaney did know I was spending the week alone. We had talked about it last week.

"Why did I ever buy this old house?" I asked out loud to myself. I would never admit it to my mother, but I had admitted it to myself now for at least the hundredth time since moving in. The second story always unnerved me a little, especially at night. I very seldom had a reason to go up there since mine and Ellie's bedrooms were both on the first floor of the massive old house.

Fighting to control my breathing, I rationalized the sounds. *It's just a squirrel*, I thought. *Calm down.* "How many times have you done this to yourself?" I reasoned out loud.

Shortly after moving in, I had heard a similar thump.

Frantically I had called the police just sure that someone was breaking into the top story of my home The female police officer that had responded to my frantic call had looked at me as if I was a discredit to the entire gender.

But the woman had searched the old home and not being able to find anything, she had walked heavily down the stairs and told me to have the trees cut if the thumps were going to bother me anymore. She had made it pretty clear with her expression that she expected not to be bothered like that again.

Maybe letting my mom win on the issue of the house wouldn't be such a bad thing after all, I thought to myself and for a brief moment, I was mad at that realtor all over again. Next time I bought a house, I would be much savvier and I would get a different realtor. I sighed again. I knew the anger was misplaced. It wasn't his fault that he was such a good salesman and I was a complete sucker. He was just doing his job.

Samuel, who had trailed me in from outside, stood like a statue beside me, his ears at attention. He had heard it too. His only movement was a small inclination of his head to the right accompanied by a low whine.

As much as I hated the thought, I knew that I had to go up there and take a look around. Walking into the living room, I grabbed the panic button for my alarm system from an end table where I always kept it when I was alone in the house and proceeded to climb the stairs to the second story.

"Calm down," I kept reasoning to myself. I had made this climb many times since the first squirrel incident and everything was always fine. It would be no different this time. I really needed to get those trees cut back. I liked squirrels, but this was just getting out of hand. I would call a tree trimmer tomorrow I decided.

Making it to the second story landing, I peeped around the corner into the hallway and to no great surprise, there was nothing there. I always kept the hall light on and it illuminated every nook and cranny in the long hallway. That was definitely not living green, but I am just way too chicken so the hall light stayed on upstairs every night. Obviously, the presence of a hall light wouldn't do any good if I did have an intruder, but it made me feel better regardless.

There were three large bedrooms upstairs, all filled with the old rickety antique furniture that the previous owners had left.

My imagination went wild thinking of all the places someone could be hiding in the rooms. But I walked into the first one finding nothing amiss. I didn't go so far as to look under the bed and I was proud of myself for that bit of rationality, but I did check behind the doors.

The second bedroom was essentially the same but I noticed the air temperature in the room was a little cooler, just barely perceptible. Almost like one of the windows had been opened for a couple of minutes. Walking over to the floor-to-ceiling windows lining the southern side of the house, I pulled back the lace curtains and checked all three.

Unexpectedly, I found one was unlocked but all three were closed, not even opened a crack. Maybe there was more of a draft when the lock wasn't in place, I decided. Now I'm a stickler for window and door locks so I knew that I hadn't left it unlocked. It was probably Ellie, she loved to play up here pretending to be a princess among the white antique furniture. I would have to remind her to lock the windows when she finished playing.

Turning to leave the room after securing the window, I felt the hair on my arms raise and a cold chill chased the length of my spine. I froze in place momentarily, but then skipped out of the room as quick as I could.

Standing in the hallway with my back against the wall facing the bedroom, I could see the reflection of the room in the dresser mirror on the wall opposite me. Nothing seemed out of place and nothing moved except the ceiling fan and the faded white lace curtains ruffling gently in its breeze.

Yet I couldn't shake the feeling I was being watched. The closet door was cracked open slightly and a shaft of light reached into the dark space, shining on nothing in particular. I tried to get my nerve up to go back into the bedroom, but I just couldn't do it even though the momentary terror had passed quickly enough.

Finally rounding up what nerve I had left, I checked the third room; finding nothing, I quickly ran back down the stairs.

Samuel was still standing in the entryway watching me as I raced down the stairs. He had not trailed after me, which was very odd behavior for him. I hadn't noticed before, which was good because I probably would have lacked the courage to climb the stairs if I had realized he wasn't behind me. His ears were still cocked forward and his hackles were up.

Knowing that there was no person upstairs since Samuel wasn't afraid of anyone, I rationally chalked it up to squirrels and walked back to the kitchen to stir the sauce.

An uneasy feeling clung to me, but there was nothing out of place, nothing missing, and nothing to indicate that someone had been or was in the house. The doors were locked while I was out riding and the second-story windows in the old house were really too high for the average criminal to bother trying to reach.

Even if someone wanted to climb up, it would have been almost impossible to do it quietly or without hurting themselves. An easy reach for squirrels that could walk the long limbs of the old oak trees like tightropes, but the branches that got close enough to the house certainly wouldn't hold a man.

Letting logic be my guide, I took a deep breath and put the thumps out of my mind. Giving the sauce a quick stir, I poured a glass of raspberry fruit wine and headed into the living room, where I took a seat on the old but comfortable couch.

Samuel had given up on watching the stairwell and rejoined me in the living room, laying spread out just to the left of the couch. I flipped through a few magazines and polished off the glass of wine.

I was just about to get up and pull the spaghetti sauce off the burner when a sensation so familiar and so menacing swept over me that the hair on my arms literally rose and the overwhelming, irrational fear washed over me. Again. The exact same fear I had felt in the woods and upstairs, but this time it was so much more intense that the other episodes paled in comparison.

I've been scared before but it was definable moments with definable fears. Suspicious people in parking lots, unexpected visitors at the door of my house, or near-misses on the interstate. But there was nothing definable about this fear except the degree of it that washed across every sense of my being.

Feeling my heart skip and my breath catch in my chest, I froze instantly in place by instinct alone. There was no conscious thought to the act and time seemed to stop as if I was an observer in my own horror story and I could step outside my body for a moment and watch the scene as it inched by me.

Unable to move or utter a word, there was little else I could do other than sit there and let time drag by me. And although I had no idea what the danger was, I knew it was emanating from one direction. I could feel it behind me, but I couldn't find the courage inside myself to turn around and that was the most frightening feeling of all. The feeling threatened to suffocate me, but breathing provided no relief.

As the seconds ticked by, the fear became more and more palpable and my hands started to tremble. The tremors crawled up from my hands to my forearms and up my shoulders then radiated downward into my chest and abdomen. My legs were shaking at this point as well and I knew I was going to die because I could feel death in the room.

I would have said that as a physician, for the most part I was pretty familiar with death. But I realized now that in reality, I knew little about it. Comfortable death, the kind that carries the old and infirm away, the kind of death that brings peace, that kind of passing I knew something about.

But my gut told me that my death, the one that I would die tonight, was going to be the definition of violence. It was hatred, rage, and jealousy all rolled into one and there would be nothing peaceful about it except that it would eventually be over.

Having been fully focused on the terror coming from behind me, I finally took note of the spasmodic barking coming from my left. Sparing a glance, I could see Samuel was making a stand. Foam spattering from his mouth, eyes wide, hair standing up like a mantle around his neck, he looked rabid. He was not moving forward, but he was not backing down either.

In the next second, silence took over the house and Samuel lay on the floor, his paws jerking spasmodically as his eyes rolled up. I still had not moved except to take that quick glance at Samuel.

Feeling an unusual sensation to my right, I glanced forward and it was then I saw him out of the corner of my right eye. Sitting on the couch not two inches away from me, leaning forward with his elbows on his knees in mockery of my own stance, he looked straight ahead as if he were merely a spectator and not the cause of this terrible scene.

Automatically, I jerked back and as far away from him as

I could, not quite making it to the end of the couch. It was then that I opened my mouth to scream for the first time. My lips were dry and very little sound came out at first, but eventually I worked the paralysis out of the muscles of my larynx and the terror was released. It did no good as there was no one to hear me. The nearest house was at least four miles away.

Maybe he knew that or maybe he didn't care. At that point, I wasn't sure. Having lost all of my breath and the ability to create any more sound across my raw vocal cords, I could do nothing more than lay there and watch him, death itself, observe me. He must have scrutinized me for only a minute or so, but it felt like an eternity.

Finally he spoke, and the normality of his voice was incongruous with the terror he inspired. "I was afraid you were going to end up like your dog so I am glad you quieted before I had to break your neck too. Noise like that can drive me to early violence. My hearing is so sensitive and I would not want you to ruin my meal. I am voraciously hungry tonight."

I was about a sentence behind him the entire time, each word sinking in a couple of seconds after he said them. Confusion hit me when he mentioned food and I looked automatically into the kitchen at the spaghetti sauce I had been cooking.

I should have pulled it off of the burner by now and it was starting to burn on the bottom of the pan. I could hear the quiet sizzle that would soon get louder and the pungent odor of the burning sauce was now filling the house.

Realization and a new-found hope hit me suddenly. In a few more minutes, it would start smoking, setting off the fire alarms, which were tied into the house's security system. It was the only part of the system, besides the panic button, that was active even when the system was disarmed.

The panic button! Hope glimmered but then faded just as quickly as there was no way to get to it now. I had put it down on the stand at the bottom of the stairs a few minutes earlier. I had laughed when the alarm representative had told me to always keep it in my pocket.

"You never know when it just might save your life," he had quipped cheerfully as he handed it to me. The idea had seemed a little overboard at the time, but now it became evident that the overly happy alarm man was brilliant.

But I still had a chance. If the smoke alarms went off, the fire service would be dispatched immediately. It was the only agency that could not be turned back with a code word. The trucks would come until the return was ordered by the fire marshal and I had met him before, usually when I was cooking, and he was always very thorough. No turn-around orders from him until he had surveyed the scene with his own eyes.

Maybe I would survive after all. Turning my head slightly to the right, I could see the alarm on the ceiling. The urge to watch for that first glowing red light indicating it had been triggered became almost impossible to ignore, but I pulled my eyes away from it as quickly as possible, vowing not to spare it another glance. It was certainly my only hope, however small it might be.

Thinking desperately of any other possibilities, I remembered the gun my ex-husband had left me, but it was locked in the safe. Fighting the urge to glance back at the stove, which might give me away as easily as the fire alarms, I turned my attention to him instead of what might save me.

My eyes fell first on his mouth. His lips were pulled back in a full smile, framing one-half inch paired fangs on each side that stood in sharp contrast to where his canines and incisors should have been. They were shiny, wet, and sharp at the tips. His lips were arched and colored a deep red, standing out sharply against his very white teeth.

I lost track of time as I stared at those fangs, having a hard time getting past them and the barriers that my mind was throwing up. Only partly believing what I was seeing, I finally was able to look up into his eyes and despite looking human, there was little that could be called human about them.

Deep green like the pastures of May before the rain has become scarce, the irises seemed to have more depth than usual, the pupils were darker and wider. Cold and hard, I could see in them his eagerness for what was to come.

I'm a rational person and not prone to flights of fancy. I believe in God, but have never believed in any other kind of supernatural. I live and exist in a very real world. But what was sitting across from me was not human. That fact I knew beyond a shadow of a doubt and the hope that had been building in my mind drained out of me in one moment, replaced by despair. The fire marshal would show up, but I would already be dead and he would probably die as well for all his trouble to come here.

He must have recognized when my logic had been replaced by reality and he began to slowly lean towards me. Attempting to move as far away from him as possible, I shifted in response, only to realize there was nowhere to go but forward. Without thinking about it but acting on pure instinct only, I jumped forward, trying to evade him.

Logical thought would have kept me sitting on the couch not believing what I was seeing. Instincts are usually stronger than logic but they did me about as much good as logic would have. I made it only a couple of feet before he reached down and caught my right instep in his left hand and in one quick jerk, he lifted me completely up in the air and slammed me back down onto the floor.

I hit the floor solidly on my back, the air knocked out of my lungs, but I just managed to keep my head from whacking the hard surface. Lacking oxygen to put up any fight, I lay there struggling for breath as he loomed over me, blocking the rest of my vision. Slowly, he dropped to one knee, I was sure he did it slowly to prolong the terror, then he dropped down to his hands to where he was suspended over me. His every movement seemed calculated to cause as much fear as possible.

My breath had returned and I began to scream until he pushed the air out of my lungs again by dropping his body onto mine. He was heavy, heavier than his frame appeared. There was little opportunity to struggle as he had pinned my arms over my head and I had to use what little air I could get in to maintain my hold on lucidity. I'm not sure why because I probably didn't want to be lucid through what was coming, but it was a self-preservation step that my autonomic system was in charge of and I couldn't stop.

He switched both of my wrists to his left hand and with the other he brushed my hair off my right shoulder. With a flick of his wrist and essentially no effort, he ripped my t-shirt at the shoulder. He paused then for just a moment, looking into my eyes, as he he slowly lowered his head, his eyes unfathomably cold as they locked onto mine. I couldn't look away.

Fangs grazed my neck and seemed to follow the course of my carotid from my clavicle up, yet he didn't bite. His movements were slow and lazy; I was sure he was playing with me. I lay completely still, not knowing what might or might not provoke him and unwilling to chance anything either way.

For a brief moment, he paused in his movements before grasping my hair with his free hand, bringing it to his face and inhaling. "What a myriad of smells you are." With a savagery that was sudden in its intensity and surprising given his former stealth, he pulled his head back and then flung it down suddenly, driving his fangs into my neck, through the muscles covering the carotid artery.

I felt the spasm of the muscles in my neck first because of the speed and then I felt the slice of his fangs through my skin almost like an afterthought. Kind of like a nurse who is really good at giving shots. You feel the medicine being pushed into your muscle before you ever feel the needle.

The pain was not as intense as I expected but within a few moments, my vision began to tunnel. I could feel his muscles contracting against my skin as he swallowed. My last coherent thought was of a small trickle of blood collecting in my hair.

TWO

The bleating of the fire alarm seemed exceptionally loud, but perhaps it was the massive headache banging in my head that added to the sound. Confused at first, I spread my hands out beside me attempting to determine where I was.

The lights were off and only a small shaft of light wrapped into the room from underneath a door. Continuing to palpate my surroundings, I recognized the smoothness of the silk bedspread that covered my bed. I started to sit up but the muscles in my back and legs were burning and I decided it wasn't worth the effort.

Reaching up with arms of lead to run my fingers through my hair, I felt as though the left side of my neck was numb and tingled ever so slightly. I only noticed because of its contrast to every other part of me, which was aching and burning. Sudden remembrance made me gasp out loud and tracing the contours of my neck, I couldn't find the puncture wounds that I knew should be there. I ran the sensitive pads of my fingers over the skin again and again till the skin on my neck became sore, but still I was unable to locate the wounds.

I doubted my sanity for a moment, questioning what I thought I had seen. But focusing on the tingling in my neck, I was sure that I hadn't imagined any of the evening. I simply didn't understand it especially the fact that I was still alive. Why was I still alive? Death had been inescapable, I was sure of it.

As I became more aware of my surroundings, I realized there were voices coming from the foyer; a smooth, calm voice and the rough gravelly voice of the fire marshal. I knew the last one well as I had set off a lot of fire alarms in the short time I had lived here.

This would probably be my last opportunity for help and I suppressed a twinge of guilt knowing I would probably get the marshal killed as well. I slowly got up off the bed, being as quiet as I could. My pain faded to the back of my mind as I made my way as stealthily as I could into the foyer.

From where I stood, I could see the monster talking to the fire marshal. He had his back to me, his left hand was resting on the top of the door, his right hand resting on his right hip. He looked casual, nothing like he had a short while before.

I didn't think he had noticed me and I brought my hands up to signal nine-one-one to the fireman, but he turned, still very casually, and stopped me with one sentence. "Our daughter will be home very soon, in a week actually." He smiled at me as he said it, cold and menacing, and I felt my blood run cold from my head to my toes, my hands dropped uselessly to my sides.

"Well, I'll be getting out of your hair now. It was nice to meet you. Tell Ellie I said hi when she comes home." Leaning around whatever kind of monster it was that stood in my entry way, the marshal, not realizing that I was in any danger, waved politely and reminded me to be more careful with my stove.

Dropping his voice lower, I heard him add, "I bet you're glad you don't have to eat her cooking much anymore." The fire marshal was laughing to himself at his joke as he walked back to his truck across the lawn, unknowingly leaving me to face certain death alone.

Standing became difficult and I fell to the floor as I began to hyperventilate. How did he know about Ellie? How did he know she was coming home soon? Now my survival became unimportant, I only cared about Ellie. He must not be here when she came home. I would need to be dead by then and he would need to have moved on. I didn't think it would be hard to accomplish, but I needed to make sure of it. How was I going to ensure my own death?

I tried to bring my breathing back under control, but I was terrified so I had little success. Without looking away from me, he shut the front door behind him and walked over to me. Kneeling down beside me, he sat for a few moments, simply looking at my face. Slowly, my breathing calmed and I knelt there looking back at him. "What are you?" My voice cracked and produced little sound.

"What do you think I am?" he questioned me. I sat looking at him dumbly. The only answers that came to my mind seemed ridiculous and I couldn't make myself put them into words. "Twenty-first century thought tells you I cannot exist," he noted, smiling at me sardonically.

"You can't," I mouthed back. Before I could finish the last word, I was staring at his fangs, glistening, and razor sharp, centimeters from my eyes. My brain didn't even register his movement, it was so fast.

The fangs were just as impressive the second time I saw them and I felt my heart rate go up just by seeing them. His full lips were pulled back from them slightly, giving me the full view.

"I would not think you would doubt me so soon after you encountered these?" His voice was a whisper, deadly yet smooth.

Managing to pull my eyes away from his fangs and search out his gaze, I had to tip my head back to look up into his eyes. The movement exposed my throat and noticing this, he ran the back of his hand along the path of my left internal jugular. Chills ran down the entire length of my spine, but I forced myself not to move, thinking of Ellie.

He needed to kill me. The sooner the better. Surely then he would not wait around for six more days. A poor plan I knew, but I didn't have a better one. "I won't doubt you anymore," I whispered back. Then I reached up and slapped him full in the face with as much strength as I could find.

He didn't flinch despite me having used every last ounce of muscle. I didn't even leave a hand-print on his face nor did he seem to be angry. His gaze remained level, no emotions were evident in his expression. Trying again, I doubled up my fist and hit him square in the jaw. The same. No emotion, no reaction at all except one whispered word.

"Ellie." From his mouth, her name was like salt in a wound and I froze, my hand in midair.

"Leave her alone. She's just a baby. Kill me, do whatever

you want to me. I'll cooperate. I'll give you anything you want, but leave her alone. I've got money in the safe and a car. Just kill me and go. Please!" I was begging.

Grasping his shoulders with both hands, I pulled myself up so that my face was level with his as I continued to plead for my daughter's life. Offers that I wouldn't have ever thought I could have put into words rolled off my tongue until I could think of nothing else with which to bargain.

He said nothing, did nothing. He seemed to be waiting for something but I had no idea what. Finally, he smiled. His face was friendly, but his eyes were mocking.

"I'm immortal and a nomad. I have no need of money or cars. The only need I have is blood, which you and your daughter have and I plan to take. You have nothing to offer me in the place of her."

His voice died away, but my mind clung to his mention of being a nomad. I was right about that part. He would be unlikely to stay here for a week if he killed me soon. My mother wouldn't bring Ellie to the house if she couldn't get in touch with me. I thanked God silently for her cautiousness now. It would probably be my saving grace. The only protection I could offer Ellie now was my mortality. I would have died a thousand times for her, but I could only do it once.

Letting go of his shoulders, I bent forward on my knees in a position of prayer and began to pray in earnest. I noticed in my periphery that he had sat down as well and was watching me with a trace of humor on his face.

"Yes, pray for your life. Pray for my immortal soul too if

you can spare the words. Pray for your daughter. Pray that yours and her deaths be quick. Pray to me that I might grant you this kindness," he intoned softly and mockingly. He bowed his head and closed his eyes. I continued to pray while my left hand snaked out to grab the edge of a nearby pine knickknack shelf, bringing it crashing to the cool wood floor. A crystal vase, my prime target, shattered into hundreds of sharp shards.

The majority of the shelf had landed on him and as he looked up, I noticed that there was no surprise on his face. He must have picked up on my movements. Quickly before he subdued me, I grabbed a shard of the fallen glass, but he only laughed thinking I considered it a weapon against him.

His expression went cold as I shoved the glass as hard as I could into my left brachial artery, buried deep in the bend of the elbow, and jerked it to the right with a slicing motion. Hot, bright red blood spurted out as my aim had been good. I stood up while I still could, not wanting to die at his feet.

He was on his feet now too, his eyes focused on the red flow dripping onto the floor, making a red lake at my feet. His fangs were extended, lips curled back, eyes hot. I had him; he couldn't resist my death wish now.

I was losing blood quickly since I had severed a fairly large artery, I knew I didn't have much time and I tried to take a few steps towards him before the blood loss took my vision.

In one second, he was there. Grabbing my left arm, he wrenched it up and placed his mouth over the pulsing artery.

Swallowing is a complex act, one that we all take for granted every day, and how strange that I should think about that in the last few moments of my life. Watching him drink for about half a minute, I began to sink down onto the floor and he followed me down. My last act as a mother was to look to the mantle and find my daughter's face there; I focused on her image while he drank, until I felt nothing and the world went black.

THREE

Honey-colored hair hung down, cutting off my line of vision. I breathed in the sweet scent of apples emanating from the shoulder-length locks framing a heart-shaped face. Her forehead against the bridge of my nose, a small mouth planted a kiss on mine then pulled away so I could see her almond-brown eyes staring back at me. A giggle escaped her cupid mouth and little hands cupped my cheeks.

"Mommy, come make me some eggs." Happiness spread through me at the sound of her voice. I started to get up and follow her as she bounced towards the kitchen, but the aching in my head cut through my dreams and brought me back to reality.

Lying on the living room rug, I found myself staring up at the dimmed lights. It was night outside and I could still see a piece of the moon through the window from where I was.

I reached up to touch my forehead and noticed I was covered with a thin sheen of sweat. Dizziness with even that small movement nearly overwhelmed me, followed by a wave of nausea. If I thought I had been sore before, I had absolutely no idea. I attempted to lick my lips, but couldn't find enough moisture.

Listening to the tick of the grandfather clock, I lay where I was, unwilling to move. The clock chimed 1:00. That meant the night was only half-way over and I was still alive.

The chimes an hour later brought me back from the restless sleep state and I realized that I had lost another hour. Rolling over to my side, I managed to lift my upper body up onto my elbow. Winded, I lay there for another couple of minutes before making it to my knees and another couple of minutes until I managed to pull myself to my feet using the divan for support. Bile rose in my throat and I choked it back just in time. My knees buckled, but I ended up in a sitting position on the divan rather than back on the floor.

Sitting there, I began to search the room for my captor. He was not in my line of vision and straining my ears, I couldn't locate a sound out of place. The hum of the refrigerator and the tick of the clock were all I could make out until the heating unit began its cycling.

Still trying without success to find the moisture to lick my lips, I knew I had to get off of the divan and try to make it to the kitchen and get something to drink. I needed fluid so I leaned as far forward as I could to gather momentum more easily, then pushed off with everything in me.

Somehow, I made it into the kitchen and to the refrigerator without going to my knees again. Pulling the refrigerator door open was like an Olympic feat and I had to stand there a moment holding on to the door to recoup for a minute before I went any further.

Looking through the disorganized shelves, the orange juice and peanut butter seemed the most likely choices because of their iron content. I made the mistake of grabbing them both at the same time, and they slipped out of my fingers and landed on the floor. Using the refrigerator as a brace, I slid down it to sit on the floor and picked up the orange juice. Tilting the container up, it was like the nectar of the gods on my lips and I drank several gulps before I cautioned myself not to drink it too fast. I slowed down and tried to sip it. I desperately needed the fluid volume, but knew it could come back up just as easily.

Needing some solid food to settle my stomach, I set the juice down beside me and reached for the peanut butter jar. Thankfully, I had not screwed the lid on too tightly or I wouldn't have been able to open it. Scooping it out with my fingers, I ate it as quickly as I could, not bothering to waste the energy to get a spoon.

Hypoglycemia and dehydration were making me tremble, but after finishing off the carton of OJ, I started to feel better and best of all, still no sign of the vampire. He must have left me for dead and I smiled at the thought.

Vampire. Hearing the word echo in my mind made it seem all the more ludicrous, but I was at least five units of blood short by looking at my nail beds so I knew I wasn't crazy. Tell that to the police, I thought to myself.

Laughing out loud with a slight hysteric tone at the thought of calling the police; the idea of notifying them suddenly took on a new urgency. I began to crawl towards my cell phone, which of course was on the other side of the kitchen. It was less risky than standing up and I was more likely to make it if I crawled.

Hesitation hit me half-way across the floor. What would I

tell the police? That my house had been broken into while I was making spaghetti and I had been held captive by a vampire?

It crossed my mind to not call the police because what could they really do to help me? I quickly dropped that idea. I had bruises, I had the gash in my arm. My dog was dead. I certainly looked as though I had been attacked so I would leave the story there.

The police could take me to a hospital tonight and tomorrow I could start looking for a new place to live. He was probably long gone, but I wouldn't take any chances. Vampires couldn't come out in the sunlight, right? At least I didn't think so. All I needed to do was to survive the night. He would never find me again.

I resumed my slow crawl across the floor with a little more energy. I had about eight feet to go to make it to where my cell phone sat on the counter. The rough tile was wreaking havoc on my knees, but I labored on till I made it to the counter.

Reaching up with both hands, I pulled myself up on my knees, my right hand inches away from my cell phone. One more second and I would have had it in my hands.

Coming seemingly out of nowhere, he wrapped a hand in my hair and with a quick jerk of his wrist, he pulled my head around and threw me backwards. I landed about ten feet away, hard on my back. I felt his hand lace through my hair again as he dragged me from the kitchen and into the living room. With a sudden release of his hand that I wasn't expecting, the floor came up to meet my head very hard.

Bright lights exploded in my vision and a hard wave of nausea hit me, but still I didn't pass out. Searching vainly in my peripheral vision, I looked for him but didn't see him. Intertwining my fingers in the carpeting, I managed to pull myself up to where I was resting on my forearms.

About four feet away directly in front of me, he sat stock still, staring at me intently. He held a pose that for most men would have been uncomfortable. His right leg was partially stretched out to his side, his left leg bent and supporting most of his weight on the ball of his left foot. He looked halfway crouched and halfway poised to leap, but he simply stayed there and so I simply rested as well, waiting for my head to quit spinning and for the lights to stop flashing behind my eyes.

My chest ached from the impact of the tile, my head pulsed with a probable concussion, and every muscle in my body felt as though it had been torn away from the ligaments that were holding me together. I shook from fear and sheer physical exhaustion. My body surely couldn't survive this much longer.

It is interesting the things that go through your mind during a crisis. During my nights as an emergency room physician, patients had often recounted small details that their brain had noticed during car accidents or other life-threatening events. Always fascinating to me, I would wonder if they remembered these minute details only after the fact when their mind had a chance to reenact the event, or did they really take such quick notice when the event was occurring.

Now I had answered my own question. Because even though I sat facing the physical manifestation of death, I was able to focus on his every feature.

Physically speaking, he was not terribly imposing except for that half-crouched position he was holding, and despite everything, I realized he was very attractive. Reasonably tall, he was probably just a hair over six feet. Dark brown wavy hair, with what looked light sun-streaked highlights, fell in long locks to the base of his neck. It swept back off of a smooth forehead, except for three or four locks that strayed down to partially cover his eyes. Intense green eyes, evenly spaced, with dark, thick arching eyebrows stared back at me. The whites were clear and the pupils exceedingly dark, which even though it sounds like a cliché really did remind me of the old well at my family farm back home.

Glistening and dark, his pupils mesmerized me, threatening to pull me over the edge and into him. Dilated and wider in diameter than human pupils, I couldn't help but stop and stare at them. His skin was light and smooth and his red lips, full in the extreme, almost leapt off his face. The contrast between their color and his skin was sharp. On a woman, it would have been considered garish, but he carried it well. He was not slight but not heavy either and his arms underneath the thermal he was wearing were corded with lean muscles. The denim that encased his thighs also showed the notching of hard muscles.

He was wearing light gray and black tennis shoes with a lot of wear to the point that most of the tread had given way

to a smooth rubber sole. He was handsome and in some
ways beautiful, but not so much that he looked feminine. He
was all male, not human, but all male.

Lifting my gaze back up to his face, I could see he knew I
was appraising him. The corners of his mouth lifted in a
sardonic smile that wrinkled his skin only slightly and I
wondered how many other women had stared at this same
man and saw that humorless smile before he ripped them to
shreds. My heart rate picked up a little at that thought.

"Your name." His voice was so quiet as to almost be a
whisper and the innocence of the words coming from him
after the previous mocking threats caught me totally by
surprise. It was not a question, more like a command
though not threatening, but even so I sat there dumbly for a
few moments. Never looking away from his face, I watched
as he lifted one eyebrow up in surprise that I dared to
withhold the information he wanted. I gathered my wits up
before he could speak again.

"Annalice," I found myself whispering back, unable to lift
my voice above his.

"Hello, Annalice. What a lovely old-fashioned name you
have. It matches your house. I spent some time upstairs
looking around. Hope you didn't mind." His voice was low
and almost calming and I didn't know what to say so I just
continued to sit there staring into his dilated pupils.
Doubtless mesmerizing, but not hypnotic like in the movies.
No loss of free will, but definitely hard to look away from.

He sat back at that point and stretched out both legs in
front of him, leaning casually back against my couch

without breaking eye contact. "Do you accept what I am now?" he asked quietly.

I nodded very minimally, my subconscious subduing my movements, suspecting that sudden or large gestures might bring him hurtling across the small distance at me. I knew I had to die to protect my daughter, but since my previous attempt had failed, I just couldn't seem to find the strength at the moment.

"You know how our encounter will end. You have proven that, but I do hope the time of prayer and theatrics is over. You cannot force my timing as I am in control of myself. Your blood will not control me and spilling it will not bring this to a quicker or different ending."

His words hit me like a ton of bricks. I felt a black cloudy haze of fear for Ellie's life form in my mind. It clouded my vision and left me nearly paralyzed, hampering my ability to breathe let alone acknowledge the creature sitting across from me. My eyes glazed over and I dropped my forehead into the carpet as I focused on breathing in and out. Other than that action, I had yet to acknowledge his words, but instead lay there in silence.

Finally looking up at him, I found that he had looked away and was staring at something to my right. Out of curiosity, I followed his gaze and with a sickening realization saw he was staring at Ellie's picture.

"She is beautiful." His voice was icy now and held a perverse undertone. I noticed then that he had a slight southern accent. Those pretty words wrapped up in that slight drawl only added to the effect.

I felt his gaze on my face, but I hadn't been able to tear my eyes away from Ellie's face. Her innocence stood out like a beacon to me. Surely there must be something he wanted, something I could use to bargain with. But was it possible to bargain with the devil? "Let's make a deal," ran through my head but I had nothing to offer except my death and I couldn't even control that.

As I sat there, my mind grasped at straws. Was there no way out for Ellie? My mom would never bring her here if she were unable to get a hold of me. That I knew for certain. And she would call. She always did, frightened that I, her only daughter, lived in what she considered the remote parts of the world surrounded by dark forests. Mom had imagined every kind of evil lurking in those woods. Well, probably not this kind, I admitted to myself but she was not far off since the outcome would be the same. She would never dream of driving to the house without a definite game plan and so he would never get her or Ellie.

Unable to stop it, a slight smile of satisfaction spread across my face and with a little defiance, I met his eyes.

"I can find her. I will find her. That is what you were thinking about, right? Stupid human to think I cannot track down one insignificant child." His voice held some anger now and his face went hard. "I already know so much about you. Give me twenty minutes in a house and I can tell you almost everything about a human. So naïve to think your home is really that private. I know where your mother lives. Or at least I know the general direction."

He smiled again and continued, "You do not give up. Still

looking for some way out for your daughter." He nodded his head in my direction as he went on, "You love her. An endearing quality." He paused there for a few seconds, letting the words sink in. "I have killed many people. Couples, entire families, friends. Very seldom does anyone truly sacrifice himself for someone, even a family member."

He paused again and I could still feel his eyes on my face, but I had closed my eyes, my confident smile gone. I didn't even acknowledge that he was speaking to me at all.

"As it turns out," he intoned, "you do have something I want. Nothing material like money or cars, mind you. Something that is much harder to give."

This caught my attention and, opening my eyes, I allowed him to catch my gaze once more. I stared into the deep wells of his pupils, rimmed by the intense green irises. These were the words I had been dying, literally dying to hear. His eyes, so riveting, compelled me to come to him and although I didn't move, I didn't try to look away either. This was what I wanted, something to bargain with and I would happily lose my soul in those eyes if there was a way out for my child.

"What?" My voice was cold and hard and the word came out as a demand. His chin lifted slightly at what must have sounded like defiance to him.

"Your cooperation." Startled by his answer, I looked at him in surprise. I'm not sure what I was expecting but that certainly wasn't it. I had already split an artery so if that wasn't cooperation, I didn't know what was. Did he mean cooperation where Ellie was concerned? I felt nauseous again and my head ached harder at the thought of what he could mean. I felt my hands form into fists and didn't even try to keep them at my sides.

"I will never willingly give her to you," I hissed the words across the short distance separating us.

A slight smile touched his expression and he laughed out loud. "You have made yourself abundantly clear regarding your daughter and lucky for you, it is not her that I really want."

I was starting to get more angry than scared now, which was dangerous since he could kill me as an afterthought. "Then what is it? Tell me and let's get on with it. There's nothing I won't do to protect her so spit it out. What is it?"

I searched my brain trying to remember every vampire movie I had ever watched. What did they need? I could think of nothing I had other than blood that he might want. The fear for my daughter's life and my dwindling patience combined allowed me to pull myself up onto my knees. Reaching over, I hauled myself over to him. "Tell me, you son of a whore!" I spat the words into his face.

With lightning speed and with only a blur caught by my eye, his hands held my face and throat with a crushing force. "My mother was no whore." His voice rang with rage. His eyes flashed with the emotion in his voice as his hands continued to crush against my bones. I was sure they would snap at any moment and my vision was starting to tunnel at the lack of oxygen.

"She was a good woman." His voice was softer with those words, his face gentler and his hands relaxed slightly, just enough that I could breathe shallowly.

I saw in that moment a trace of humanity, the first that I had seen in him. As both a mother and a daughter, I could understand his pain. His grip loosened and I pulled myself out of his hands, falling backwards on the floor.

"It was you that I was trying to insult, not your mother." My voice was raspy from the force of his hands. I tried not to let my voice shake too much, but I couldn't control it completely and if he noticed it, he didn't show it.

"Yes, I sometimes forget that semantics have changed over the years." The rage had left his face just as suddenly.

Taking a moment to calm my voice, I went on to the main point. "How can I cooperate?"

He had me now and he knew it; the victory showed on his face. "Occasionally, I long for a short period of human company. Very short, mind you. To understand, you must know something of vampires, our cravings, and you must know something of me. Blood is my main objective. It controls my every thought. I crave it, long for it and there is nothing more important than finding it. However, I do have other desires."

Here he held up a finger for emphasis. "Although they are all colored by the desire for blood. I am essentially a loner as all vampires are, I believe. A nomad as I said earlier, roaming night after night rarely doing anything more than skirting the human world except to feed. Occasionally, it grows mundane and I choose a human with whom to spend a few days. To reacquaint myself with humanity, it helps me understand my prey better. Keep up with the changing of times and the human race itself. It is good for our kind to be able to drop our guard from time to time and be known for what we really are. To not have to conceal our most base desires if only for a few days. I do this very seldom, but it seems that now is a good time."

"I will benefit and so will you and that is why I have chosen you. You have something I want and I can give you something that you want. Please do not think it is because you are special or different from the thousands of other humans I have killed. You are not different. You are not special. You will most certainly die when our time is up. You are alone, however, and will be alone in your home for some time; so it provides a convenient opportunity. I give this opportunity to you in exchange for your daughter's life. Do you accept the terms?"

I studied his face looking for a hint of what he was really thinking as he spoke, but it might as well have been cast in stone. I wasn't quite sure what he was saying or maybe my mind just refused to accept what he was offering. After our previous encounters in the evening, I was fairly certain that I understood the talk of blood, but could I cooperate and be his companion? And what did that even mean? I was sure there would be more to it than I was capable of realizing in my current condition.

I started to speak but he held up his hand, placing his right pointer finger on my lips, cutting off my questions.

"Do you accept the terms? Your cooperation in exchange for your daughter's life? It is a simple question. Yes or no? The specifics will be explained later. And by the way, I killed old lady McElhaney. Ripped her throat out and left her dying body to rot. You are totally alone." He waited now for my answer.

My mind was on what he had said about Ms. McElhaney. I realized he must have overheard the conversation with my mom on the phone. It all came together then. The sensation of panic and terror that had chased me from the woods and then what I had felt upstairs had been him.

"Yes. Of course. Anything for her." I nodded my head as he pulled his finger away from my mouth.

I grasped his hand as he pulled it away. "But answer me this. Why didn't you just kill me in the woods?" I was curious. None of this made any sense. "You didn't know I was alone until you heard me talking to my mom." Having many more questions, I started to ask more as he pulled his finger out of my hand and placed it back over my lips.

He clearly didn't like my questions but answered anyway. "I surveyed your house out just before dawn on my way to my resting spot for the day. I could hear only two defenseless hearts beating and one of those was a child. I wanted to take you then. To wake you with my fangs at your throat."

He reached over with the other hand to run one cool finger down my neck while he spoke, his right index finger still on my lips. Both of his hands were on me as if we were in an embrace. "That is the best time, you know. You would have smelled so much more human after an entire night in your bed before you covered your skin and hair with all of the fragrances human women are so fond of. But I would have been pressed for time. I would have had to spend the day here and I could not take the chance that some nosy human would come poking around, despite the isolation here, while I was incapacitated."

He casually lifted his shoulders now when he spoke further like we were talking about the weather. "So I was fairly certain that you were essentially alone. I decided to let you sit and I would come back the next day. Besides, why would I want to kill you in the cold dirt of the woods when I could defile you and kill you in the comfort of your own home?"

The bleakness of his words startled me and I knew my shock was evident on my face. He was enjoying it. I felt a pit in my stomach, cold and empty.

What had I agreed to? Giving him my blood, my body, or something more important? Would he drain my soul as well? It took only a second for me to realize I would give up anything for Ellie so it didn't really matter; he could have it all. Pulling his hand away from my mouth, I whispered, "Defile me then." In return, he flashed me another predatory smile.

The chiming of the clock made me jump slightly at the first strike; it chimed five in the morning. The heavy oak that housed the mechanism of the clock gave it an ominous resounding boom that echoed throughout the emptiness of the house. The clock had been in my family for at least three generations, but I had never noticed before how lonely it sounded. It now reminded me of a death knell.

This hell of a night would soon be over but I still wasn't

exactly sure how it would end and his face still held that smile. A smile that confidently said he had won.

"So let me explain the rules of our engagement," he began. "You are mine during the dark of the day, which means you will sleep when I sleep. You will do as you are told without question. Most importantly, you will contact no one and you will not leave this house unless accompanied by me. I expect to not have to repeat myself and, remember, any disobedience will make our agreement null and void. Ending your own life intentionally will also nullify our agreement. Do you understand?" He waited now, prompting me to answer with the full weight of his eyes on me.

Nodding my head yes, I vaguely realized I did have several questions, but I suppose my thoughts were racing too quickly for them to be coherent.

"Then I will see you at the setting of the sun." His voice was low when he spoke.

He was suddenly standing before I realized his movements and reaching down, he grasped my hands and pulled me quickly to my feet. My head swam with the sudden movement, but I was locked in his grip so I didn't falter. Leaning down, he placed one cool touch of his lips to the back of my right hand and then he was gone. A second later, I heard the back door close and I was alone.

With his leaving, I also lost control of my legs and I sank back down to the floor. I knew it had been pure adrenaline that had kept me going for the last couple of hours. But now I had nothing left and no reason left to even attempt to regain my footing so I just lay there. It hurt to think and I attempted to completely empty my mind.

It didn't work because my every thought was of him or of Ellie. Like watching a movie, each bad moment replayed itself like poorly scripted drama scenes from a horror film.

And like many poorly made horror films that I had watched, this one couldn't keep me awake either and I eventually fell asleep. I don't remember drifting away and how I remained asleep is beyond me with the images of what I had experienced still playing through my mind.

They were even worse in my dreams. More distorted and slowed down even further in that eerie way that is only possible in dreams. But despite the images flashing through my mind, I slept deeply and it took the incessant chiming of the clock striking noon to rouse me.

FOUR

Awareness came before the opening of my eyes and I knew it was noon because of the glare coming from the picture window in the living room. I was tempted to stay there and not move as I couldn't see any point to getting up, but even when you know you are going to die, you still have to contend with the bladder, so move I did.

Pulling myself up to a kneeling position, I gave myself a minute to let my spinning head slow down before I stumbled into the bathroom. To my surprise, I managed to make it to the commode without passing out by using both hands to steady myself as I walked. It was still a relief to sit down even if it was only a toilet.

After several minutes of convincing myself, I got up to the bathroom sink. Luckily it wasn't too far away. Looking into the oversized mirror, I gasped a little at my own appearance. I looked like hell and that was putting it mildly.

Reaching up to pull at the snarls in my hair, I took a second to pull one of my lower eyelids down. Paler in color than it should have been, I was surprised to find that my inner lid still held any color at all. An old school method for determining a blood count. Not terribly accurate, but at least it gave you an idea if someone was anemic or not.

Turning on the faucet, I reached both hands into the cold water, splashing it up onto my face and then running my fingers through my hair trying to tame it down a little. Looking back in the mirror, I couldn't tell much improvement.

The vanity of the situation hit me then. Primping in front of a mirror when my killer would be returning in less than six hours hardly made sense. What did it matter if I looked like crap? Like most women, I had spent numerous hours in front of a mirror and for what? It had been wasted time. He was here for blood and not the way I looked. So deciding not to waste the few remaining hours of my life that I had left, I gave up on my hair.

My stomach was twisting with hunger and the dizziness was on the verge of becoming incapacitating so eating became a priority. I walked towards the kitchen, passing through the living room on the way, not paying attention to where I was stepping.

Feeling my left foot drag through a thick wetness, I paused with my foot in midair knowing without looking what was clinging to my foot. Looking down to confirm my suspicion, thick maroon blood clung to the entire length of my foot. My blood.

My gut reaction was to scream as the viscous liquid enveloped my skin and now dripped slowly from my sole back into the coagulated pool beneath me, but honestly I just didn't have the energy. I waited for the expected bile to rise in my throat, but nothing happened.

Since the bloody mess didn't discourage my appetite, I walked on into the kitchen marking the tile floor with one-sided bloody footprints all the way to the refrigerator.

Grabbing the handle, I swung open the fridge and reached in automatically for the eggs. Carrying four to the stove, I quickly cracked them onto the griddle, tossing the shells into the sink, and turned it on. They were scrambled in a matter of minutes. Spooning them onto a plate, I walked outside into the sunlight. It was still cool, but looked like it would warm up to at least 60, I thought.

Lifting my face up to the warmth of the sun and into the light breeze, I let it it race across my face, turning my head side to side to catch the sun rays on both sides. It felt good to stand outside in the sunlight after the horrendous night. Realizing for the first time in a while how beautiful the daylight was, I looked up into the sun a moment. Closing my eyes, I reveled in the golden light that penetrated my eyelids for a few moments more.

Eating the warm breakfast, I looked out across the pastures, still brown from the winter, and focused on the horses in the pasture. I could just make out the small herd standing at the far southeast corner of the pasture closest to the border of the forest. They were sunning themselves just as I was.

Continuing to survey the property, I realized how normal everything looked. Nothing appeared out of the ordinary. No one would have ever believed that I had lived out a fantasy-land nightmare.

I had stood on this same deck yesterday just hours before my assault by a mythical creature. Now in the light of day, it was easy to forget what had happened and believe that I had made the entire thing up and that I would be here to see the coming spring. My mother always said, "Everything looks better in the daylight."

But I hadn't made this up and I hadn't dreamed it. The bloody footprints and my dead dog were proof enough to confirm I wasn't losing my mind. Despite the brightness of the sun, it could no longer penetrate the haze of darkness overtaking my mind, knowing that spring was coming and I wouldn't be here to enjoy it with Ellie.

Thinking of her brought to mind the promise I had made to the vampire last night. Was I mentally strong enough to stay here and wait for his return? Could I actually keep myself from contacting my mother? Not say goodbye to my daughter?

And that was where I knew that I had to draw the line. Yes, I was strong enough to die for her. I had the strength to leave them wondering what had happened to me. But I wasn't strong enough to leave without some sort of goodbye. I would have to find a way to tell her how much she had and would always mean to me.

I wanted to tell her how proud she had made me and how much happiness she had brought to my life. Tell her to listen to my mother. If I had listened to her, I wouldn't be sitting here contemplating goodbyes.

Turning on my heel, I walked back into the house to think about this some more. Absentmindedly, I reached down and rubbed my left arm, expecting to feel the self-inflicted cut, warm and swollen like a fresh wound should be, but there was only the smooth skin of my inner elbow.

Looking down, I didn't believe my eyes at first. The

laceration was gone. Not healed with a visible scar but just gone. Walking over to the window to get a better look in the bright light streaming in, I stared intently at the spot where the cut should have been, but the skin of my inner arm was completely flawless. I hadn't imagined the cut as the blood was still on the floor. But looking down at my arm again confirmed what I had already seen. The incision was completely gone.

Hurrying to the bathroom, I looked into the mirror, but my neck was as baby smooth as my arm. No puncture wounds not even any bruising, the same as my arm. But I distinctly remembered the sensation of his fangs piercing my skin and hearing him swallow my blood. Just as I remembered watching his mouth close over the flow of blood from my arm.

Turning around, I pulled my shirt over my head and looked at my back. Dark red bruises covered me from my neck to my hips. Turning back around as I pulled my shirt back on, I jerked the sleeve up on my right arm. Deep red bruises along with fingerprints could be seen traveling up my arm, but where his lips had touched me, my skin was flawless.

Leaving the bathroom, I went back to the kitchen. It was well lit, easily the cheeriest room in the house, and the sun alone calmed my frayed nerves. I was safe as long as the sun was shining. Pulling out a bar-stool, I sat down, resting my arms and head on the cool bar.

For the first time today, a split-second thought of Ms. McElhaney flashed through my mind as I walked back to the kitchen. It became impossible to stop the flow of images through my head. I could see her lying dead on the floor with the homemade quilt lying ruined and bloodied beside her, or her body spread out across the old iron frame bed. She had no close family and it would take the few neighbors there were out here a few days to notice her absence.

I wanted to call the police and notify them of her death. It was the ethical thing to do and I knew it. It seemed so unfair for her to be decomposing in her home. Reasoning out loud, I talked myself through the conversation with the police. It didn't take long to realize that no matter how the call was made, the police would quickly show up here looking for information. Her house was littered with my phone numbers and pictures of Ellie as we had become close to her since we had moved here.

Maybe I should call her house to see if he was lying, I thought to myself. My hand was on a wall phone a full second before I decided that was a bad idea. My number would be on her caller I.D. and I knew in my heart that he was telling the truth. Calling her house wouldn't help her or me now.

Letting my hand fall away from the phone, I began to pace in the kitchen. My previous dizziness had been pushed to the back of my mind while I was thinking about my sweet elderly neighbor. Panic truly hit me for the first time. I had been a fool. What was I still doing here? Could I escape and shouldn't I try?

The answer now seemed shockingly clear. He was gone,

at least for the day, and I had wasted a lot of very valuable time. I should call my mom and drive as fast as I could to get to Ellie tonight. I could make it by nightfall.

My mind screamed instructions and my body obeyed. I had the house phone in my hand with mom's number partially dialed. Terror and a near loss of reason caused my hands to shake and I was unable to finish dialing the number. It was as if I had finally used up the last of my sanity reserves and I could handle no more.

I knew that I was about to lose myself in the grip of panic and I used what small amount of mental reserves I had left to bring my rapid breathing under control. I forced myself to breathe in slowly, count to three, and then exhale just as slowly. Feeling my heart rate drop in response, I gripped the phone with all my strength and forced my hand to hang it back up, at least until I could think this through more clearly.

Sitting back down in the kitchen, I ran my hands up over my face and through my hair. The muscles in my back ached at the motions. My hair felt grimy and I suddenly felt very dirty.

Uncertainty clung to me. Logic told me to leave but my gut instinct screamed for me to stay. Nausea returned with my indecision and a thin sheen of sweat formed on my face and under my arms, adding to my unclean feeling.

Deciding to wash my face again, I walked back through the living room, my eyes landing on Samuel for the first time. I had forgotten him as I had been so focused on my own problems. Tears sprang to my eyes as they swept over him.

Kneeling down beside him on my knees, I knitted my hands into the fur around his neck. It had always been the thickest there and one of his favorite places to be scratched. Even though the faint stench of death was just beginning to become apparent, I couldn't keep myself from dropping my head against his. The tears flowed down my face and onto his. He had been my guardian and friend for several years. He had let me cry on his shoulder numerous times during the worst moments of my life.

Now I was crying on his shoulder one last time. The tears came until there was nothing left. I cried not only for the loss of my pet, but also for the loss of my future and my life.

Lifting myself up off Samuel, I stood up, taking a second to dry my eyes on the backs of my hands, and then leaned down to pick him up as I refused to drag my beloved friend.

He was heavy and the lack of muscle tone made it even harder to carry him, but I managed to get him to the door. It took a while as I had to lay him down to open the door and then pick him up again, my back muscles burning in response.

Walking out on the deck, I struggled to get him down the steps. I nearly dropped him, but somehow managed to stay upright with him in my arms. Thankfully he had always been on the small side for a German shepherd.

Standing for several minutes deciding on the best place to bury him, I finally decided on the garden. It wasn't like I would be using it this year and since I had broken the ground up already, it would be an easy place to dig the grave. So with the decision made, I walked to the garden and placed him gently on the grass at the edge as I couldn't stand to get his fur dirty.

The shovel I got from the barn felt clumsy and foreign in my hands. It took about an hour to dig Samuel a shallow resting place but it was the best I could do as my strength was quickly giving out.

Wrapping him in a small but thick horse blanket I kept in the barn, I placed him in the small hole. It only took a few minutes to cover him up and I packed the dirt down as best as I could with the flat side of the shovel.

Staring down at the grave, the shovel slipped out of my hands and I waited for more tears to fall, but I found I had no more at the moment. My beloved Samuel's interment left me dejected and I felt desperately alone. Glad that he had not suffered, I could not keep from wishing that he could have kept me company while I waited to die.

Feeling dirtier than ever, a bath became a priority. While burying Samuel, my indecision had grown and I was now even less certain of what to do. Reasoning that my mind would be clearer if I were clean, I left the garden and went straight to the bathroom. The tears that I had been unable to cry now streamed uncontrollably down my face.

FIVE

The hot water wrapped around my skin like a blanket as I slipped down into the tub. I had gotten the water as hot as I could take it, hoping to ease my aching muscles from where the vampire had thrown me around.

Red as a lobster, the jets of the tub punched at my skin until that pain began to overtake the muscle cramps. Although the water couldn't erase everything that had happened, my mind did clear a little and I was able to think more rationally.

It was close to 4 p.m. If the vampire lore I knew was correct, most of which had been gathered from the occasional movie, he would return sometime around sundown. It was mid-February so the sun would be setting about 5:30 p.m. That meant I had about two and a half hours until he returned.

Should I use the two and half hours to make a run for it? Try to drive to Ellie and pull her out of my mom's arms and get as far away from here as possible. Leave my mother to face his wrath?

It didn't seem probable that I could convince her we were being stalked by a vampire and we all needed to go into hiding. The psych facility would be getting a call if I told her that story. Then I would be hiding from the police as well as a vampire.

But as much thought as I put into that scenario, I knew I couldn't leave my mother to face him. It would be better to be dead than to know I had betrayed one of the two people that had loved and raised me and whom I loved more than anyone in the world besides Ellie. Mom deserved better.

I contemplated telling her the truth for a short time longer, knowing all along that it was a dead end road. Mom, most of the time immensely practical except where this house was concerned, would never buy into that story. Not that I could blame her. It sounded ridiculous even to me, sitting here in the daylight in my bathtub.

Sliding deeper into the tub, I let the water run over my head and through my hair. Reaching up, I fanned the long locks out with my hands and rinsed it out of habit. I scoured my scalp and then scrubbed myself from head to toe.

Remembering his mouth on me, I scrubbed at my neck again until the skin felt nearly raw. Giving up because I couldn't make myself feel clean no matter how long I scrubbed, I leaned back into the tub, trying again to focus on the best solution to my problem.

What about a priest? Was there some sort of exorcism for vampires? And once again, was I willing to risk that person's life to see?

Could I kill the vampire myself? Another improbable plan, I felt, given the speed of his movements I had witnessed. But of all the plans that I had worked through in my mind, killing him seemed the safest for everyone else involved. If I didn't succeed though, it would still leave Ellie at risk. He probably wouldn't feel obligated to hold to our agreement if he felt I had betrayed it.

A chilling thought occurred to me for the first time. What if he didn't follow through with his word and went after Ellie despite his promise? I mean, how much could you trust a vampire?

The more I thought about my situation, trusting a vampire seemed like the most absurd plan of all. Hadn't I felt the air change just by his entering the room last night? Didn't my hair stand on end? And here I was, sitting in my house, like a fly in a spider web waiting for him to return. To be his beck and call girl until he killed me, hoping that he would keep a promise to me, his intended victim, and not kill my family.

Panic seeped into my mind once again while I had been running this scenario through my mind and now I was under its control, feeling its heaviness beginning to suffocate me.

I shot up out of the water, splashing it on the walls and onto the floor with the force. There wasn't much time. I needed to pack some clothes for myself and some food. I didn't want to be stopping to eat once I had picked up Ellie. She had clothes at my mom's house. There was money and a gun in the safe.

Grabbing a towel from the linen closet, I barely had made a dent in the water beading on my skin before I was pulling on my jeans and t-shirt. My hands were shaking as I attempted the combination on the safe and it took three tries for my trembling fingers to get it right. Finally, the lock released and the door swung open on the hinges. I reached into the dark of the safe, my hand landing on the gun first.

Grabbing the small amount of emergency cash I always kept, I stuffed the money in my back pocket and pushed the gun into the waistband of my pants. Jerking the hangers violently, I pulled a few warm clothes out of my closet including a thick down-filled coat and shoved them all into an overnight bag.

I was in my car in less than ten minutes. The clock in the car shone like a beacon in the dark garage reading 4:45 p.m. forcing my mind to register how close I was cutting this. Pushing the garage door opener on my visor, I waited impatiently for the door to open and was pulling out just as the edge of the door cleared my car.

Jabbing my finger down on the locking mechanism, I didn't give the old house a second look as I roared down the driveway that turned into the winding dirt road.

Taking each curve too quickly, my wheels spun rocks and dirt into the trees covering the road. Since the dirt road dead-ended in my driveway, it was unlikely I would meet another car. My nerves were frayed and my eyes strained around each curve, half-expecting the vampire to be standing in the road waiting for me.

It was still light out, however, with the late afternoon sun having taken on the dark yellow color rather than the clear light of midday. Coming from an angle, the sun shone through the trees casting long shadows from the neighboring forest across the road, adding to my fear and desperation.

Reaching the end of the eight-mile dirt road, I sat facing

the busy highway, left turn signal on, watching the passing cars filled with people. They were probably returning home from work or going to eat with their family or to visit friends. Normal people living normal lives and I so badly wanted to join them.

To turn the clock back and appreciate the mundane, to take my mom up on the offer of going with her and Ellie. Why had I not listened to her? Why had I stayed at that old house, cut off from the outside world for all intents and purposes? If only I hadn't been so stubborn.

The clock flashed 4:55 p.m. The eerie red numbers glowed more brightly as the light outside began to dwindle.

Driving wildly, I had made it to the end of the dirt road in a record ten minutes. I so badly wanted to punch the gas pedal and take off after Ellie, rejoin the land of the normal, but I couldn't make myself do it. I couldn't risk Ellie's life on the chance he couldn't find us.

Despite my previous impulsivity, I knew I had to go back. There was no true way out for me except to return where fate had placed me. He was the way out and when he had consumed me, then and only then would it be over.

4:57 p.m. Reaching up with my left hand, I turned the blinker off. My heart was reacting to it like a metronome. Very little time remained and so making a U-turn, I began the long drive back to my personal hell.

5:05 p.m. I pulled back into the garage, the door closing behind me with a heavy finality. I had driven back to the house with an even greater urgency than I had left it. Inside the house, I placed the gun and money on top of the refrigerator. Grabbing a juice bottle out of the refrigerator, I downed it quickly without stopping for air.

5:10 p.m. I sat down in the middle of the living room floor, the ceiling fan turning lazy circles over my head. I could smell the coagulated blood in the corner of the room, the ceiling fan blowing the foul scent around the room, making the bile rise in my throat. It wasn't the blood per say that was making me sick. But it smelled like death, which I had smelled many times. Only this time the stench belonged to me.

If I survived tonight, I made up my mind to clean it up tomorrow. I couldn't convince myself that he actually meant to keep me alive for a week. I wasn't sure that I even wanted him to. It reminded me of being on death row. Was there any point to being given a few days to live?

5:12 p.m. I could see the digital clock from where I sat on the floor, its red light glittering in the dark reminding me of my date with the devil. As if I could forget. My mind kept asking the strangest questions. Should I meet him at the door? What should I wear? Would he want to talk and what would we talk about?

5:15 p.m. Gold and red rays from the setting sun caught my eye out the window. The sliver of sun that remained shimmered behind the mountains off in the west and I could see the moon beginning to take shape in the dusk.

One lone star just barely visible on the horizon to the left of the tallest mountain peak caught my attention and I watched it get brighter and brighter as the sun completely set into the horizon. The walls of the living room that had been awash in the gold and red hues of the sun were now dark and I realized I had forgotten to turn on any lights, but I couldn't convince myself to move or to care.

5:28 p.m. I sat there in the dark still focusing on the one star I could see out the window. It helped me to keep my breathing steady. "Starlight, starbright, first star I see tonight. I wish I may, I wish I might have the wish I wish tonight," I whispered into the dark. The childhood rhyme played over and over through my mind. I finished it with a silent plea for Ellie's life every time.

5:42 p.m. Still nothing. I would go crazy, I was sure of it. The house was now completely dark with only the light of the moon shining through the windows yet still I sat there.

I brought my knees up and laid my head in the circle of my arms on them. My blood pounded in my ears pushed by a heart that had been racing ever since I had stepped back into the house. The roar of blood proved I was still alive, but I had no confidence in how long it would continue.

5:50 p.m. The hairs on the back of my neck stood up and my heart paused for what felt like an eternity before it began to pound all the faster, blood pumping harder than I would have given my heart credit for before now. The same terrifying fear I had experienced the evening before came over me and I felt like an ant under the microscope in the sunlight. Sweat was beginning to form under my arms and breasts and my hands were clammy. Feeling a slight breeze rustle past me, I knew he was there.

Fingertips, cool and smooth, lightly traced circles up and down my neck. I didn't move, didn't say a word, scarcely breathed, until cool lips replaced the fingers then I involuntarily jerked back. I didn't get far for I was quickly caught in the grip of his left hand holding me steadfastly in place while he moved his mouth up my neck. Stopping at the base of my jaw, he parted his mouth to let his teeth graze lightly against my skin. Involuntarily, I tensed up expecting those fangs to slice through my skin.

"This will be nice, I promise," he whispered into my ear. "I am pleasantly surprised you did not run. I thought it likely I would have to track you and Ellie down. Instead, I find you are a lady of some honor. Tell me, did you do exactly as I told you?" His voice, soft yet rich at the same time, held no hint of anger.

Panicking for a moment, it occurred to me I wasn't to have left the house but I did when I buried Samuel and when I ran. He had to have noticed Samuel was gone. Would that break our agreement? He continued to stroke my neck with his face, lightly nipping as he moved.

"You are making it very hard for me to take this slowly with your heart racing like a jackrabbit. Again, did you do exactly as I said?"

I hesitated briefly again. "No... no. I buried my dog. He was beginning to stink. What you said didn't cross my mind when I found his body this morning." My voiced strained with the attempt to keep it from quivering.

"Is there anything else you need to tell me? Remember, my senses are much more accurate than yours and I will know if you are lying. Be careful with your words, Annalice. They determine your fate."

Again, I hesitated. "I did think about leaving but turned around in the garage." My breath rushed out with the words and I left out the part about driving to the road. I didn't think he could read anything else from me since my heart was already hitting nearly one-eighty. My skin tingled with icy fear as I waited for his reaction.

I was essentially blind in the dark, but I could feel him all around me. The fine hairs on my arms stood up in response to his presence. It was also as if his coolness was in such stark contrast to the warmer air of the house that it provided a line of demarcation between him and his surroundings.

His breath cool against my neck, his hands began to retrace the circular patterns over my upper arms from my shoulders to my elbows. I started to relax in spite of myself and he laughed quietly in the dark.

Wondering what he found funny, it occurred to me he could feel my muscles becoming slack in his hands in response to him, or maybe he thought my terror over Samuel was funny. Either way, the laugh had a mocking edge to it and I could feel myself tightening up all over again.

"Since you have been honest, I will honor our agreement. But do not make another mistake. I would consider that willful disobedience." Without meaning to, I exhaled in response to his words and, feeling relieved, I nodded my own agreement

In the next second, he was gone and back. I barely had recognized his movement before he was leaning over me, bathed in the soft light of an old lamp whose shade was off-white and muted by the low wattage of the bulb that lit it.

The room had always appeared cozier in this light and almost as if he had willed it, I looked up into his face. The mood of the room suddenly took on an entirely new feeling as his intent was clearly written in his expression.

I began to clamor back, struggling to gain my footing, a handhold in the plush rug. I made it about six feet before I realized he hadn't come after me. His lack of movement brought me up short.

I studied him for a moment from where I had stopped in my escape. He was sitting in a relaxed position on the floor; his face was smooth and emotionless, appearing to be uninterested in whether I ran or not.

And then I realized that there was no reason for him to chase what couldn't get away from him. He had all night and knowing that in order to save Ellie, I would eventually come back to him. I had nowhere else to go

He was looking at me, probably enjoying my terror and the play of my emotions on my face. Getting up on my knees and then standing, I walked purposefully back to him and dropped back down again in front of him.

For a couple of minutes, we sat just like that no movement, no words. It was then I decided there would be no more tears, no more cowering. I was doing this for Ellie and my mom. I would do it right. Whatever he had planned for me, I would take it. I wouldn't give him the satisfaction of seeing my terror. If I had nothing else, I had my pride and with my mind made up, I looked up full in his face.

If he noticed the change in me, he didn't acknowledge it.

His eyes were dilated and it was extremely difficult not to stare into them. So I decided not to try. What did it matter either way? And so I let my gaze get caught. Maybe it would make what was going to happen easier to bear if I was taken in by him.

He stared back at me with eyes that I suspected had seen thousands of moments just like this one, his face softened by the muted light. With exaggerated slowness, he took a long lock of my hair and spiraled it around the fingers of his left hand. It stood out dark against the white skin of his hand.

Rising up on his knees, he leaned in over me. I stared now at the sculpted muscles of his chest outlined through his soft blue t-shirt and followed the sharp line of his muscles down. His hips were narrow and his legs long and corded.

Looking up from his body just as his lips brushed mine slightly, I saw him pull away. In a slow sensuous movement, he pulled his shirt off and dropped it on the floor next to us.

Dropping his face closer to mine again and with more intensity, he kissed me a second time. Re-wrapping his hand in my hair, he jerked my head back rather forcefully until I was looking up at his face.

He was beautiful yet masculine; I could see that more clearly tonight and I didn't try to look away. His features couldn't have been more perfect except there was no warmth in his eyes.

There was a lust, however, clearly evident in every feature of his face that could not be denied. It emanated from him like a hunger. I wondered then if he was as attractive as I thought he was, or if I was responding to the sexual heat radiating off of him. It didn't really matter, I knew, the end result was the same, but I couldn't help but be curious.

Taking me by surprise, a wave of heat radiated out from deep within my core. Ashamed by my reaction to him, I rationalized that it was impossible not to react to the combination of his beauty and his evident desire.

But something wasn't right. I'll admit it had been a while since I had felt any great passion, but now in a matter of a few minutes I felt like I was on fire from the inside out. The heat had changed to a mild ache and a hunger that I simply couldn't put into words. Hunger for everything. Everything that I had ever craved seemed to be running through my mind. Food, alcohol, sex, money. I wanted it all and I wanted him.

Motionless, I sat in front of him, not really knowing how to deal with what I was feeling. His mouth was on mine again, his lips were hungry for more than just blood. Reaching up with one hand, he pulled my shirt away with a single motion of his wrist.

Still not moving except the heaving of my chest, which I couldn't stop despite my best efforts, I felt his arms reach around my back. The cool skin of his chest grazed mine for a millisecond as he unhooked my bra easily before pulling the straps slowly off my shoulders as he leaned away from me.

I felt totally exposed and I tried to look away from him, but he grabbed my face, holding it in place. Feeling a deep flush start at my cheeks and spread down onto my neck and my chest, I could do nothing but stare back at him. His eyes were so piercing that I couldn't even shut mine. I had never felt so ashamed as I both hated him and wanted him at the same time.

His hands grasped my breasts, kneading them harshly and I watched as he leaned down and lightly licked my left nipple. I jerked and my back arched, pushing my breast farther into his mouth. I felt a slight sting as he lightly bit, his eyes never left the single thin line of blood as it ran down my body. I felt its warmth tracing down the contours of my abdomen and I tried to brush it away, but he caught my hand in his first.

Pushing me back into the carpet, he started where the blood trail ended on my lower abdomen and used his tongue to follow its path back up to the wound on my breast. Wrapping his tongue around my breast again, he gave one long draw before he moved on to the right side. Again he bit me lightly and then began swirling his tongue around my nipple until it was hard and firm. I continued to arch to him against my will. Lacing my fingers through his shoulder-length hair, I tried to hold him where he was and he didn't fight me.

My entire body ached with desire for him and the knowledge that something was wrong didn't change how badly I wanted him. I shouldn't have been responding to him like this, but I couldn't stop. Worse yet, I didn't try to stop.

When he pulled his mouth away, I gasped and arched my back towards him again, begging him to help me. To put an end to this hunger that was eating me from the inside out.

Dropping his full weight on me, he fanned my hair out around my head, exposing both sides of my neck. It seemed his mouth was everywhere simultaneously. I couldn't keep track of where he was or where he was going to be next. He alternated between soft kisses and sharp nips as he touched every part of my skin. He drew blood many times, but could have only taken small amounts since he moved on so quickly.

My skin tingled wherever his mouth touched me and soon there was a tingling line all the way down my belly. My skin burned with desire for him; wrapping my legs around his body, I tried to force him to me as the hunger continued to gnaw away at my sanity.

When he returned to my mouth, I wrapped my tongue around his. I wanted to consume him, so strong was my hunger. His desire seemed much more urgent now and I was dizzy with lack of oxygen when he finally lifted his mouth from mine.

Grabbing my hair once more, he pulled my head to the side. His mouth was hot from the heat of my blood and I felt his fangs serrate my skin more deeply this time.

With each bite and each beat of my heart, the hunger surged through my system more strongly than before. I could feel it spreading across my breasts and then down my abdomen and into my legs, all the way to the tips of my toes.

Bucking against him, I begged him again to finish this, to help me, but instead he pulled himself away from me and my grasping hands. Taking my neck in a firm hold, he lifted me slightly off the ground. Arching my breasts up to him again, I struggled in his grasp.

He was laughing now and although it registered he was laughing at me, at that moment, I simply didn't care.

"What is it, Annalice? What do you want?" His voice was mocking but did nothing to stop my desire.

Breathless, I tried to answer. "You, please. I can't take it anymore. Please."

"Who do you belong to?" His full lips smiled down at me as he asked.

"Why are you doing this to me? I'm yours. Please just end this. I know you can." I was breathless after only a few words.

Reaching for him, I pulled his mouth back to mine. I could taste my blood on his tongue and I bit him in return, grazing his tongue with my teeth. He pulled away abruptly as a small drop of his blood hit my tongue.

Still holding me slightly off the ground, we stared at each other for a millisecond before I was suddenly shoved back down into the carpet. Pushing my thighs apart, he pushed into me so hard that I thought my hips would dislocate.

Wrapping my legs around him, I pulled him in to me as deeply as I could. He was hard and thick and I struggled to pull him in further. His strokes were long and slow to begin with, but quickly became harder and more rhythmic.

I orgasmed at least three times before losing count. Sinking his fangs into my neck, he came forcefully into me. With his culmination of pleasure, I lost all rational thought as my mind floated in a haze.

I felt no pain at all from his bites, it was as if my body was under the control of some stimulant and every sensation had been converted into pure pleasure.

My hands were on his back and I could feel the muscles contracting along the length of his spine before he collapsed onto me. As I lay there underneath him, his chest against mine, he drank slowly from my neck. I could hear and feel each swallow. His lips were soft against my skin and the intimacy of it was almost overwhelming. This was singlehandedly the most erotic moment of my life and the muscles of my legs shook with the after-shocks.

Opening my eyes with the cool rush of air against my bare skin as he pulled away from me, I found him staring at me, an amused expression on his face.

"I told you it would be nice," he observed as he rolled away and then was gone.

Not moving for several minutes, I lay on the carpet as the high slowly wore off and the shame at what I had just committed came over me. Like a crackhead coming down, I thought to myself as I ran my fingers through my very disheveled hair. I had behaved just like a crackhead. And the sensation hadn't gone completely away with the orgasm. Hunger and thirst still hovered at the edge of my thoughts along with the desire for him.

Reaching down to grab my clothes, my eyes took notice of his clothes lying beside mine. Dropping my t-shirt back onto the floor, I surreptitiously grabbed his while glancing over my shoulder to make sure he was nowhere around. I could hear the shower running from my bathroom and so I turned my attention back to his clothes.

His thermal t-shirt was soft like it had been worn many times, but it was clean and the tag was from a very expensive store. Grabbing his jeans next, I hastily ran my hands down into each pocket finding nothing except a couple of hundred dollars bills and a ten. There was no identification of any kind. No license and no wallet. No keys. Not even any scraps of paper.

"Find anything interesting?" His voice unnerved me and my hands flew up slightly causing me to drop his jeans. The money floated down to the floor.

I could feel my face flushing with embarrassment as I turned to face him. He was standing in the door of my bedroom, water running in rivulets down his naked chest and abdomen to catch in the very low-slung towel.

"J...just trying to find out your name," I stammered back at him. Looking down at the floor so my eyes wouldn't hang up on the dark hair trailing down to parts of him that I couldn't get off of my mind, I grabbed my clothes and walked towards the bathroom, feeling the need for a shower as well. He was gone from the doorway when I made it there and I was again wondering where he was and how he could move so fast.

Opening the bathroom door, I was brought up short at the sight of his pale skin through the glass shower door. It's just not every day you find a vampire in your shower.

It was the first time I had truly seen him, without his clothes on that is, in normal lighting. He seemed oblivious to my presence so I took the opportunity to study him

From where I stood now, he looked human. His skin was most definitely pale, but not such that it would stand out in casual passing. Physically he was in great shape and had the appearance of a man who had been accustomed to hard work, with tight muscles and essentially no body fat. He appeared to be in his late twenties as there was not a touch of gray in his hair and his skin was unwrinkled. Remembering his body on mine, I could feel the flush of shame crawling across my face again.

What had he done to me? It made absolutely no sense at all that he could create that response in me no matter how good-looking he was or how skilled he was at sex.

Basically a scientist at heart, I considered my response from a clinical standpoint. I doubted that it was any kind of hypnotism or outside mind control. But something had definitely happened.

My skin still tingled wherever his fangs had penetrated as did my mouth and lips. Was there something in his bodily fluids? Reaching down, I could feel the evidence of his climax and I even tingled there. I didn't have any time to consider it further as he stepped out of the shower. My face flushed again when our eyes met.

I'm sure my reaction to our encounter wouldn't be considered normal by any stretch of the imagination. I couldn't even take any solace in believing that I had been forced after the way I had responded. It was almost as if I had taken a neurostimulator like dopamine or something. And then it hit me. I had acted EXACTLY like a crackhead, or a meth head, or a sex addict, or an alcoholic, or a gambler.

Or all of the above.

"I do love a good shower," he declared offhandedly, bringing my attention back to him as he reached into the linen cabinet for a towel. The bright red of the towel against his skin made it appear even paler. For the first time, I questioned why I had picked such an obscene color for my bathroom décor.

"I rarely occupy a human home, but I certainly make use of the shower when I do. One of the greatest inventions of the human race, if you ask me," he noted as he continued to towel off.

"What's your name?" The words were out of my mouth before I realized I had thought them let alone spoke them. He hesitated momentarily before continuing to rub himself down. If I hadn't been studying him so intently, I probably wouldn't have recognized the hesitation.

"I have no name. Names are unimportant." He didn't answer any further.

"Really. Then why did you ask for mine?" I continued. He grinned slightly at the edge in my voice. His answer was irritating and I couldn't keep the tone from creeping in.

"I already knew it, Annalice, just as I knew about Ellie and your mother's whereabouts. The name itself is unimportant but you telling it to me is a sign of submission. A sign that you recognize my possession of you. But I have no need of a name as you possess nothing of me."

With the silence broken, it was easier to persist. "I just need to call you something. You must have had a name when you were human."

At the mention of his former living state, his face froze in an angry scowl for a split-second before answering. "You will answer me, not call me." Turning scornful eyes on me, he whispered silkily, "Unless you plan on moaning it into my ear later?"

His sarcasm was well played and I felt myself get hot again from the intensity of my embarrassment and I dropped my gaze as I couldn't stand the humiliation any more. When I opened them, he was gone.

Angrily I threw open the shower. When I stepped out twenty minutes later, I felt a little better. After putting on clean clothes from my closet, I went back into the living room. The lights were on and he was sitting on the couch, flipping through one of my magazines. The activity was so ordinary that it seemed surreal.

Looking up, he placed the magazine down and leaned back into the couch. "My name was Asa. I suppose it will do no harm for you to know it."

Asa, I repeated it in my head. Not a name I had commonly heard. "How could it possibly hurt for me to know your name?" I couldn't help but ask.

Sighing softly before speaking, he finally answered, "I often forget how you humans today think. It is one of the reasons I choose to spend some time with one every few years. When you live as long as we do, it is easy to become outdated. It can happen in only a few decades. I have not taken a companion since the late eighties so you should feel honored I have chosen you."

Pausing with a smirk on his face, he waited for a reaction,

which I didn't give him and so he continued on. "Names are quite powerful. Humans today do not seem to realize that your name is a window to your soul. However, since I am lacking a soul, I suppose it can do me no harm for you to know it. It was a nice name, do you agree? My mother named me after my uncle. Do you know what it means?" He looked at me questioningly.

Seeing me shake my head no, he continued on. "It means healer or doctor. My mother took a lot of pride in the names of her children, mine especially meant a lot to her since it belonged to her youngest brother. She placed it upon me at birth, hoping it would imbibe me with the spirit of charity and mercy. I certainly turned out to be a great disappointment. Therefore, I rarely use it but please feel free to call me by it if it makes you more comfortable." He made a small bow in my direction as he returned to his magazine.

"Superstitious, huh?" I murmured absentmindedly while walking towards the kitchen. "I would say that puts you being born at least before the 1930s." Trying to act nonchalant while I probed for information, I waited expectantly for an answer that never came. When I turned around, he was gone without even a footstep.

Hunger was still gnawing at my insides and the main thought on my mind now was food and something to drink. It occurred to me that he probably had plans for me that didn't entail eating so I should eat when I could.

The reaction to his bodily fluids hadn't completely abated. It was weaker for sure, but my every appetite was still raging stronger than it should be even given my current situation. Despite my disgust at my previous reaction, I knew it would take little action on his part to have my knees quivering again.

Since it seemed likely I would end up on my back again, I took the opportunity to search for something to eat before my stomach ate through itself.

Certain that I was dangerously anemic, I searched for something both quick and high in iron. Finally giving up, I reached for the peanut butter again, a reasonable choice.

Pulling up one large spoonful after another, I ate each one as quickly as I could while mulling over some questions that were eating at the back of my mind. The main question being why did I not feel worse than I did?

For someone who had probably lost four or five units of blood, I didn't feel half bad. A little dizzy, but otherwise I didn't really have many symptoms.

Turning it over in my mind, I ate at least a quarter of the peanut butter and was still not full. Then it hit me again. I was still like a crackhead. It all came back to his spit. His bodily fluids must also contain adrenaline-like substances in addition to neurotransmitters. That's what was keeping me going. He was injecting me with a stimulant every time he bit or kissed me.

But why? What benefit did that provide to the biting vampire? Did it help keep the victim alive so they could be a victim longer? Was it protection for the vampire in some way?

Lost in thought and pondering this question, I was still eating peanut butter when the fine hairs rose on the back of my neck and traveled down my spine. The terror didn't make it to my knees this time before I was able to bring my mind under control. Turning around slowly, peanut butter jar still in hand, I was face to face with my attacker again.

Standing only a few inches from me, his presence was nearly overpowering and it took my constant attention to keep my breathing steady.

"I had almost forgotten about feeding you, I was so interested in feeding myself. Where should we take you to eat? I know you could prepare food, but let us not waste the night and I doubt this," he stopped for a moment to pull the jar out my hand, "will keep your strength up. I will feel cheated if you do not survive the week. Besides, being out in public with you will also give me the opportunity to study the humanity around me."

As hungry as I felt, it sounded like a good plan to me. "OK," I quipped quickly and grabbing the keys to my car off the counter, I walked out to the garage with him following behind me.

Walking to the passenger seat, I tossed him the keys without any warning. Just as I expected, he caught them without any effort but with a puzzled look. Since he was clearly used to being in control, I had expected him to want to drive.

"I never became proficient at driving," he noted, walking to the passenger door and tossing the keys back to me, which I just barely caught.

"Why not?" I asked, shocked that anyone, vampire or human, had never learned to drive.

91

"I have never seen the point. My movements are much more discreet and less traceable without a car."

Getting into the driver's seat, I motioned to his seat-belt out of habit. He looked a little confused, not knowing what I was trying to point out. Leaning over across him, I pulled the strap across his waist and buckled it into place. My hand was still on the buckle and our proximity was close.

In a split-second, his hand was on the back of my neck, his voice low in my ear. "Your concern is so kind."

Aiming my most condescending look at him, I replied, "I'm not that kind. I would actually like to see you go through the windshield but it probably wouldn't kill you. And I don't want to get stopped and watch you kill a cop. So put it on. Please?" I added hastily as he raised an eyebrow at me and I remembered who was in control.

SIX

It was about thirty miles to the nearest restaurant, one of my favorites. Putting the windows down once we were on the main road, the wind blew through my hair and cooled down my tingling skin. I felt so much more free whipping around the curves that weaved through the darkened mountains, even though it was an illusion. I was still a captive, but the cedar smells of the cold forest we were driving through combined with the breeze off the mountain took it off of my mind to some degree. The night was cool but not cold and it would have been a great drive if he hadn't been sitting beside me.

Turning up the radio that was tuned into an old seventies station, I drove faster than I would normally have done. Usually I was a calm driver. With Ellie depending on me, I always tried to play it safe. Maybe that weight was somewhat lifted off of my shoulders because I had done everything I could for her.

My fate was up to Asa now. If I died in a car accident tonight or by a vampire's fangs in a few days, the difference was minimal. And so for the first time in my life, I let the horses underneath the hood of my Camaro really run.

It was exhilarating. My captor never said a word, just sat staring out the window as we twisted sharp turns one after the other.

Unfortunately, the road leveled out and my short-lived feeling of freedom came to an end, but on the flip side that meant we were closer to town. My stomach was aching as we pulled into the parking lot. I was sure I had never felt so hungry in my entire life. The restaurant was a sight for sore eyes.

Asa indicated with one finger towards the most distant end of the parking lot. Pulling into darkest corner, I shoved the gear shifter into park and walked quickly to the front door of the restaurant, not bothering to see if he was behind me. I knew he was, I could feel him back there.

Ellie and I spent as much time around these tables as we did our table at home so I automatically headed towards one of the more comfortable ones that I was used to in the back of the restaurant. It was quieter back there and I often sat there when I was on call so my pager wouldn't annoy the other guests seated at the tables around me. I didn't bother to pick up the menu as I knew it by heart. One of my favorite waitresses, Lisa, waved as we sat down and immediately headed in our direction.

Feeling self-conscious for no reason, I pulled my hair down around my neck hiding the no-longer existent puncture wounds and smiled in return.

"What'll it be?" Lisa asked as she made it to my side of the table first.

"I'll take a quarter pounder, fries, and a large diet coke. No wait. Bring me the real thing." I ordered the first cravings that came to my mind.

Lisa laughed. "That's not usually on your diet." She was

looking at me a little incredulously.

"I've been donating blood recently so I have free reign to eat some protein. I'm just following orders." I laughed back at her.

"For you, sir?" Lisa asked, turning her attention to Asa.

"Water only. I did not donate any blood today." The vampire smiled politely at the waitress.

"Sure thing, I'll get the order in ASAP." Lisa, turning on her heel so that only I could see her face, gave me a wink and mouthed, "He's hot," as she headed into the kitchen.

Lisa had taken care of Ellie and I for at least two years; she was one of the few waitresses that survived the high turnover of the restaurant. It crossed my mind, but only briefly, to get her attention about my predicament. Better not bring her or anyone else into this, although I was sure she had gotten a good enough look at Asa's face to give a description to the police when the investigation into my death began.

That thought took me a little by surprise. How would it happen? Would he drain me and leave my body in my house or would he destroy the evidence? I hadn't given this any consideration. Which would be better for Ellie, to have a body to mourn, or to live with the one-in-a-million chance that I could still be out there somewhere?

A body to mourn, I decided. It would hurt more to begin with, I suspected, but it would end quicker and she could get on with her life.

The need to know his plans became intense and I couldn't quit thinking about how I would die. "Are you going to leave my body so my family can bury me, or are you going to bury me somewhere and leave them wondering about my fate? I need to know." The force in my voice brought his eyes quickly to my face, away from the other people he had been studying.

"I cannot leave your body, drained of blood for the authorities to find, of course. I never leave evidence of my existence for anyone to find," he explained indifferently and then turned his attention back to the other patrons in the restaurant.

"What about Ms. McElhaney? What about her body?" I retorted just barely above a whisper.

"I did not drain her. Her death appears no different than any other brutal assault. But you... You, I will drink until not a single drop of blood can be expressed from your veins." His voice was low and matter of fact.

His nonchalance angered me and it took all of my control to keep my voice level and low. "My daughter will need closure. No one is going to find my body and say to themselves, 'A vampire crime! I knew it. They do exist.' Surely if you're going to drink my blood, hold me hostage for a week, and finally kill me, you can have the decency to leave something for my family to bury. Make it look like I cut myself or fell or something!" I hissed the words at him.

His hand suddenly crushed mine underneath the table hidden by the lacy cloth covering it. His reflexes must have been lightning-fast because I never saw him move and I doubted anyone else did either. I bit my lip at the pain.

"Do you not yet realize that your life and your daughter's

D . L . A T H A

happiness in the scheme of my existence mean nothing? Your human life is like an evaporating mist. A blip in my long life. And besides, I have no decency! Your family will be blessed to be alive. I give them nothing more." His anger took me by surprise after his feigned civility. I knew he was a monster, but I had temporarily forgotten.

We were staring at one another intensely. At that moment, Lisa walked up to the table with my order, thankfully, and he released my hand, giving me the chance to break our eye contact. Looking down at my hand cradled in my lap, it was already starting to swell and the shape of his fingers could be seen in a blotchy red pattern on my skin.

Lisa had always been perceptive, knowing just by the look on my face if I'd had a bad day at the hospital. She placed my plate down quietly on the table. Reaching out, she touched my shoulder. "Let me know if you need anything else, Annalice."

Looking up, I made eye contact with her. "I'm good, Lisa. Thanks." I gave her my best "everything's fine" smile that I usually reserved for hospital administrators. I didn't want her becoming collateral damage. She had two little kids herself.

After she had walked to a neighboring table, I tried to focus on eating. Luckily, the hamburger wasn't so big that I couldn't hold it with one hand. Realizing again how famished I was, I tried to ignore the monster beside me and focused instead on the food. He had resumed studying the faces in the restaurant.

The hamburger was heavenly and I ate every little crumb then started on the massive order of fries. I never ate fries, it was like eating a small heart attack, but what did it matter now? I wished I had eaten more of them over the years. Draining my coke, I signaled for a passing waitress who stopped to refill my glass. I drained it again and waited on another.

Lisa passed back by this time with another Coke. "You want some dessert? We have key lime pie tonight, since you're splurging?" she asked, taking my empty plate and setting the ice-filled glass down on the table.

"Yeah, I do. Bring me a piece to take home too, Lisa. OK?"

She looked at me in amazement. "Wow, you must have made some kind of donation!" She laughed as she walked away.

"You have no idea," I muttered to myself.

We sat in silence as I ate. Dipping a French fry into a large pile of ketchup, I sucked the ketchup off before chomping down on the fry. He eyed me speculatively with raised eyebrows, but didn't say anything. He must have expected me to be repulsed by anything that remotely looked like blood.

"So do vampires eat any food at all?" I asked as I waited for the pie, pushing the rest of the fries away.

His voice held annoyance when he answered. "Why do you ask these questions, knowing that I am going to kill you? Do you think by acting interested in me I will decide to spare you in the end? Do you think you are the first human that has feigned an interest in me to try to save their skin?"

"Do vampires have no curiosity?" I jabbed back. "And I promise that the 'you're going to die part' hasn't escaped me."

The silence resumed as I waited for my dessert. I could find nothing else more interesting than him in the room and so I let my attention fall on him completely. He seemed to be staring off in space, not in my direction, so I took the opportunity to appraise him head to toe again for the second time, but this time with his clothes on.

I have to say, he really looked human. No one in the room, I noticed as I surveyed the crowded restaurant, was paying us any attention other than the occasional female whose eye he caught in a quick lustful glance. He didn't stand out in any odd way, he was very handsome, but other than being very fair-skinned, he didn't look scary or overtly threatening when his fangs were hidden. But I knew from experience he could easily turn that side of himself on or off at will.

Tonight he was wearing a dark blue thermal pullover with stylish blue jeans and boots. I hadn't noticed before but he was wearing a ring on the fourth finger of his right hand. It looked silver but it could have been platinum or white gold and the design, nearly worn away, was unrecognizable to me.

Several locks of his hair had fallen back across his eyes, adding to his absurd sex appeal as it gave him a look of innocence. I noticed he caught the eye of every woman that walked by our table on her way to the restroom. Apparently, a couple of the women needed to use the bathroom several times during the course of my dinner.

I had a thousand questions for him and I was burning with curiosity now that I had resigned myself to my death. Why should he not answer my questions? I could see no harm in it.

Feeling my eyes on him, he turned his regard back to me. "Fine. What do you want to know? I will answer a few of your questions. A few so you better make them good ones. It seems you are going to stare holes through me if I don't. But make no mistake, I am not going to become sentimental about you. You may come to know me, think you understand me, and I will still kill you. It seems a cruel trick to play on yourself."

"Don't worry. I have no illusions about you, just questions. I'm a doctor, you know. Very practical and naturally curious especially about scientific anomalies such as yourself." I spoke quietly. He laughed slightly and with a slight bow of his head, he prodded me forward. "How old are you?"

Taking a slightly deeper breath as if this question annoyed him, he answered, "I was born sometime in the year 1831. I died in 1858." The smile that was on his face moments ago was now gone.

" Why does that question bother you so much?" I questioned in between a long draw of my soda.

Giving a slight sigh, he answered, "It is inevitably one of the first questions a human will ask. It gets tiresome after a while. You are all so predictably obsessed with age. Surely, Doctor, you can come up with a more interesting question."

As any woman in her thirties can understand, that answer was irritating to say the least and I sighed back at him. "For someone who will never age or die, don't you think you're being a little judgmental?"

By that time, my second pie had arrived and deciding to go ahead and really splurge, I sank my fork into it with a little force, throwing back a large bite before saying anything else. "I thought you needed me to help update you on the twenty-first century. Is that really true because you haven't asked much of me except for blood and sex?" I grabbed another bite of pie and waited for him to answer. He didn't answer immediately so I continued on. "How many humans have you held hostage, killed, and why do vampires have sex anyways, and why would you possibly care about remaining up to date?"

He was staring at me now like I was insane. "You are quite morbid for a human and you are certainly the most brazen hostage I've ever had. Perhaps that explains why you have no mate at your home."

Did he mean that as a jab or was that just an observation? Raising my eyebrows at him, I waited for answers.

Tapping his right index finger absentmindedly on the table, he began. "Can you imagine what it is like to exist in a world that is ever-changing but never change yourself? I was born in a time of lamps and candles where the world went to sleep with the night. Then I became a nightwalker and learned to live in the night, in a land of darkness by becoming part of the night and blending into it. And now you humans have lit the night up. At first, it was just the occasional dim lighting in the homes of the wealthy, but now it is entire cities and sometimes I feel like I cannot escape the light. And now, you have even recreated the sun."

He paused here for a moment when the waitress refilled my drink again. When my glass was full and the waitress gone, he continued. "I am a nomad but every few decades or so, I realize that I have become so outdated that I must make contact with a human to remind me of our differences and why I will never be like you again. To learn again how you think and act. I fear that at some point in the future, the night will no longer provide shelter for my kind as it will be as brightly illuminated as the day." He stopped now, studying various people in the restaurant again and I waited, but he didn't resume.

"How many? Human hostages that is?" I questioned, my voice urging him to continue.

Raising his eyebrows slightly, he brought his lips together in a little smile before responding. "At most, I have revealed my true nature to less humans than I can count on two hands. I killed each one of them. These deaths I remember specifically, but as to how many humans I have killed in my existence, I do not keep a record. I do not have to kill to feed and so I do not always kill. If I had not found you in such isolating circumstances, chances are I would have drank a little and you would have lived, if I had even chose to feed from you at all. But you were too convenient. You can thank your choice of housing for your death."

I supposed the old saying 'mother knows best' certainly

fit here. I cursed myself mentally again for my lack of practicality.

His voice brought me back to the present. "Now before you decide that I have a conscience after all, you need to know the only reason I do not kill every time that I feed is simply that I do not want the authorities to become involved. And there are plenty of times that I kill simply for the thrill of it. Although it is unlikely they would find me, I do not see that it is worth the risk."

He paused here as the waitress that replaced Lisa came to place the ticket on the table. Reaching into my purse, I pulled out some bills and handed them to her, indicating that I needed no change so she wouldn't come back. When she was gone, I nodded for him to continue.

Smiling at me suddenly, he leaned in close. "As for sex, lust is lust whether it is for blood or sex. We carry the same desires from our human life into our vampiric life. Combine our lust for sex and blood and you have a powerful stimulant. Essentially, they are the same to us. It is hard to have one without the other. But you already knew that, Annalice, since you fucked me like a common whore today with your blood on my tongue."

His eyes were intense and I could clearly see the desire on his face. I felt a flush explode on to my cheeks. I would like to say it was solely because I was embarrassed, but unfortunately I could also feel my own lust for him kick in. It didn't provide me with any affirmation of my character.

Standing quickly to gain some distance from my own lust, my chair scraped roughly on the concrete floor, balanced precariously for a moment, then finally crashed to the floor. A hush fell across the restaurant as if someone had dropped an entire serving tray. I could feel Asa's eyes on my face.

Looking down at him, I could see anger that I had brought attention to us evident in his expression. Smiling politely at the surrounding tables, I turned and walked out to the car. I didn't hear his chair move or him get up but by the way my skin was crawling, I knew he was behind me.

We were about twenty feet into the parking lot before he jerked me around and delivered a resounding slap to my right cheek, sending my head ricocheting backwards. Knocking me to the ground, I didn't have time to catch my breath before he had jerked me to my feet again. He was so angry that he was shaking slightly. Glancing around the parking lot, I was happy to find no witnesses either to the abuse or the sad state that I was in. I, at least, wanted to die with some dignity left.

"Now you worry about making a scene, but I know there is no one around; no one to see us because I have already checked, because I am not a weak stupid human," he hissed at me, pulling my face around to look at him. "Are you truly committed to this, Annalice, because I have my doubts? Maybe you are not as committed to your daughter as I thought." His voice was low but harsh.

Trying to apologize, the words only half-way came out, such was the force of his grip on my face. He didn't listen, but instead began to drag me towards my car.

We had parked on the edge of the parking lot, my Camaro pulled in facing the restaurant, and behind it nothing but a grown over lot. Despite my fear and having learned my lesson, I didn't fight as he pulled me across the desolate space, bypassing the passenger door of my car.

Sure that he had lost all patience with me, I was certain he would kill me now. Although I didn't fight, I couldn't keep from crying and he wrapped a strong hand around my jaw, muffling my tears.

A few steps past the door of my car, he swung me around, forcing me across the trunk. A moment of relief washed across me as I realized he wasn't dragging me into the bushes to kill me. The relief was short-lived when it occurred to me he was going to put me in the trunk.

Unable to control myself, I begin to cry harder and even his hand couldn't muffle the sound completely and so he slapped me again.

Losing consciousness briefly, I came back to myself just as I felt the fabric of my panties rip as he jerked them off of my body. My pants were already down around my ankles and I was still bent across the hood. In my surreal state, I could see the restaurant a hundred feet away or so and it was like I was looking at a different world, another reality.

I could see people leaving the restaurant, smiling and waving goodbye to their friends. No one looked or even glanced in my direction as he knocked my feet apart with one foot and I didn't try to get their attention. I had made enough mistakes for one day.

I wasn't prepared or ready for him this time since we had exchanged no saliva, but still he pushed into me with force enough to cause me to cry out if I had been able to breathe.

His weight constricted my respirations to the point that I was forced to focus solely on breathing as he stroked forcibly into me.

Tears continued to roll down my cheeks as he took me against my will. Pulling my hair to one side, he bit into the back of my neck. I could feel blood run in a small rivulet down my back as his strokes got faster and faster. Finally, I felt him stiffen and the car shook slightly with his orgasm. As he stepped away from me and was no longer holding me up, my legs gave way and I sank down onto the cold pavement, my knees striking the ground hard.

Kneeling down beside me, he whispered into my ear, "You asked the questions. If you do not like the answers, quit asking. I am giving you a second chance, Annalice, because I need this and so far you have been a fun date. But I suggest you not make mistakes like that one again."

Shaking like a rag doll, I was finally able to nod at his back as he walked around the car and out of my line of vision. I heard the passenger door open, then felt the car settle down with his weight. Using the bumper, I pulled myself up and resting against it, I pulled my jeans back up as well.

Taking a deep breath, I let myself have a moment to calm my trembling hands before rejoining him in the car. It was going to be a long ride home both from my humiliation and the now-familiar hunger, induced by his fluids, setting in.

We did not speak as I pulled out of the parking lot onto the highway and as each mile rolled under the wheels of my car, the silence became heavier until I felt I would suffocate under its weight.

As I had expected, the trip was longer and lonelier. Maybe it was that there were fewer cars on the highway, making it seem darker. Or maybe it was knowing that I was again leaving all semblance of normal behind as I returned home to my reality now. Blood and violence.

At some point, I had started to think of each day as a number; day one and so forth. I was fast approaching day two. It was about midnight now and there were only four more days for me to live.

I continued to drive, turning off on the lonely dirt road that would eventually end in the circular drive at my house. No words were said by either of us so it gave me plenty of time to think.

My mind continued to stray back to the fact I would be dead soon. I didn't think I was morbid, surely most humans my age would be thinking as I was. My past life now seemed so short and I thought about all the things I would miss. Mainly, Ellie growing up, her first prom, first boyfriend, graduation, choosing a college, her wedding, and finally, her children. Every time I thought of Ellie, it was with a mixture of regret and jubilation that even though I wouldn't be with her, she would be alive and allowed to grow up.

And try as I might, I couldn't help but feel the loss over the things I would never get to do. My twenties had been spent pursuing medicine and then in raising a child and building a medical practice. There had been no time for many outside interests or romance, hence my divorce, and

107

now there never would be.

I looked over at the man beside me. No, not man Vampire, monster, aberration. I'm not usually a person of much hate, but I hated him. I hated him with every ounce of me. I hated him for taking me away from my daughter, for putting me in this position, for raping me, and making me want him.

I had done nothing to deserve this. The rage boiled inside me and it felt like I would explode from the intensity of it. I almost felt like I could touch the emotion shimmering along my skin like currents of electricity.

For a split-second the rage was so intense that I forgot how weak I was compared to him and considered reaching over and breaking his neck. But Ellie's face flashed in my mind and that is what saved me. I tried valiantly to push the rage to the back of my mind and after what seemed like an eternity, I managed to control it enough that my heart began to slow its race and the currents of electricity I felt running along my skin stopped.

"What were you thinking that made your heart race?" he asked, breaking the silence. I was surprised since I had been the one asking all the questions this evening.

My first impulse was to lie, but what did it really matter? I doubt he would be concerned that I wanted to kill him. He had probably grown used to that reaction over the years.

"Well, honestly, I was thinking about all the life I was going to miss out on and how I wanted to kill you. I'm sure you have had life enough for the both of us and it's simply not fair."

I heard his low throaty laugh but didn't turn my head to look at him. I knew he would be wearing that condescending smile.

"You could not kill me. I am immortal. An unfair match for an ordinary human. So far, you have done well at accepting your lot. Except for that little mistake at the restaurant, but I taught you a nice lesson for that, right? It is what it is, Annalice. Do not forget what you are getting in return for your compliance." He spoke into the quiet of the car. "Let us make this civil, Annalice. No drama or theatrics. It can be pleasant and I can promise you a painless end."

I had nothing to say back to him, but I supposed I should be grateful that he was promising me a quick end.

I made the final curve in the road and the house stood eerily in the moonlight. Pulling into the garage, the heavy overhead door let down behind us. I felt like I was pulling into a crypt. I knew his gaze was resting on me. I could sense it without even looking over at him, but I couldn't stop myself and turning towards him, my eyes locked with his. The hunger was easily visible and that was the best word to describe it. He was hungry again.

Jumping out of the car, I hurried towards the door. I, at the very least, wanted to be in the house before he fed again and not pinned down to the seat of my car.

Just as I was topping the last step into the house, his hands wrapped around my neck, jerking me around and throwing me back across the hood of the car. I slammed into the metal and the force caused me to instinctively close my eyes for a split-second.

Opening them, I found myself looking into his dilated gaze. His nostrils were slightly flared, lips parted and pulled back over the doubled fangs that were fully extended. They glistened even in the semi-darkness of the garage.

Taking my left wrist, he brought it up to his mouth and kissed the inside gently. Then, holding my hand in his other hand, he extended my wrist joint and bit cleanly through to my radial artery. Though it is a very sensitive part of the body, it hurt only for a few seconds.

He drank more deeply this time, long swallows over about a minute. Dizziness began to cloud my mind and I dropped my head back on the cold smooth metal of the car. He brought his head up and a drop of my blood escaped the corner of his mouth, his tongue flicked out to catch it before it dropped.

Leaning down, he whispered into my ear, "You are going to be a hard one to keep alive. You bring out the worst in me. I doubt you will last the week. Sleep well, my dear." In the next moment, he was gone.

I lay there on the hood for a few moments, partly because I was too weak to move and partly because I half expected him to come back. But he didn't return and finally I let myself slide down the hood until my feet were touching the floor. Taking a few seconds to steady myself, I walked into the house.

The old wall clock struck one just as I walked into the living room. My heart paused in its beating as I was so startled. Exhaustion was all that forced me to make it to my bedroom and I collapsed on the bed. I was asleep before my head even touched the pillow.

SEVEN

I dreamt of the sun. Bright, hot and shimmering. I had never seen it so vast or brilliant. The sky was a deep gemstone-blue and the golden orb took up at least a quarter of it with no clouds to shield the Earth from the power of its rays. It was mid-July or at least from the slant of the sun on the creek water and its intensity, I thought it was mid-July. The creek wound lazily through the Ozark mountains, the deep green of the trees reached up from the cliffs overhanging the water to touch the sky, creating the illusion that the world consisted of only the river in the valley, the trees, and the sun. There was no noise from the outside world and I lay back on the hot rocks that had been baking in the sun all day.

It was almost painful yet I enjoyed the sensation after climbing out of the cool water of the creek. The heat dampened by the water worked out the kinks of my muscles brought on by swimming after Ellie. We had made two trips back and forth across the stretch of water running between two sets of rapids and I was tired and sore.

She was a good swimmer and although I listened intently while resting on the rocks for her laughter as she played with Samuel in the water, I wasn't actually worried about her. She was like a fish and had been swimming since she was two. The world always seemed perfect when we were here.

Opening my eyes, I trailed the edges of the cliffs. Unbroken by anything except vegetation and the occasional cedar tree that grew precariously in the cracks marking the cliff surface, I saw nothing out of place. But still I searched. For what, I wasn't sure but inwardly, I knew something wasn't right.

Sitting up, I scanned the surface of the water as I realized the sounds of her laughter were gone. A pit opened in my abdomen through which the entire creek could have poured. Starting to panic, I again ran my eyes over the cliff edges out into the distance until I could see them no more.

Instinctively, I knew the water wasn't the danger and jumping to my feet, I ran to the water's edge and dove in. Needing to reach the cliffs, I swam with as much power as I had but, as usual in a dream, rather than cutting swiftly through the water, it was like swimming through molasses. I finally made it to where the water and the cliffs met. Reaching up and catching hold of a crooked cedar, I pulled myself into a path cut through the cliff by the slow trickle of a millennium-old stream.

We had climbed it many times in the summer when the stream had dried up at its source from the power of the sun. This time of year, the moss had dried out and the footing wasn't terribly slick. Somehow, as in most dreams, I had a sense of the terrible lying ahead yet couldn't stop myself from following it. I couldn't stop this nightmare from occurring even in my own mind.

I continued to scurry up the slope. Grasping at every

small tree or shrub that presented itself, I managed to pull myself to the top and haul myself over the edge. Winded but now standing on the cliff, I went back to scanning the windblown edge, this time with a bird's eye view.

West to east, I strained my eyes and finally saw her. Standing with her back to the edge of the diving cliff, her long soft tresses blew gently in the breeze of the sunny day. Here, the cliff arched out over the creek, a local jumping spot for lots of kids over the years. It was a short fifteen-foot drop into the creek at one of its deepest depths as long as you dove out far enough.

But I had no fear of the dive. My fear was of the animal I knew she faced. Her arms were pulled up defensively in front of herself and one leg was positioned farther back as if she might turn and dive at any moment. Starting towards her, I stopped abruptly as I realized the sun was gone from the sky, replaced by the cloudy gray skies of a February day.

Looking down from the cliff's edge to the water, the placid waters had been replaced by the river's winter current. Strong enough to carry vehicles from bridges and drown the most able bodied swimmer foolish enough to test its strength. The warm balmy air was gone and now felt cold against my still wet skin and swimsuit.

Looking back at Ellie, I hurried towards her and what she faced so defensively. Knowing what it was, I was unable to put it into words, to make myself think the word. Making my way across the distance standing between us, I stepped out to reach for her on the diving rock. "Ellie, take my hand," I cried out above the wind. But she remained frozen on the edge of the rock.

Looking around, I still couldn't see what had frightened her so terribly, but when I faced her again, I felt the terror rise up in me as well. The same hair-raising fear that had become a part of my life now and I couldn't even dream normally.

It was him, the vampire. Turning back to Ellie, I reached out to her with my hands, not allowing myself to stroke her cheek or one lock of her hair for fear I would cling to her.

"I love you. Forgive me and forget me." Smiling at her one last time, I jumped forward and shoved her off and over the cliff edge. Instinctively, she turned in midair and dove neatly into the gray churning waters below.

I wasn't afraid for her for I knew she was in no danger now, and leaning over the cliff edge, I watched my beautiful daughter dive into the now sun-kissed summer waters of the river. Without looking back, she rolled over onto her back and looked up into the blue July skies. She was laughing as she swam back to a waiting group of friends where they picnicked with my mother on the heat-soaked rocks.

I laughed with her and paused for a moment before turning my back on the tranquil summer scene back to the dark and miserable cold day that awaited me. Wet and shivering, with gray skin and blue fingernails, I faced the damp sunless skies and the vampire waiting at the tree line.

I awoke, clammy and cool with the cold sweat of a nightmare to the point that even the low setting of the ceiling fan rose gooseflesh on my skin. I lay there unmoving for a moment, hoping my memories of the images would finally take on the quality of a dream and lose some of their reality. It didn't happen.

The dream had brought to my consciousness what my mind had not dealt with until now. I had seen Ellie as she would be in a few months when I was gone from her life. Would she understand? I doubted it, but the images of her playing happily in the water gave me some peace that even if I wasn't here, her life could and would go on.

I desperately needed to say goodbye to her. Somehow. But exactly how I would accomplish that I couldn't yet decide. I knew I couldn't call Ellie. My mother would answer and she could pick up trouble a mile away. She would know that something was terribly wrong and she would come. I'm a bad liar and I couldn't fool her. But somehow I had to find a way.

And I wondered if it was a purely selfish need or would it help Ellie as well? It would be risky and I needed to think it through more clearly. I still had three more nights.

Right now, I needed to focus on surviving the day and that was going to take nutrition and possibly a blood transfusion. I laughed inwardly at the thought. I bet that would throw him off a little. Reaching for the bedpost immediately before standing, expecting to have to steady myself after the amount of blood I had lost during the night, I caught it in my right hand but discovered quickly that I didn't need it. I felt pretty good. No dizziness or nausea this morning and no tired muscles.

The only bad sensation was a mild ache in the bones of

my legs and chest. I must be making new blood cells, I rationalized to myself. Confused but not wasting much brain power on how well I felt, I headed into the bathroom to take care of the necessities and get a shower.

After rinsing off in the hottest water I could tolerate as it took the edge off of the bone pain, I stepped out and dried off. I slipped fresh underclothes on and then followed them with crisp scrub pants and a V-neck tee and headed back into the bathroom to brush my teeth.

My mother had always touted the importance of a clean mouth in the worst of situations. It was her firm belief that brushing your teeth could improve your outlook on any situation by at least fifty percent. It was a belief I shared and so after squeezing a generous amount of blue paste onto my brush, I brushed with fervor as I considered my situation.

I was working hard on the left lower teeth when I noticed again how unscathed the skin of my neck was. Lifting my wrist up to look at the most recent puncture wound, I inspected it under the bright light of the vanity. No trace of his penetration of my artery, not even any bruising. How was that possible?

As an ER doc, I knew trauma inside and out and bruises have a fairly predictable timetable. I should have had bright bluish purple contusions yet looking in the mirror, there were none. No puncture wounds, no bruising, and no redness. Yesterday I at least had bruises from where he had thrown me around. Now those were gone as well.

My skin was perfect and as I remembered back over the last two nights, I realized there had been little posttraumatic bleeding. I sat down on the edge of the tub and began pulling a comb through my hair. It was long and the events of the night had left it so tangled that the water hadn't even made much of a dent in the knots. Lost in thought about the lack of bruising and bleeding, I pulled the comb slowly again and again through my disheveled hair.

How did he puncture a vessel, drink free-flowing blood, stop the bleeding, and heal the tissue? There had to be a scientific explanation, I was sure that it wasn't magic.

Drinking free-flowing blood was the easy part. Leeches and ticks did that all the time. It was a protein in their spit. The medical field even used leech saliva therapeutically when patients had clots.

But reversing the process had to be trickier. His saliva had to contain an anticoagulant to keep the blood from clotting and a protein that was activated secondarily to clot the wound, as well as growth hormones to repair the damage.

But why would his body go to that much trouble? Evolutionarily speaking, DNA was not altruistic. There had to be more benefits to his spit for him.

I continued to think about this as I put the comb on the bathroom counter and walked into the kitchen to find something to eat. Pouring a large glass of milk and grabbing a left-over muffin from a few days gone by, I sat down at the kitchen table and continued to mull over the possibilities.

Clearly biology begets survival of the species. So how did this help him? I was now pretty certain his fluids also contained neurostimulators. Blood coagulation, tissue growth hormones, and neurostimulants no doubt allowed the prey to live longer, requiring fewer victims and therefore the ability to blend in more. My theory still seemed to be missing something, but I couldn't seem to put my finger on what that missing element was.

Walking into the living room to rest my overactive mind, I slumped onto the couch. When you're a prisoner in your home, you realize how boring a place it can be. Even in this roomy old house, I felt as if the walls were closing in on me.

Absentmindedly and out of habit, I reached for the remote. Looking at it in my hand, it occurred to me I had lost touch completely with the outside world. A war could have been going on and I would have had no idea.

Flipping on the TV, I hastily turned to one of the national news channels, jabbing at the next channel button when any image of violence popped up. I just couldn't take that right now.

Finally landing on the news, I had seen all of the national headlines in ten minutes. Nothing too exciting, just the usual stuff and just as violent as the fiction so I turned to Discovery Channel. At least people probably weren't going to die in front of my eyes.

Tossing the remote control down, I just sat there for a few minutes lost in thought. Something in the dialogue on one of the educational channels caught my attention and I listened intently to a Ph.D. discussing how the Internet was changing the face of American civilization.

The Internet. I hadn't even thought about it until now. Not a huge web surfer, I had let it completely slip through my mind. I doubted Asa would be checking my search engines. He probably didn't even know how. Perhaps others out in the real world knew something about vampires. Getting up quickly, I hurried to the computer and pulled up my favorite search engine.

At first, I typed in vampire and blood-clotting. Forty three thousand hits. I spent about an hour going through the first sixteen pages. Mostly it was about vampire bats and their ability to keep their prey's blood from clotting. Nothing that helped me very much.

Deciding to try a less specific search, I tried vampire. Over three million hits. *I certainly don't have that much time,* I thought irritably to myself. I spent another couple of hours and only got through about one hundred pages. Again, nothing much of any value. Usually my eyes gave out after that much time on the Internet but today I gave up first, deleted my search, and went back into the living room. My eyes felt surprisingly good, but my bones were still aching.

It was about three in the afternoon. Glancing around at the taupe walls, I felt more claustrophobic in the house. I really needed to get outside for a while, but remembering his warning, I decided the sun room might be a safer alternative.

Grabbing a drink as I passed through the kitchen, as dehydration seemed to be my constant companion, I went to the opposite end of the house and walked into the glass-enclosed room. I had always kept the blinds closed when the room wasn't in use for energy purposes, but also the exposure from all of that glass always made me a little nervous at night.

Reaching the cord for one of the blinds, I gave it a strong tug. The vertical blinds turned quickly and the dimness gave way suddenly to extreme brightness. Sharp pains stabbed at my eyes and I clasped both hands tightly over them, my eyes squeezed shut behind the palms of my hands.

Slowly, I moved my hands and opened my eyes cautiously, adjusting to the light. I had never suffered from light sensitivity before now. My head ached at the sudden onslaught of what to me was the most brilliant light I had ever experienced.

Finally after several minutes, I was able to open the other blinds, forcing myself to endure repeated episodes of the stabbing bright light each time. I was desperate to feel like I was outside in the sunlight even if it was just an illusion.

I sat staring out the windows with my eyes squinted, wishing I had some sunglasses. I couldn't remember where a pair was off the top of my head. My bones were aching harder now and I couldn't convince myself to get up and look for a pair.

Did the ache in my bones and the sudden onset of sensitivity to sunlight have anything to do with the vampire? It seemed likely since I had never had a reaction like that to the sun before. I stretched out on the wicker couch thinking about everything that had happened to me. About the puncture wounds that disappeared and the fact that I was actually feeling better than I really should be after all of my blood loss. The neuro-transmitters were obviously doing their job.

Lying on the couch, my eyes fell on the crystal handle of the ceiling fan that turned above me. Ellie had picked it out at the local hardware store, laughing at the facets glimmering in the overhead lights of the store.

Catching a ray of the sun, bright light reflected suddenly into my eyes, causing me to turn my head suddenly into thick cushions on the couch while my stomach lurched at its brightness. "Great, I'm turning into a vampire," I groaned out loud to myself.

In the span of a couple of seconds, all of the missing pieces fell into place. The biology of his saliva now made perfect sense. The point was to keep the prey alive long enough to convert them. Most of the victims would die, but occasionally one would make it through to become a new vampire. Maybe I was the one.

Vampires had once been humans according to all of the legends I knew. Was it possible that I was becoming a vampire? According to the common myth, it was the vampire's bite that turned a human. Was that happening to me?

I had a sudden burst of hope. Not that I wanted to be a vampire because that couldn't be less true. But if I did become like him, would I not at least stand a chance at surviving him? As a human, I had essentially no hope of standing against him.

Would I rather be a vampire than be dead? I could watch Ellie grow up, at least from a distance. Would I still think of her as my daughter? Would I look at her the same or would I be the same soulless creature Asa was?

Did he choose to be this way or did it come with the territory? Had he given up his soul to become what he was and would I do the same by choosing that life?

For surely, if what I was postulating were true, I would need to increase my exposure to him. It would be a conscious decision to become a vampire. I would have no excuse in the afterlife if the rumors of vampires and their lack of souls were fact and not fiction.

I stayed there on the couch attempting to logically think through the hundreds of questions that were turning themselves over in my mind until I noticed by the waning light that the sun was beginning to set. I slipped off of the wicker divan and moved to sit right in front of the largest window. The room had been lit by the natural light only and I made no move to turn the lights on, but continued to sit in the dark as I had the night before.

I couldn't see the setting sun as the sunroom faced south, but I watched as the shadows grew across the yard and pastures until they weren't just outlines of the forms in the yard but overtook the forms themselves, their previously distinct lines blending into the darkness. A few stars appeared in the sky. I didn't know which direction Asa would come from, but I stared intently into the dark, hoping to catch a glimpse of his return to my house and my life. I needed and wanted to learn more about him.

My night vision was stronger as I could distinguish more characteristics farther out in the pasture than I had ever been able to before tonight. I did catch the movement of what looked like coyotes near the tree line and even thought

I saw a rabbit hidden in the taller grass at the junction of the lawn and the pasture. But I saw no movement from Asa nor did I sense he was in the house yet.

I continued to sit looking out the window, contemplating my possible conversion to a vampire, convinced it was a scientific event. I was sure that there was nothing magic about the process and the most reasonable explanation was that this was a viral process.

As he had bit me, he had spread the virus through his saliva. The virus spread from one cell to another, that's why it was not an immediate conversion. Possibly a retrovirus, one that incorporated itself into the human DNA, forever changing the person into essentially a different species.

Wouldn't Asa know what was happening to me? Had he ever spent a long enough period of time with a human to allow the conversion to take place? From our previous conversations, I knew he was pretty superstitious and I suspected that viral genetics weren't his strong point.

But obviously he had been turned so he had to know how it happened, right? But if he knew I could change, why would he be taking the chance? Wouldn't it have been better to just kill me and move on quickly? Or was it possible he didn't know how he was changed? And this was as new to him as it was to me.

Waiting now had a new edge. It was still fear but now with a touch of anticipation. Hoping to beat him at his own game, doubt played simultaneously with the possibility of survival on the edge of my mind.

Could I really beat him physically? Emotionally, he had

the upper hand on me and even if I was turned before he killed me, he had age and experience on his side.

Information became a priority and I vowed to myself to find a way to draw it out of him, and tomorrow I would spend more time on the Internet. Surely back in the recesses I could find something to help me. Where there was fiction, there had to be fact.

The dining room clock struck seven, bringing me back to the present. He still wasn't here and I began to get nervous. Was he not coming? What would happen if he didn't? Maybe he had moved on. Had I been inoculated to the degree that my immune system couldn't recover and I would still turn? I had so many questions and no answers.

I left the sunroom and walked back into the kitchen, grabbing a couple of colas as I passed the fridge. I downed one quickly, carrying the second in my other hand. Regardless of what happened, I wouldn't have to count calories any more. I smiled at the thought and drank the second soda just as quickly as the first.

Having nothing to do but wait, I walked aimlessly through the house. Ending up in the den, the piano caught my gaze and I had the sudden urge to play it. Sitting down, my hands flew over the keys to a few popular songs. I hadn't played in a few days, but despite the lack of a warm up, I played with pretty good precision. Must be a side-effect of the virus.

I was half-way through a metal ballad when I experienced the familiar terror the vampire brought with his presence. The hairs on my neck and arms stood up; my sixth sense knowing that the predator was behind me. My hands stopped in midair and my breathing, as well as my heartbeat picked up, and I had to fight to bring them under control.

Letting my hands drop back onto the keys, I resumed my playing knowing that he hadn't moved. I could feel his gaze on my back, but didn't stop until the song was over. Slowly I turned around and found him sitting in a period piece of furniture.

The chair, which had come with the house, was an antique and most of my friends who had sat in it found it to be very uncomfortable. Asa, apart from his clothes, looked like he belonged in it. We sat looking at one another for several moments but didn't speak.

Finally, I turned back to the piano and played one of Chopin's Nocturnes. Night music at least seemed appropriate for him. As I played the piece, I contemplated how to become more exposed.

I was fairly certain, or at least as certain as one could be about vampire physiology, that his saliva contained the virus. No doubt his blood did as well. Probably every bodily fluid did to some degree, some fluids holding higher viral concentrations than others.

Finally, I decided the best course of action was to simply be exposed to as many bodily fluids as possible. How to seduce a vampire became the million-dollar question.

Just thinking about it made me nervous. I slowed the tempo of the nocturne to give myself more time to devise a plan. My hands were sweating and my heart was pounding.

I was sure he could hear it; I could almost hear it myself.

Luckily Chopin had spared no paper on this piece and its length gave me time to get ready for what I was about to have to do.

I could still feel him behind me although my hair was at least no longer standing on end, but the sensation that his eyes were burning straight through me and my scheme remained. He would surely realize what I was doing, but it wasn't exactly like I had anything to lose. There was only one way to find out and so playing the final chord of the piece, I turned slowly around to face him.

Sitting on the piano bench, I stretched my legs out in front of me and leaned back on the keyboard, pulling my arms up to rest beside me. I flashed what I hoped was a seductive smile at him. "You're late so I thought maybe you had moved on." I had a fleeting wish that I had put on something more appealing as the scrubs certainly left much to be desired in the wardrobe category.

His face held that smile of his that was both sadistic and seductive at the same time. "I had to stop and eat first."

He smiled even more when he said it so I guess my face showed a little of the surprise I felt. So he had already fed? That had to be a really bad sign, but it almost seemed as if he was baiting me. I decided to play along.

"So I guess that means I get a night off from being the main course?" I asked as nonchalantly as I could while I turned back to the piano, trying to act disinterested. But he was beside me before I could finish turning and pressed my back up hard against the keyboard.

"Tonight you are the dessert. I am in no hurry for the next three evenings to come to an end so I really must be careful."

"I think slow is what I have in mind as well," I murmured, to him as I leaned in to him, lifting my face to his. Pressing my lips to the coolness of his, I kissed him gently, but made it clear what I wanted. Reminding myself mentally of my goal, I pushed him back into his chair, placing my arms on either side of his head.

Parting his lips with mine, I ran my tongue over his lips and then over the tips of his fangs. Tasting sweetness on them, I suppressed as a shudder as I realized that the sweet taste was his newest victim's blood.

Sensing in his body language that he was about to bite me, which would cut my exposure too short, I pulled away and began to trail light kisses down the right side of his neck as he whispered into my ear.

"You must have enjoyed our time together. Can you not wait to experience that again? I must have left you wanting more," he murmured into my ear.

"I want some more all right," I whispered, continuing my onslaught of his throat and switching to the other side. Stopping only long enough to grasp the hem of his shirt, I pulled it off quietly laying it on the floor beside us.

Not taking my eyes off his body, I kissed along his chest, following the line between his pectorals. His skin was cool to the touch, but when I looked up, I could see the growing lust in his eyes. Feeling it in my bloodstream as well, I knew I would soon run out of time, and I would be as hungry as him.

Leveling my most sincere expression at him, I told him, "I decided if I'm going to die, I might as well have as much fun as possible. I've been single a while and I had forgotten what I was missing."

Placing my lips back on his, I kissed him as languidly as I knew how. "The other night was amazing," I whispered into the pale skin of his neck as I finally broke contact. "I'm not sure how you were able to do that. I was terrified, yet I couldn't stop myself."

He laughed slightly, low and throaty, at my comment. "It is my bite. It drives human women wild. And the more I want them, the more they want me. Practically begging me to kill them."

His words repeated in my mind. He was right in a way, except it wasn't the bite. It was the saliva again. Pheromones or sex chemicals, whatever they were, they allowed women to experience his desire and orgasm. Pretty impressive spit. I remembered that I had begged a little too the first time.

His hands were everywhere now and although he hadn't bitten me yet, I knew that his growing excitement was leading that way and I couldn't help but shiver slightly with the anticipation.

Reaching back up, I entwined my hands in his thick hair again and pulled his mouth back to mine. I slid my tongue quickly and harshly across his left fangs, creating a small gash that quickly oozed salty blood.

I felt the change in him almost instantaneously. The semi-control that he had commanded over himself moments before vanished as quickly as I had spilled my blood in his mouth.

I massaged his neck and shoulders while I straddled him, his lips warming to the temperature of mine until I felt I couldn't tell where I stopped and he started. The kiss became harder and more insistent, his tongue curling around mine. And as I expected, the cut continued to bleed although slowly because of how small it was. I had done the right thing as he couldn't pull his mouth away from mine.

Pulling away from him as the cut finally sealed over, I could now see his fangs more clearly as his lips were pulled back for the first time tonight. They were more extended than they were earlier. I couldn't look away from the sharpness of them as he lifted my right arm to his mouth.

As he kissed the inner aspect of my elbow, chills started at my neck and raced down my back. I shivered in expectation despite myself. His arrogance concerning human women was well deserved. Still watching me, he pierced the soft skin overlying my brachial artery and I gasped at the pain. Several drops ran down my right arm and landed on the ivory piano keys below, brilliant red against the sharp white. He brought my other arm up and did the same thing. There was a quick sharp pain with each bite, but now his pheromones had reached critical mass in my cerebral circulation and all thoughts of pain, or anything else for that matter, were gone.

My blood flowed like a gentle tributary down both arms and he followed it with his mouth, consuming it as he made several smaller bites along its path. Reaching up with one hand, he easily pulled my t-shirt apart at the seams. I was wearing a newer red bra. I had thought of the irony when I pulled it out of my closet. It accentuated my skin nicely. He sucked his breath in slightly.

"How I love that color," he murmured to himself. Pulling it slowly off of my shoulders until my breasts slipped out, he dropped it to the floor with one hand while he cupped me with the other.

He removed my panties just as easily and lifted himself off the chair to push his pants down. My eyes slid down his muscular abdomen. Pulling myself up on him while I looked up to watch his face, I slid myself down the length of him. He gasped slightly and I did too as a thousand nerve endings seemed to catch fire internally, spreading down my legs and simultaneously up into my lower abdomen. Starting to move up and down, I had only just begun when I climaxed so thoroughly that I had a few heart palpitations.

Certain that the enhanced sensations were part of the conversion process, I questioned whether or not my circulatory system could handle the change. But I didn't have time to consider it long for he started to move himself. His strong strokes brought me to climax over and over until finally, with quite a bit of force, I felt him shudder and come inside of me. When he was finished, I nearly collapsed onto him and without thinking, I rested my forehead on his shoulder. I half expected him to flinch from my unintentional casual contact, but he didn't and I continued to rest. For the first time, I noticed he had a scent. I hadn't noticed it before. He smelled somehow manly and spicy at the same time. Always suffering from allergies, I had never had a particularly strong sense of smell, but apparently that was changing now.

Sitting up, I took in a deep breath through my nose. I could smell the scent of sex and the slight mustiness of the old house. Smells that I had never particularly noticed before tonight. Glancing down at him, I saw he was looking at me intently.

"You made me lose my breath. I'll be okay in a couple of minutes," I lied, telling him the first plausible excuse that came to my mind.

"I have that effect on humans. I always make them lose their breath, one way or the other," he replied with a slight smile on his face. Then he pushed me off into the floor. Hitting my head on a nearby bookcase as I fell, my vision tunneled. I tried to hang on, but lasted only a second or two and then everything went black.

EIGHT

I awoke not immediately knowing how much time had passed. Finding myself in a different room than where I last remembered was very disconcerting and it took a few minutes to reorient myself.

When I finally recognized I was in my bedroom, I sat up and swung my legs down. My feet touched the carpet and shock caused me to jerk them back before they were even flat on the floor. A multitude of increased sensations had burst onto the soles of my feet and I was unprepared for the heightened sensorium. I had never realized how thick and soft the carpet was and putting my feet back down, I ran them back and forth through the carpet until they were warm from the friction.

I recognized the now familiar warm stinging sensation again in my mouth and now enveloping my throat and continuing on down into my abdomen, almost like I had swallowed whiskey. I reveled in the sensations for I knew I was making progress.

Getting up, I walked into the living room and found Asa intently studying my cell phone. I had a moment of panic before I realized that I hadn't called Ellie.

Looking up at me as I walked towards him, he pointed towards the phone, saying, "Teach me."

I nodded slightly, feigning disinterest. My head hurt and I

wanted to scream at him for throwing me on the floor, but I was so happy about the ongoing conversion that I was able to hide my anger at least momentarily. I taught him the basics in a matter of minutes, my heart dropping as he realized how much could be hidden on a phone. I wasn't surprised when he crushed it easily in his hands.

I sounded almost cheery when I told him, "I didn't have anything to hide, Asa." Smiling at him, I put the cell phone in the trash and began to look for the car keys. "I'm absolutely starving. Can we go eat?"

Looking at me reprovingly, he asked, "Do you not eat during the day? You should be keeping your strength up for me."

"Thanks to my new vampire hours, I party all night and sleep most of the day, and besides, I'm not much of a cook. So, come on, let's go eat, please. I mean, let me go eat. That way, I'll have plenty of energy for you to suck out." I smiled at him as I said it and he gestured towards the door but didn't look happy about it.

Grabbing a jacket off of the back of a chair, I folded it over my arm, still feeling too warm and tingly to put it on. Walking into the garage, I was surprised to find Asa waiting at the driver's door of my car.

"Tonight, I am going to refresh myself with driving," he told me, "but I forgot to get the keys."

Sighing, I took one last look at my car while it was still whole and tossed him my key ring. Sliding into the passenger seat was a new experience. It had been a long time since I had ridden with anyone else, let alone a vampire.

I gave him directions to a city located in the opposite direction from where we had previously gone. He didn't want us to be seen together repeatedly by the same humans so I chose a steakhouse to the north side of the county. But by the looks of things, we were never going to make it there.

"We're as slow as a funeral procession," I groaned out loud, but mostly to myself. I must have really been developing a morbid sense of humor because I laughed out loud at my unintentional joke. "At this rate, we won't make it by dawn and you'll burst into flames in the sun. Go ahead, slow down some more."

Continuing at his snail's pace and still never even sparing me a quick glance, he muttered, "You humans act invincible, which makes no sense given the fact I can snap your bones with one hand." His voice held a shade of anger.

Now it was my turn to be snide. "For someone who's invincible, you drive like you're made of glass," I retorted back at him.

"You ARE made of glass so be careful," he shot back, making it clear he was tired of my driving commentary.

Silence ensured as we made our way through the mountains. Coming to a straight stretch as we exited the foothills, I gestured at the two-lane road that would lead us into town. An old country store, just about to close, marked the turn off.

I was angry, restless, and emotionally labile which seemed a new constant for me. "Please pull in here. I'm so thirsty, I don't want to wait till we get into town. It's a pretty long drive still," I tried to ask politely, but it sounded a little strained. I wasn't used to having to ask anyone's permission for something as simple as a drink.

Surprisingly, he did what I asked without saying anything. He very carefully parked and reaching for the door handle, I started to get out of the car but before I could, he pulled me backwards into the seat.

"Do not draw attention to yourself." His voice was hard and the grip he had around my arm was even harder. He wrapped one strong hand around my neck, cutting off my breathing. I nodded with as much movement as his grip would allow. Slowly, his hand relaxed and pulling my arm out of his grip, I stepped out of the car, slamming the door angrily behind me.

This old store had certainly seen better times. The building was squatty but long. The interior had never been well lit and the paint on the walls might have been bright forty years ago. Now it was dingy and the old concrete floor was cracked with age. But with age sometimes came nostalgia and that is what had kept this place open through the years. A woman in her mid-seventies sat behind the counter appearing to be oblivious to my presence, but I knew better. She had, like any blue-haired southern woman, eyes that wouldn't miss a thing.

I walked up to the counter with two twenty-ounce sodas and a couple of candy bars; she rang me up without saying anything but the amount. I handed her a ten and she counted out my change.

Never making eye contact but instead unnecessarily

bagging my snack food, she asked, "You need any help?"

I cringed slightly at her words. She must have noticed our exchange in the car.

Drawing attention to my situation hadn't been on the agenda for the night and I did my best to sound calm and reassuring as I answered. "No. I'm good. We were just playing mostly. But thanks." I could tell she didn't believe me, but there was nothing else I could do so I wished her a good evening and walked back out to the car.

Asa was still sitting in the car, with the windows rolled down and the engine off. I knew he had been listening to see if I had said anything to the clerk.

Getting into the car, I twisted the lid off of one of the bottles and drank until I had emptied over half of the bottle without stopping.

"You seem exceptionally thirsty," Asa commented, studying me too intently for my taste.

"Well, I have to replace my blood volume. I'm just being careful so I don't get dehydrated. I don't want to shortchange you," I told him before starting to drink again.

Starting the car, he pulled slowly back onto the road and drove towards town. I finished up the bottle of pop and started on the second while downing a candy bar. He was right. I was extremely thirsty and hungry. I had also felt shaky over the last few hours, a symptom of low blood sugar. Pretty certain that my body needed the extra sugar for the cellular conversion, I ate the second candy bar too.

Having eaten two candy bars and two sodas, I felt full for the moment. Getting food off of my mind for the first time in a while, I suddenly realized how claustrophobic I was. I so badly wanted to stretch my legs and get outside for a little while. "Do you mind if we stop for a little while so I can get some exercise? There's a hiking trail up ahead that goes into the mountains that would let me stretch my legs. The restaurant will be open for a while."

He shrugged his shoulders in indifference and I pointed out the trail as we got close. Stepping out of the car as soon as Asa had parked, I reveled in the slight breeze blowing in from the mountains. Reaching up, I rubbed the back of my hand across my forehead; I was startled to find I was sweating and my skin felt a little warm.

Realizing I was running a fever, I considered turning back to the car, but instead pivoted to face the trail into the mountains, not wanting to give Asa any cause to suspect anything other than anemia was bothering me. Taking a deep breath, I rubbed a few chills off my arms with my hands and began walking.

The cool breeze lifted my hair off my neck as it trailed down onto my back, causing chills to race along my skin where the light sweat had built up. My heartbeat had increased slightly to the point it was just at the cutoff to be called a true tachycardia. My joints and muscles stills ached slightly, but I forced myself to walk fast enough to not slow my ascent into the hills.

I knew this trail well. It was one that Ellie and I had climbed many times. Part of the Ozark Highlands Trail; it would eventually take us to a large overhang that was big enough to camp in. Legend said Native Americans had lived here and by the looks of the place, I had no doubt. A workout on a good day, I struggled to climb quickly enough that Asa wouldn't recognize my weakness, but his perceptive ears were my downfall.

"Your heart is racing." He made the statement with a tone that was accusing, which caused my heart to race even more with fear that `he recognized what was going on.

My stomach dropped to my knees. Of course he would know. That's why every other human companion he had in the past had died. They were never allowed to complete the conversion.

Not planning on giving up, however, I stopped in the trail and turned to face him. "Of course my heart is racing. I'm walking up a mountain with very little blood. That's also why I'm sweating and breathing heavy. For someone who's killed a lot of humans by exsanguination, you sure don't seem to know the signs."

Crossing my arms across my chest, I tried to look exasperated as I waited for his response. Although he was walking about twenty feet behind me up the trail, he now caught up in the blink of an eye.

"I kill so quickly that there is no time for signs," he intoned with his unblinking gaze leveled at me.

"What about your other 'companions'?" I asked, making quotations in the air with my fingers. "Didn't they get weaker the longer you stayed?"

He had walked past me now and I turned and had to hurry to catch up to him, which accelerated my breathing even further.

"They were not as lucky as you," he answered back and then was gone. I couldn't see him or hear him and so I stood in the path for a moment not quite knowing what to do. Finally, I decided to just keep walking. It felt so good out here in the cool of the night that I vowed not to let him ruin it.

"Lucky my ass," I muttered under my breath as I resumed my walk.

The path was rocky but thanks to my newly enhanced night vision, I was able to make my way a little better than I would have in the past. I followed the trail around until I came to the Indian cave; heading inside its damp coolness, I rested until my heart rate had dropped a little closer to normal.

The muscles in my legs grew somewhat stiff as I sat there so I left the cave and continued on the trail. I kept walking without seeing a trace of him again. Coming to the vista at the peak of the mountain, I sat down on a rock and focused my vision on the points of light out in the distance. About twenty miles away, I could see the lights of several towns. Even at this height, they still looked fairly bright; maybe it was because of the contrast of the dark black of the mountains.

I was lost in thought when I felt the hairs on my neck and arms raise, accompanied by the pure terror of his presence and I knew he was there. Not having breath to spare on him yet, I didn't speak. Honestly, I had little to say for once. The night was beautiful and even though I was technically dying, I could still enjoy it. I didn't want his mouth or mine to ruin the peace of the moment.

Of course, that didn't last long but for once it was the vampire that broke the quietness. "My former human companions died fairly quickly. I realize now it was most likely because it was too much of a mental and physical strain on them and they were unable to adjust. It is likely you will die more prematurely than I desire as well, although thus far you have outpaced them all. I wonder why that is?" He was looking at me while he spoke.

I could feel his eyes on my face so I turned to look at him. "Maybe you should make an effort to not knock me unconscious by throwing me to the floor or consider not wrapping your vice-grip hands around my throat. That might increase my shelf life."

Laughing at my words, he answered back, "I suppose if I want to keep you around for much longer, I will have to be more careful with you. So I shall endeavor to not throw you around or choke you. As far as blood drinking goes, I will attempt to slow it down a little too, but unfortunately that just comes with the territory and at least I will get pleasure out of that sort of death. I would not derive nearly as much enjoyment if you simply hit your head and fell over dead. But tell me, why do you want to live longer? Why have not you just given up like the rest? You are going to die so how do you find the strength to go on with this charade?"

Turning towards him, I found he was staring at me with wide dilated eyes showing true interest now like I was the weird freak in a science experiment and not him.

"Tell me about the rest?" I asked, as interested in his

response as he was in mine.

"You first," he insisted, "and if your answer satisfies my curiosity, then possibly I will answer your question."

Honestly, his questions didn't deserve answers, but this charade, the one I was living now was my only chance. I nodded at him slightly, indicating my intent to play along. "This so-called charade is my life and therefore I don't intend to waste any moment of it. Even if those moments are with you. Besides," and I gave him my most serious expression, "I'm still trying to find a way for this weak human girl to kill you." I ended my words with a smile, hoping to make him think I was just joking, but I couldn't have been more serious.

"Now it's your turn. What about the rest? What happened to them?" I asked, desperately wanting to know. "You said you killed them all."

Leaning back against the trunk of an old oak tree in the dark, he now had all the appearances of a vampire. With his pale skin that stood out in contrast to the dark of the night, he looked slightly eerie. His eyes looked almost empty they were so dilated, and his mouth, so red in the lighting of my house, looked dark in the night, giving him a very leering smile.

"Yes," he nodded slowly, "all five of them. My first was a young man, an attorney. I was crueler to him than the others. I think it was my great jealousy at his station in life, the same one that was robbed from me. He broke under the stress within the first two nights and tried to escape."

He laughed a low menacing laugh and rubbed his hands

through his hair before continuing on. "He went during the day and I had to track him. This was before automobiles so it only took four hours, but I was furious. So furious that I took my time with him. He did not die well, which was good for me. I needed the release."

Anxious to try to learn something from his previous conquests, I settled back into the hard curve of a rock and listened.

"My second was a woman. Beautiful and delicate the way wealthy women were back then. It was the 1880s. I found her along a small river in Louisiana. She had slipped out of her father's house for a moonlit dip one summer night with her young man. Unfortunately for her, I beat him there. I did not bother to wait around for him. I will never forget her pale skin, nearly as pale as mine, against the dark blue of her satin gown. There was nothing she could really teach me; I just wanted her. I carried her back to a crypt where I had spent a few nights. I promised not to kill her suitor if she would cooperate. And I kept my word; I did not kill him, although he probably would have preferred it. I remember seeing a picture of him in the paper, he swung for her death.

"I tied her up and gagged her just before dawn every day. She was perfectly safe in the crypt, but I came back after the first evening to find her babbling. Her mind never came back so I snapped her neck a couple of nights later. Her blood was still good though. The madness had no affect on the taste." He paused here with an amused expression on his face.

It was all I could do to not choke at his last words. He was definitely superstitious. That poor girl. I could commiserate with her terror. At least I was trapped in my own house and not some wet, rat-infested crypt.

It was getting chillier now and even my low-grade fever couldn't keep me from feeling it. Noticing for the first time that he was wearing a jacket, I looked at it enviously, my own jacket forgotten in the car.

"Can you feel the cold?" I asked, pulling him out of his thoughts.

"It does not feel cold to me, but I can detect the change in temperature," he answered back.

"Then why do you wear a coat?" I turned to look back down at the valley below.

"That is a foolish question, Annalice. Why wear clothes at all? Except to fit in, of course. I would look odd, do you not think, if I were dressed inappropriately in February?" For once, his voice didn't hold complete contempt even though his words did.

Leaning forward, he slipped his arms out of his jacket and handed it to me. "I can see that you are cold."

I reached for it willingly as I was starting to get pretty chilly. "How chivalrous of you," I murmured quietly, sliding it over my shoulders and pushing my arms through the sleeves. It was fairly large and I pulled it tightly around me. Looking up at him, I caught a quick flash of anger on his face, but then it was gone just as quickly.

"Not to let you think that I am being kind, I just do not want you to catch your death of cold. I would much rather deliver it myself." His voice was like silk when he said it, but was it possible that I had just seen a moment of actual kindness?

"So tell me about the third," I asked, trying to get him back on subject.

"Again you are really very morbid," he noted, turning to face the view from the mountain. "Of all the humans I have kept, I will admit that you are the most entertaining. The third was another young man. It was somewhere around the twenties to thirties. I was in Oklahoma. Cars were not quite common yet and the Great Depression was going on, so the law was lax and drifters were so frequent that no one looked at me that peculiarly when I walked the night. I had been traveling most of a month, going nowhere in particular, when I came upon this small ranch one evening sometime after midnight. It was owned by this very handsome young man. He was not wealthy, but not poor either. A very eligible bachelor during that time period.

"He was gone when I arrived and I helped myself to his bath while he was out. You should have seen the look on his face when he stepped into his bedroom and found me lounging on his bed. I played with him for a while, letting him think I was mortal. He fought quite admirably. He pulled a gun and shot me, at which point I fell down. I am a pretty good actor when I want to be and I let him walk up on me. I kept my eyes open and kept perfectly still until he leaned in over me. I am sure you can imagine what happened next."

I looked over at him when he stopped talking. I most

certainly could imagine what had happened next and in my mind's eye, I could see the look on the man's face when he realized his shot may have been true but his reality was not.

"How long?" I asked quietly.

He shrugged. "Just a few days. Long enough for him to teach me how to drive, use the telephone. Things like that, you know, the necessities of the time."

The light breeze picked up slightly and chills raced across my skin, which was burning up now with a raging fever. My head and throat ached from the viral process and every joint in my body throbbed with pain.

"What did you do to him?" I asked, not because I wanted to know, but it would keep my mind off the pain and might help keep me resolved to see this through to the end. No matter what that might be.

"Why do you want to know? How does it help to torture yourself like this?" His exasperation was obvious in the tone of his voice.

"You say you don't care so why do you mind telling me?" I retorted, just as irritated.

He laughed bitterly now. "How correct you are. Fine. He begged for mercy, but that is just not in a vampire's character." He paused now and my breath caught in my throat.

"Breathe, Annalice, I did not torture him. He was obedient to our agreement so I showed him what mercy I was capable of, which was to kill him quickly. I drained him and buried him in the hills of his homeland. Torture affects the taste anyhow."

"But not enough mercy to spare him? He couldn't have hurt you. Do you realize that?" I asked, unable to keep the emotion from my voice. I could picture all of these poor people just like me and I was angry for all of them. I hurt for all of them. The loss of their lives and now mine seemed terribly unfair. His low voice broke the train of my depressing thoughts and despite how badly I felt for his prior victims, I couldn't keep from turning my attention back to our conversation.

"You humans come closer to finding out the truth behind every mystery each year and with those truths, the power to do something with the knowledge. I cannot chance letting anyone know of my existence. That is just the way it is. Surely your analytical mind can understand that."

Despite how much I wanted to deny that truth, I couldn't. If I were him, I wouldn't want anyone to know about me either. But I hoped that I wouldn't become the monster he had let himself become.

"Yeah, I guess I can. I can't say that I understand why you need to kill them. It's your decision to spend time with them and let them know what you are. You could get the same information by pretending to be human and developing relationships that don't end in their death," I answered, trying to keep my voice calm and even since I suspected my words were a little inflammatory.

"You hypocritical human. Humans drone on and on about being accepted for what you are, including all of your faults and flaws, but you extend the same courtesy to no one else. Your governments even try to rewrite history to hide the evil that your race has committed and you judge me for wanting a few meaningless humans to really know who I am, what I really am!"

His voice was razor-sharp with anger brought on by my answer. And although I didn't move for fear that my slightest movement would put his rage into action, I couldn't control my tongue.

"I don't answer for all of humanity. I answer for myself and take responsibility for my own decisions. It seems that you should do the same." I half expected not to finish my sentence before he ripped my throat out, but to my surprise he simply sat there, listening.

"Responsibility is a quaint human concept that no longer applies to me. I am not a human. I am a predator and predators do not question the need to kill. We simply do it."

I didn't say anything back to him after that for quite a long while. Honestly, my fever was too high and I felt slightly nauseated. That along with the ache in my bones kept me silent. I had no idea what kept him silent and, honestly, I just didn't care so long as he was.

Leaning back again into the crook of the tree, I stared off into the view from the mountaintop. Small pinpoints of light could be seen scattered throughout the mountains and off in the distance, groupings of lights representing the small rural towns could be seen trailing through the mountains, until ending in a bright area representing the city we had been heading to when we stopped at the country store.

I watched the lights now starting to glitter slightly through the fog that was developing in the valleys below. It was beautiful up here and I couldn't convince myself to leave. The thought of going back to my prison made me feel even more ill deep down in the pit of my stomach.

"Fifty years ago, that valley would have been darker than the night at this time. I would have never dreamed it would have become this popular." His voice coming from the darkness and combined with his stillness seemed disembodied and it startled me. It was the first time he had offered information without me begging it out of him.

"What became this popular?" I questioned. My curiosity was really going now and I looked at him intently.

"Electricity. I still remember the first time I saw it. I had gone to the World's Fair in Chicago and these brilliant lights were strung up through a village that had been built inside the fair. Back then, the lights had more of a golden color and they were beautiful. Looking back on it, I realize the lights were not as bright as I remember, especially compared with the lights of today. But at the time, they seemed like a miracle to me, but terrifying as well. I realized the potential of humanity that night. You should have seen the inventions, the Ferris wheel, the Tesla Coil!"

Hard to believe that he was offering this much information willingly, I listened intently and despite myself, couldn't help but be fascinated.

"You should have seen it, Annalice. You probably can not possibly imagine in the great age of technology that you were born into how amazing electricity was the first few times I saw it. It was like seeing the sun again for the first time in thirty years. I was a little afraid that those miniature

151

suns might burn me, but after I realized they were not that strong, I could almost feel hope again. Not hope that I would ever fit into the human world, but it did seem almost possible that I might at least have a daytime.

"And the Ferris wheel. I stood under it looking up at it for at least a solid hour. Each time it turned, I kept expecting a human to fall to their death, but it never happened. Spinning around and around, effortlessly and never tiring. That single machine was more amazing to me than the steam engine had been when I was alive. Everyone there was shocked to see it. It was massive. I finally dragged myself away from it."

"What happened to your hope?" I asked quietly from my position against the tree. When he didn't answer me immediately, I tried to be patient hoping he was just coming up with an answer.

The silence lasted for several more minutes before he finally answered. "The Tesla coil demonstration. That was truly terrifying. I could feel the current deep down in my core. It was like my entire being was vibrating with it. Any creature that could build that was dangerous by definition and I was right to fear them."

He was again silent and I tried my hardest to relax against the cold surface behind me. The trunk of the tree was scratchy and I could feel it even through the coat he had given me. It seemed my nerve endings had doubled in number or their ability to sense. My skin was still burning and overall I just felt unwell. It was like having flu on steroids and my unwell feeling of had significantly worsened throughout the course of the night.

His voice continued on in the darkness, "I was so scared and angry of what you humans could accomplish. And knowing I would never truly be a part of that world ever again, I left and spent several days in the ground. Did not bother to come out. But when I did finally emerge from the dirt, I was even angrier. I killed many humans for several nights. Mostly men and slowly. I wanted them to suffer. I guess because I was so outraged at the men who had created the machines I had marveled at a few nights before. I had realized the true threat of humans for the first time."

He went silent then, and resting my head against the tree, I stared at the stars, mesmerized by their beauty despite how bad I felt. Not moving, I just rested, no longer interested in conversation. I had heard enough of death and murder.

My head started to spin and ache and even the far-away stars seemed excruciatingly bright. If I had seen this in one of my patients, I would have bet money they had meningitis. Finding it hard to concentrate, I tried to follow my train of thought. It was logical I would have a form of meningitis. The virus would need to cross the blood-brain barrier, the membrane that separates the blood from the fluids that surround the brain, in order to infect my central nervous system.

Would I survive this? I wasn't sure. The conversion process itself might kill me long before Asa did. But there was nothing I could do except watch the stars with what was left of my energy. Hoping he didn't realize or understand what was happening to me, I wished on the brightest star that I could find. I watched that star until its brightness seemed to be tattooed onto my retina permanently and it became a blurry glowing orb. It was the last image I remember seeing.

NINE

I awoke with a start, my arms brought up defensively and my hands splayed open to protect my very sensitive eyes from the glaring light pouring through the windows of my bedroom. For what seemed like hours, my eyes adjusted slowly and I could eventually look in the general direction of the sunlight so long as I didn't look directly at it.

Sitting up slowly in bed, I noticed I was in my robe and the bed was made neatly around me. Not remembering how I came to be back in my own bed, I felt very confused. But the answer was quick to be found in the form of a note on my nightstand.

In an elaborate cursive handwriting, Asa had left me a message. "You were quite ill and fell asleep. Your body felt afire. Eat and drink today for you need the nutrition. I shall as previous return tonight and hope to find you breathing still. Our time together has been too short and I do not like to be cheated out of what is rightfully mine."

The message was cold. Yet he had carried me home, dressed me in my nightclothes, and put me to bed. Could it be another sign of compassion like his offer of a coat? His actions pointed to yes, but looking at the note again, I couldn't completely convince myself he had any ability to care left in him.

It didn't matter, I told myself as I got out of bed. I had

survived the night and that was all that mattered. And things were looking up. I was like a new person compared to how I had felt the the night before. Checking my skin, it felt cool to the touch and my headache was gone, along with the nausea.

The worry of what would come next ran across my mind, but I pushed the thoughts away knowing it wouldn't help to borrow troubles from tomorrow when I had enough of them for today. No, it was more like taking one hour at a time, I realized quickly. Tomorrow was an eternity away.

I was brought out of my reverie by the overpowering sound of the doorbell. What had always been a low-key alarm now sounded like the trumpets on judgment day. My hands came up to cover my ears automatically and stayed there for the entire duration of the bell, which seemed to last forever. Why had I ever picked such a pretentious door alarm?

Terror rippled through me as I realized the implications of someone being here. The vampire would no doubt smell the new scent, putting them and me in danger and jeopardizing my entire plan. But nothing could be done about it now as I couldn't mask their scent or change the fact they had been here.

I stood stock still, unsure of what to do. Should I answer the door and act like everything was fine or sit quietly on the floor hoping that whoever it was went quickly on their way?

Trying to think logically through the situation, my thoughts were cut short again by the unnaturally loud chiming of the bell. Well, so much for my unwanted guest just going on their merry way.

Insistence was one of their strong qualities, I thought to myself, when the doorbell rang for the third time, accompanied by a sharp rapping on the door and a twisting of the doorknob.

Ignoring them was clearly not an option and I walked towards the entryway. Realizing on the way I still had my hands over my ears, I brought them down, trying my best to relax them against my sides even as I felt the vibrations, yes, felt the vibrations of the doorbell before I heard it again. Reaching for a pair of sunglasses from a nearby shelf, I was happy I had found them before I had to face the sun that would stream in when I opened the door.

Gritting my teeth at the intensity of the alarm, I swung the door open angrily. "What?" I spoke loudly without meaning to, but it didn't elicit any surprise in the expression of the man I faced. His finger still hovered over the doorbell and it quickly jabbed at it again, bringing on the clamor of the bell again.

I was surprised, not expecting him to ring the door again, and couldn't stop myself in time to keep from reaching up to cover my ears.

"Oh I'm sorry. I didn't mean to punch it again. You startled me." My unwanted visitor smiled politely down at me. He was lying. I had seen the quick little sarcastic smile pop onto his face when I covered my ears.

Despite my overly sensitive hearing, I attempted to be as polite as I could. "Can I help you?" I was nearly sick with fear at his being here, but I was curious too. Who was he? A salesman. He was wearing a suit. No, a Jehovah's Witness, I decided quickly. That made much more sense but all the sadder because invariably they were the nicest people. They were irritating and all, but to be honest, anyone who spends their free time attempting to save your soul can't be all that bad. And as we always say in medicine, the nicer they are, the quicker they die.

All of that went through my mind while I waited for him to answer. My mind was clearer and that had to mean the worst of the viral replication phase was behind me. I felt so much better today and could see the glimmer of hope on the horizon. That glimmer faded out with my visitor's words.

"Detective Rumsfield, ma'am. I'm here to check on you at the request of the owner of the Oak Grove country store," the man explained while nonchalantly trying to look past me into my house.

Standing there with one hand on the door, I was stock still, not moving. He was looking at me expectantly and I blurted an answer out before thinking it through clearly.

"I'm fine. Nothing happened." My inept answer had his full attention now. He had been standing at an angle to me as if he were taking in the scenery of the old country home but now he turned to face me completely.

"So you were in some sort of danger last night?" he questioned now. He must have noticed I was looking at him quite suspiciously because he added, "I'm with the Madison County Police by the way."

Now I was really scared. I had known that old ladies' eyes

wouldn't miss a thing, but I hadn't expected her to call the cops. This was even worse than I had thought. I was so unnerved that I continued to just stand there.

"May I come in? I'd also like to ask you a few questions about your neighbor." His eyes were on me and I was sure that he, like the store owner, wouldn't miss anything either. I tried to smooth the worries off my face.

"Um, sure. Sorry. I'm a night owl so I just got up and I'm still a little foggy," I explained to him, smiling as friendly as I could. But there was no way I could let him into the house. I still hadn't cleaned up the blood from off the floor where I had tried to get myself drained.

Pulling the door closed behind me, I motioned towards the deck. "If it's OK with you, I'd prefer to sit on the deck. Helps me to wake up to see the sun."

Watching his facial expressions closely, I felt like he must have a good poker face. He didn't bat an eye at my unusual request. And I'm sure he thought it was unusual since it was only the low fifties outside. Honestly, I hadn't noticed how cool it was until I saw the outdoor thermometer out of the corner of my eye. My tolerance to the frosty air had been growing.

I turned and walked towards the back deck with him following behind. Motioning to one of the Adirondack chairs, I settled into one and waited for him to do the same.

Watching his eyes sweep across the chair and then across the rest of the deck, I nearly laughed out loud as he searched furtively for another place to sit, but could find none. Finally he lowered himself down, really down into the low-set chair and after some fidgeting, he stretched his long legs across the leg rest since there was really nothing else he could do. He looked vaguely uncomfortable and very unprofessional, which made me laugh silently to myself. Even with a death threat over my head, I had perverse sense of humor I guess.

Trying to look normal, I continued to smile at him, but it was difficult with all the squinting I was doing. The sun was burning my eyes even behind the dark tint of my sunglasses to the point I felt like they were desiccating in the brightness.

Barely able to open and close them from the lack of moisture, I could feel my eyelids sticking together each time I blinked, which was often. Vampire-like eyes were really not built for the daylight, I decided as I waited for him to speak.

Wondering to myself how long I could stay out here before my differences became obvious to the detective, I longed for the darkness of the house, where I would be more comfortable and look more normal.

"Are you okay, ma'am?" he asked, his voice shaded with concern. Certain that it was practiced, I still believed his concern was genuine, yet at the same time I knew he was suspicious of me. I mean, who doesn't let the police in when they ask?

Logically, he had every reason to be wary of me. That had put me right in the center of his radar and I knew it, but what else could I do? If he saw all of that blood, he would race back to town to get a warrant to search my house and then he would die. Asa would kill him quickly and probably in a bad way just to be perverse.

"Ma'am?" His voice was just loud enough to bring me back to our conversation. I looked back at him, still squinting. "Are you OK?" he asked again as he slipped his cell phone out of his pocket and flipped it open.

Who is he going to call? I wondered to myself just for a moment before coming up with an answer. "I'm fine. Stayed out a little too long last night with an old friend. And had a little too much to drink. I'm sure you know what I'm talking about. Now the sun's too bright and every sound's a little too loud." I laughed a little hoping it would relax him.

"I don't drink, ma'am," he answered back, his voice flat and dry and his facial expression just as dull. This wasn't going well.

"I, uh, I usually don't either but I had a couple of margaritas too many last night like I said. I guess that's why the alcohol affected me so much, you know, being such a light drinker and all." I laughed nervously despite the situation.

The look on his face told me he thought I was a lush. It bothered me a little, which was ridiculous given the fact I was being consumed by a vampire. Time to move on to a new topic, the logical part of my brain told me.

"What did you want to ask me about?" I asked, trying to turn the conversation away from my supposed alcohol use and back to his original reason for coming here.

Just as he was about to flip the cell phone closed and answer my question, it rang. "Excuse me," he whispered politely to me, putting the phone to his ear.

161

"Rumsfield," he answered, struggling somewhat to get up out of the Adirondack chair and walk towards the back of the deck for some privacy. I laughed a little. No one could get out of one of those chairs gracefully.

But my new vampire hearing had its perks and I doubted he would walk far enough away to get any true privacy. Listening intently, I didn't feel guilty at all. After all, I was trying to save his neck as much as my own.

"Yeah, I'm here now," he was saying to the person on the other end of the line. "Nervous as a cat. Didn't want me in the house. We're on her deck. I can't force my way in, Bobby. No search warrant. You know that. I'll come up with something. Ask to use the bathroom or something."

Rolling my eyes at his duplicity, I knew it would look really bizarre if I didn't let him in to use the bathroom, but it was imperative I kept him out of the living room. A puddle of blood would be hard to explain. At least now he wouldn't catch me unawares.

While he was talking, I couldn't help but take him all in. He was the first human I had truly talked to or interacted with since the vampire had arrived. I have to say he actually looked like a detective while still managing to look like a cowboy, which I didn't expect from Madison County. They usually just looked like cowboys.

Tall and lean, his sandy blond hair, streaked with brown, was cut short but not buzzed, and he had a pretty good tan on his face even for this time of the year, which made his blue eyes look like the sky. His cowboy boots were clean and his Dockers neatly pressed. He was wearing a higher end dress jacket. Nice looking, I couldn't help but notice to myself. I even wondered if it was his wife who pressed his pants.

"Sorry about that," he announced, walking back towards me. I gestured to the Adirondack chair again with a slight smile. He frowned back at me and looking around one last time for another place to sit, he finally lowered himself down for the second time. That was fine with me. The more uncomfortable he was, the sooner he would leave I hoped.

"No problem," I replied, continuing to try to appear as perky as I could despite my sun-induced hangover.

"So who was he?" he asked, leaning back into the chair and now unfortunately not looking uncomfortable at all.

"Who?" I asked back, playing dumb.

"You know who, ma'am. The man who wrapped his hands around your throat last night in the parking lot of the Oak Grove Country store. I'm sure you didn't forget him that quickly," he retorted, sounding exasperated that I would bother to play dumb.

"Just a guy that I met at a bar awhile back. He turned out to be a prick so I cut him loose. I'm sure you've heard this story a hundred times, Detective. But it doesn't matter, he's gone now." I lied as good as I knew how.

"Where does he live and what did you say his name was?" he asked, as if I was dumb enough not to realize I hadn't already told him Asa's name.

"I didn't say actually. And as for where he lives, I have no idea. I told him to hit the road and that's exactly what he did. Probably west if I was guessing. He talked a little about

163

Oklahoma one night." I waited now to see how pressing he would be.

Trying to decide if I should tell him Asa's real name, I decided it couldn't hurt. It wasn't exactly like he could be traced. "And his name was Asa. I'm sure you're not going to believe this, but I don't know his last name."

"You're right. I don't believe that so try again," he said, leveling his most stern detective expression at me. It was time to play hardball.

"I really don't know. He was only a good for a few one night stands. Good enough for sex, but not good enough to take home to Momma," I explained, leveling my best 'I'm not taking any crap' look at him.

He raised his eyebrows at me and let silence fill the space between us, but I kept my cool and didn't try to fill it for him. That was one of the first things doctors are taught when dealing with attorneys. Don't incriminate yourself. Facing him couldn't be any worse than a few attorneys I had met. At least he was on the right side.

"Ms. Creed, you may not understand the seriousness of my visit. I'm not here just because your fuck buddy squeezed your neck. There's not enough time in the day to respond to all of those calls. You should know that we found Ms. McElhaney dead last night. Her great-nephew came to visit when he couldn't get a hold of her," he told me, pulling a couple of pictures out of his pocket and leaning forward to shove them into my hands.

It was really hard to gross me out but even I was unprepared when I looked down at the photos in my hands and the surprise on my face at least appeared genuine. Looking up at the detective with a gasp, we stared at each other for a moment before I tore my eyes from his in order to study the photographs.

After my initial surprise, I could see that there was very little left of Ms. McElhaney's neck. The lacerations were all the way to the bones of the cervical spine with the platysma muscle ripped to the side. The remnants of the sternocleidomastoid muscle could be seen on either side and I was pretty sure I could make out one end of the internal carotid artery on the left.

More haunting than anything was her eyes. They were open and staring straight ahead. I knew the last face she had seen as his fangs had cut into her neck. I would see that same face again this evening and I would probably suffer the same fate. Maybe even tonight when he caught the scent of the detective.

Taking a deep breath, I tried to keep my composure but failed and shoved the pictures back to the waiting policeman. "Why did you show me that? She was my friend. Reminded me of my grandma."

I nearly shouted at him since I was so angry with him for forcing me to remember her that way, for being here, and for presuming I had been involved in her demise. But I knew that was illogical, he was just following up on leads and doing his job.

"Do you think your ex had anything to do with this?" His voice was quieter and calmer now, expecting me to be more forthcoming.

"I didn't know him that well, but he didn't really seem like a killer." I was lying through my teeth, of course he was a killer. Asa would have been proud of me though, my pulse didn't even increase.

"And you have no idea where he's gone." He said the words like a statement, not a question.

"No, I really don't. He left. Probably headed back out West where he came from. I'm pretty sure he lived somewhere in California. He seemed the type. And no, I don't know his last name." My tone was sharper as I answered him. I threw my feet up on a footstool indicating my boredom with his questioning. We sat staring at each other now for a couple of minutes.

"So you have nothing to hide?" he asked, with just as much attitude as I had answered him with.

"Are you implying I had something to do with Ms. McElhaney's death?" I shoved up out of my chair now with a lot of speed and stood looking down at him. He needed to leave and now. Nothing good was going to come from his visit and I was getting more and more antsy. Close to agitation even.

Catching him off-guard, he struggled slightly to get up out of the chair. He couldn't quite match my speed but when he finally did, he fairly towered over me. I hadn't realized how tall he was. I could see in his eyes that something about me didn't seem right to him.

"You don't seem that upset she's dead, yet she has pictures of you and your daughter all over the place," he observed, spreading his hands out in front of him. "What's wrong with this picture, ma'am? Your neighbor is dead and you just don't seem to care."

"I care. Of course I care. I loved that old woman, but there's nothing I can do about it and I had nothing to do with it. Why don't you get out there and look for the thing that did it and leave me alone!" Currents of rage ripped through my limbs as my heart raced and my breathing became irregular.

I was genuinely angry and I was handling this all wrong. I knew it, but couldn't seem to stop. I honestly meant the part about finding the thing that had done this. That would be pretty amazing.

"Detective, maybe you should leave," I announced walking towards the front steps to show him out.

"I'd like to look around your house, ma'am. You shouldn't mind. If you really have nothing to hide that is." His tone was slightly threatening, almost daring me to defy him.

"No I don't think so, Officer. This is my home. I've done nothing wrong and you're not going to treat me like a common criminal. It's time for you to go. Goodbye." He had followed behind me as I walked and we were standing on the porch where the sidewalk began.

Continuing on, he walked down the steps onto the sidewalk and turned to face me. "Actually that's exactly what I'm going to do. I'll get a warrant and I'll be back just like you are a common criminal." Taking off his hat with one hand, he tipped it at me. "Ma'am," he concluded and strode quickly to his car. I guess he forgot that he was supposed to use the bathroom.

He drove slowly down my drive, even slower than Asa. When he was out of sight, I collapsed onto the top step and rested my head in my hands. *Great, I really screwed this up*, I thought to myself.

I was upset partially because I had let him get under my skin the way he did. I should have kept better control of my reactions since I had so much at stake. Detective Rumsfield would be back all right. I didn't doubt it for a second and I would bet good money that he would have a warrant. The good old boys mentality was alive and well here, he would get the warrant whether there was evidence or not.

Knowing he would return at some point and I had no time to lose, I walked into the living room and surveyed the mess. The pool of blood was a stinking nasty mess surrounded by broken glass and knocked over furniture.

Taking a deep breath, I went straight to work on the gruesome spot on the living room floor. I had seen blood what must be a million times, but this big coagulated puddle was disgusting. I guess because it was mine and because of what it represented. The smell was revolting to the point of nausea as I knelt next to it and began scrubbing at it with some towels and a bowl of hot water.

After I had cleaned up the large pool and then the footprints, I noticed the seams of my hard wood floors were stained a maroon color radiating outwards about three feet from where the pool had been. It must have set long enough that it had drained down in-between the boards. That would be impossible to get out.

I had seen enough true crime shows to know that, but I also knew there was nothing I could do about it so I decided to do the most classic true crime cover up of all and roll out a runner carpet I had stored earlier in the year in the basement.

I mused to myself on the way to the basement that it was almost like I had kept it there for this exact purpose. I had nearly thrown it away several times, but just kept hanging onto it for no good reason. It was heavy and more than just a little bit musty, but I dragged it up the stairs easily, hoping that the detective's sense of smell would be like most people in this area and out of shape from all of the allergens.

Picking up the tall wall shelf was easier than it looked. It was really quite light, made of bamboo, otherwise I wouldn't have been able to pull it over on myself that first night. Making quick work with the broom, I swept up all of the broken glass and rearranged the surviving knickknacks on the shelves. There weren't many left since most of them had broken when I brought the shelf down.

As I was picking up the last figurine off of the floor, my fingertips brushed against photo paper and looking down I saw it was a forgotten picture of Ellie from the year before. It must have fallen out of one of my books when I was using it as a bookmark.

Without thinking about it, I rocked back onto my heels and stared at her beautiful face. She looked so happy and I really noticed for the first time just how much she had grown up in a year.

Tears started to spring to my eyes, but before they could

really get going, I shoved the picture back into one of the books and stood up. There was no time to waste on tears with Detective Rumsfield on his way back over.

I stood back to survey my work. It looked presentable at least and it definitely smelled better, even though I knew it wouldn't stand up to a deep forensics survey. Then it occurred to me that all they would find would be my blood even if they did tear the place apart. There was nothing that could pin Ms. McElhaney on me.

Gathering up the dirty towels and water, I threw the towels in the washer along with the water, and an entire gallon of bleach. The only thing that would have made it more classic true crime would have been to burn the towels and pour the water down the sink, where it could have later tested positive on a swab.

For the first time today, I thought about food when my stomach made a noise that was almost disturbing. Opening the kitchen cabinet, I grabbed an assortment of anything I could find and munched it down quickly. It seemed strange but although I was hungry, the food didn't taste quite right. Almost foreign but I knew I needed it so I ate it anyway.

I had nothing else to do now except wait for whatever was going to happen. If the police hadn't shown up, I would have still been in bed until late into the afternoon. So I lay back down on the couch and closed my eyes, not really planning to fall asleep but just wanting to avoid the brightness of the sun streaming in through the cracks in the blinds.

TEN

No sooner had I closed my overly sensitive eyes, I was opening them to the epic sound of the doorbell again. Knowing who it was immediately, I got up just as quickly if for no other reason than to keep him from ringing it again.

Making it to the door before he could ring it again, I threw the door open to find, just as I expected, Detective Rumsfield standing on my front porch with as much arrogance as one man could muster.

His long left arm was lifted up and resting on one of the columns supporting the wide overhang of the porch, the other was resting nonchalantly on his right hip. He was no longer wearing his coat and I noticed immediately that he was in much better shape than I had first realized. Tall and strongly built, I wished momentarily I could unload all that was happening to me onto his strong shoulders.

The smug look on his face said it all. He had the warrant and there would be no way around letting him in now.

"Ma'am, I have a warrant to search the premises. I'll need you to stand out here while I have a look around."

"I'll just bet you do. Call in a favor, Detective? This is bullshit and you know it." I fought to control my anger, but wasn't quite successful. Would being a vampire always mean being emotionally unstable?

Not rising to my words, he simply smiled and gestured

for me to step outside. Glaring at him as I crossed the threshold, I turned to watch him walk in and, just like I expected, he took his hat off before he went into my house. How perfectly polite.

Sitting down in the low-hung swing, I waited patiently for him to do his search. No longer alarmed, I focused on not letting the swing glide into the patch of light bending itself around the corner of the porch.

Pushing my left foot against the wall, I swung gently, listening to the detective walk around my house. He obviously chose to go upstairs first and I could hear his heavy footsteps moving from room to room. Finally, I heard him come down the stairs, pause momentarily on the landing, then walk into the living room.

He paused where he stood at the entrance into the living room. I could imagine him surveying the room, wondering if the floor runner was a new addition. He must have stood there a few seconds before I heard him lift a foot to continue on through the room. With that step, his foot made contact with a piece of glass I must have missed.

Cringing when I heard the crunch, I held my breath expectantly; I waited to see if he was going to pull the rug up to study the floor underneath his feet. But instead, I could hear him picking up and replacing the few remaining knickknacks on the bamboo shelf.

Ticking off each piece in my head as he examined them individually and then placed them back on the cabinet, I could feel my muscles relaxing when he moved on towards the kitchen. Finally, after what seemed like an eternity, he walked back out onto the front porch, placing his hat back on as he stepped out the front door.

I smiled at him from my semi-relaxed position on the porch swing, waiting for him to speak. It was very strange how I was partially relieved by his presence, but at the same time terrified he was here. Despite knowing his being here was going to open an entire new can of worms, it was still comforting to be around a human. I was really desperate, I realized, for this little touch of humanity since I might die earlier than scheduled.

"I'll need to look around outside now and I'll need you to stay here until I'm done," he instructed, looking down at me as he walked down the steps.

"No problem. I'll be right here waiting for you to get back," I replied, smiling my best 'butter can't melt in my mouth' smile.

I waited for him to return, which took about a half hour. There was very little to interest him in the barns as I expected. The buildings were old and other than storing my saddles and farm tools, I didn't spend much time there and it showed.

"Find anything out of order?" I asked as his heavy footsteps landed on the porch. Without asking, he sat down in one of the old porch chairs.

"I didn't find anything to cause me to dig deeper," he answered, folding his arms across his chest.

I started to get up to show him to his car, but his next words froze me in place.

"But I know something is wrong, Annalice. Your house is

a mess. There are empty cartons, jars, and boxes all over the kitchen. Your laundry's piling up. What's going on? Is your ex threatening you? You act like everything is fine but I can tell that you're lying."

He had that concerned voice again and I could see by the look on his face that he was sincere. His face softened while he watched me, he folded his hands between his knees and leaned towards me.

Closing my eyes and taking a deep breath, I could picture myself telling him about the vampire and I could almost hear the words pouring out of me, describing the last few days that I had spent in hell to him. I imagined him believing my ludicrous tale and I also imagined he would have a plan. A plan in which I would unquestionably survive. Together, we would face Asa and win or maybe find his daytime resting spot and kill him. In my mind's eye, I could see that he would believe me.

My daydream must have lasted longer than I realized because he brought me back to reality by clearing his throat a couple of times. I opened my eyes and looked across the short distance that separated us, knowing that my reality was set and it was backwards. The daydream should have been the vampire and reality should have been spilling my troubles on this hard-working detective.

"Detective Rumsfield, I'm fine. Really. My ex is long since gone and I'm no housekeeper. Just enjoying a little bachelorette time with my daughter being gone. Nothing to worry about. It'll be clean before she comes home and life will get back to normal. Well, except Ms. McElhaney and that just breaks my heart. She was a real sweetheart and I'm going to miss her."

Part of my spiel was a lie and the other part truth. I would miss my sweet elderly neighbor, but life would never be back to normal.

His face had tensed up at my partial truths and between gritted teeth, he responded, "I can tell you mean that, Annalice. I know you're a good person. I did my background work on you. A doctor with no criminal history at all. Not even a speeding ticket and no history at all of any domestic violence calls. I've followed you all the way back to high school. I probably know more about you than your momma and that's why none of this makes any sense. What you're hiding and why you're hiding it makes no sense to me. But you're hiding it all the same."

Silence filled the air with tension and I waited, again not offering to fill that space, to see how far his anger was going to carry him. Sensing that he was trying to remain calm, I knew he was struggling. His hunches were good, but he had nothing else to go on. I would have been frustrated too.

"One more thing," he said jabbing a long finger in my direction. "You obviously don't know much about operating a broom. There are several shards of glass on the living room floor. Interesting thing is I looked at your little knickknacks and most of them are chipped at least in one place or another. Like the entire cabinet fell over and not too long ago either, because none of the chipped parts have any dust, unlike the shelf, and you were just in too big a hurry to clean up real well."

"That doesn't sound like a crime to me, Detective. So I'm not the best housekeeper, I don't really think you can arrest me over that." Sarcasm dripped into my voice and I heard him laugh a little darkly to himself.

"Yeah, you're right but I'll be back, ma'am. Don't doubt it. And by the way, you might want to put away your saddle. Wouldn't want it to ruin." Turning quickly, he strode angrily towards his car.

Standing in the shade of the porch, I watched him walk down the old stone path towards the parked police car and the policeman waiting for him.

Pausing about half-way down the walk, he took a deep breath and stood for a second. I guessed he had something else he wanted to say but needed a second to calm down before he could. With a slight drop of his head, he turned and walked even quicker back towards me, taking the steps in one stride before thrusting something into my hand.

Instinctively, my hand closed around the stiff business card feeling the edges bend slightly in my hand. He was very close and his nearness caught me off-guard, causing me to step back quickly but he followed. He was too close.

Close enough I could smell him for the first time. The first time I truly caught his human scent, the scent that I was losing and I wanted him suddenly in an unfamiliar way that I couldn't put a name to.

Close enough that I could hear his heart beating. It sounded strong and I could hear the different valves closing, pushing his blood through the four chambers.

Focusing on it for a moment, I listened to the splitting of

his aortic and pulmonic valves when he inhaled. I gasped audibly at the beauty of the sounds, having only heard them before through the muffled earpiece of a stethoscope. It took my breath away.

Having heard my gasp, he reached out and caught both of my shoulders in his hands. Again, a need I couldn't put into words surged through me, causing my knees to go a little weak but his hands steadied me with both their strength and their warmth.

Placing my cooler hands over his, I pulled them away. "Detective," I told him quietly, "it's not what you think."

Staring at me silently for a second, he let his hands fall down to his side and took a step back. "Call me Michael and keep my card close by. It's got my cell phone and office number. Call me if you need anything, Annalice. And I mean anything."

He stopped there with a quiet sigh. I could tell he was debating whether to really tell me what he thought or to just softball his concern to me.

He must have chosen the latter because his voice was slightly softer when he resumed. "I don't think everything's OK, but I can tell you're not ready to talk and I can't make you. But I want you to know that we can work through whatever the problem is."

Tipping his hat again, he walked towards his car, this time without stopping or sparing me another glance. And I didn't watch him go this time either.

Instead, I went back into the house so I didn't have to see my last and only hope, no matter how small it was, disappear down the driveway. I was in this for the long haul and there was no other way out for me.

But this man shouldn't have to die. I was certain that Detective Rumsfield, or Michael, wasn't going to give up. He didn't believe my story and I really couldn't blame him for that. I was pretty certain he would keep surveillance on my house tonight, which was a terrifying thought. Certain he wouldn't catch Asa unawares, I knew the opposite wouldn't hold true.

It probably didn't matter. He had probably signed his own death warrant along with mine by just coming here. If only there was some way I could warn Michael, but that was simply not possible. He wouldn't believe me. I couldn't blame him. If someone had come into the emergency room with this story, I would have called psych immediately.

ELEVEN

Back in the house, I felt better and I think it was partly due to being away from the sun. With the blinds closed, it was mostly dark except those few pinholes of very small but exquisitely bright shafts of light that I couldn't seem to protect my eyes from. I thought about putting blankets over the curtain rods but decided that might make Asa suspicious so I left my sunglasses on instead.

Lying back down on the couch, I fell asleep almost immediately. I remember dreaming but could only recall images. Images of Ellie, Asa, and Michael all rolled together and tumbling over each other. I couldn't identify a cause and effect in my streaming unconsciousness, only pieces of a complicated puzzle that no matter how I tried, I couldn't get to fit together.

I awoke as anxious as my fitful sleep had been. Dreading to open my eyes, I kept them closed as I stretched, arching my back up and off the couch. Surprisingly, I didn't have a kink despite my hours on the couch.

Reaching up to run my hand across my forehead to wipe away the expected sweat after my dreams, I was surprised to find my skin drier and cooler than previously. Not cold and not a distinct enough difference that it couldn't be attributed to severe anemia.

The sun had set. I knew before I even opened my eyes

that the fiery globe that had wreaked havoc on my eyes all day had disappeared behind the mountains. I'm not sure what told me it was dark yet I knew, and I felt better with the knowledge. A slight unease that had nothing to do with the vampire or the detective had been hovering in the back of my mind throughout the entire day, and now it was gone. I attributed my lack of tact with the detective to it as well.

Not gone, however, was my anxiety for the detective's safety and that caused a fear that overshadowed the sun. Since night had fallen, Asa would be back soon and I had no false hope that he wouldn't pick up Michael's scent before he even reached the house. Certain he would plan to kill Michael, I wondered if he would track him right away or confront me first.

Given the constraints of our arrangement, I was also certain that Asa's first thought would be that I had betrayed him and so I paced the house from one end to the other, waiting for the vampire who would decide the fate of Michael and myself.

The sun was well past set and I expected him any moment. Strangely enough, I wanted him to be here even though my heart palpitated at what he would do when he arrived. I was craving him and I needed him for something, but I couldn't put my finger on what it was.

Walking into the bedroom, I grabbed up the sheets where our agreement had been consecrated on several times and buried my face in the crumpled material in my hands.

His scent was so much more powerful than that of Michael's and after taking several long inhales, I felt slightly calmer despite the fears in my mind. Rolling over on my side, I kept the sheets pressed to my face and let my senses expand outward, hoping to hear some sound of Asa's approach.

Finding it hard to concentrate because of the sound of my own heart, I couldn't help but listen to the slow thump of an organ I had taken for granted for thirty years. I also knew from its sounds that it was diseased and dying, a race against time to see if my human body could hold up long enough for the vampire one to form from it.

Sluggishly sucking blood from my lungs, I listened as my heart struggled to pump the partially re-oxygenated blood back out and willed it to keep going. Did it have the strength? Only time would tell.

Despite the fact I was dying, I did appreciate the beauty of the process. Obviously, vampires are an anaerobic species as was evident by my lovely lilac nail beds.

Part of my blood must now be vampiric cells and no longer oxygen carrying, which was in part keeping me alive and contributing to the fact that despite my failing heart and lungs, I didn't feel short of breath. My lips, once lovely and pink, were no longer as vibrant in color; explainable to Asa that I was suffering from lack of blood. I thanked the stars again that he didn't understand his own physiology.

Forcing myself to tune out the sounds of my own mortality, I turned my attention to the echoes of the house around me, only to find it alive with noises I couldn't recognize. The acuity of my new hearing was impressive, but was obviously going to take some time to get adjusted to. Loud sounds could bring me to my knees, but what was even more frustrating were all of those that I had never heard before tonight. There was definitely going to be a learning curve.

Listening intently, I could hear nothing that sounded like the approach of a vampire, or a human for that matter. Soft swishing sounds emanated from the upper floors of the house, which I eventually attributed to the smallest branches of the oak trees brushing against the house.

Footsteps, small and quick, ran quickly back and forth through a wall in the washroom, which I decided had to be a field mouse. Reminding myself that I needed to call the exterminator if I survived, I tried to suppress the sounds of the house and move out into the yard, ignoring for now the myriad of sounds that remained unrecognized.

The beginning drops of light rain could be heard landing on the trees and vegetation outside and the wind picked up a little more. Having to strain even further to catch other sounds over the din of the rain, I had to refocus and listen even more intently for some sound indicating Asa's arrival.

Sifting through the fainter sounds that existed outside the house, I could hear numerous heartbeats, all of which were either too fast or too slow to be human. The heavy thump of my horses could be heard faintly from where they stood at the back of the field. The light humming of birds' wings along with the rapid pace of their hearts could be heard in the trees that surrounded the porch. A couple of dogs barked down by the crossroads, along with an occasional car down on the highway.

Although I could hear cars distantly in the background, I couldn't make out any traffic near my house, nor could I hear the squeak of leather seats or a radio to suggest there was a parked car.

If Michael was out there, he was being exceptionally quiet and I couldn't help but let my breath out slowly in relief that at least for the moment he wasn't here. Having no false hopes that he wouldn't return, I was relieved at least that I might not have to listen to him die tonight.

I continued to focus on the night around me, listening expectantly for Asa. Why wasn't he here yet? I could still catch the scent of the detective. My smell had not improved as much as my hearing, but it was definitely greater than the average human's and Michael's scent hung slightly in the air. Just enough for me to catch it when a draft moved the air around inside the old home.

It was then I caught a new sound. Very very faintly, I could hear the light fall of footsteps coming up on the porch, but before I could analyze them to any degree, he was in front of me. His speed was amazing.

Opening my eyes, I found him beside me on the bed. Eyes closed, legs crossed in front of him. He seemed to be listening as well, either mocking my pose or perhaps he was listening for the detective like I was.

Studying his expression, I could see his rage was only barely concealed. His beautiful face was stony. A muscle in his left jaw twitched and I could see his teeth were clenched, causing the muscles in his neck to stand out slightly. I could have sworn his lips were even redder than normal. A fact I attributed to a recent feeding.

Wondering who he had drank from tonight, since he obviously had, and whether or not they were still alive, I watched him closely. The rain I had heard had left a light moist sheen on his hair and skin, adding further to the suppleness of his skin.

Feeling my eyes upon his face, he opened them suddenly and I gasped in response to the depth of hatred and anger radiating towards me. A deep green rim surrounded the black pools of his dilated pupils and knowing it would be nearly impossible to escape his gaze, I didn't resist.

Raising his left hand, he moved it slowly towards me with none of his usual speed. He must have done it intentionally for it prolonged the agony as I waited for his supernaturally strong hand to reach me. Would he snap my neck, choke out my life, or pull me to him?

Time nearly stood still, but when his hand finally reached me, he simply stroked my right cheek, slowly moving his fingers along my cheekbone just at the corner of my eye and tracing it down towards my lips.

Using only his thumb, he traced the arch of my upper lip gently before following the contour of my lower lip. He repeated it about twenty times. I sat there quietly and without moving, fearing that the slightest movement would bring his wrath without warning. But then again, maybe that would have been better than the suspense of not knowing when or if he was going to strike.

Languidly running his hand behind my neck, he pulled me towards him until our faces were even and our lips were nearly touching. His fangs were fully exposed, shockingly white against the bright red of his lips. He pulled further until I was no longer able to balance myself and would have fallen face first onto the floor if he weren't holding me. Instead, he twisted me around and back onto the bed until he was kneeling over the top of me.

A drop of water fell from an overhanging lock of his dark hair, landing on my cheek. I had watched it fall, able to follow its movement in a way I had never been able to do before tonight, until it was beyond my line of vision. With even slower movements, he leaned down further and licked it off with a flick of his tongue.

His lips moved to mine and he kissed me more gently than he had ever done, just barely grazing my lips with his fangs. His tongue tasted sweet and softly swirled around mine while his fingers traced perfect circles from my cheeks to my chin. In spite of myself, I couldn't help but relax in his powerful yet soft grip.

Lifting his face from mine, we were eye to eye again. "You little human whore." His voice remained soft despite the message in the words. I wasn't sure what he meant, but doubtless it had something to do with the earlier presence of the detective.

Trying to keep my face expressionless lest he read the wrong emotion, I fought to keep my voice calm as well when I responded. "Why do you call me that when this was part of our agreement? I do what you want and you let Ellie live. I'm only keeping my word."

His grip tightened around my face but I didn't struggle.

"You little fool. I can smell him here and I can smell your lust for him in the air. All this talk about your little girl yet you spend the time you promised to me lusting after a human man. You are obviously not as concerned about her as you act. As usual, you humans never fail to disappoint me and I owe you nothing now." He hissed his final words at me.

"Are you sure it's not fear you're smelling? I don't remember any lust while I was trying to explain to a cop why I was with a man who threatened to strangle me in a parking lot and why my neighbor was found dead with her throat ripped out. For a vampire trying to avoid publicity, you might start with not choking me in public spaces!" I hissed the words right back at him.

His hand was still wrapped around my chin but I managed to get the words out. I was so angry remembering what was left of Ms. McElhaney that reaching up, I gripped his wrist with both my hands and dug my fingernails into him as deeply as I could. I thrashed from side to side using all of the strength I had. Despite landing one slap to his cool face and a few kicks, he gave no indication as to whether or not he felt it nor did he try to stop me.

His only response was to lower the full length of his body onto mine, which stopped my thrashing easily enough for a couple of reasons. First was his sheer weight and strength, but also I was feeling the beginnings of lust, which was quite disturbing in many ways but present nonetheless. He was after all a beautiful creature, with an emphasis on the creature part. But there was also something else. Again I longed for something from him, although exactly what, I wasn't sure.

He was right about the detective. I did find him attractive but it wasn't sex I had wanted from him. I still couldn't name the desire or want that he had caused in me.

Pheromones are very powerful and Asa had clearly picked up on something that even I wasn't aware of about myself. But with Asa it was different. Yes, he was beautiful and any female would have responded to his beauty, but I was certain that a new part of me was identifying with something in Asa that I would never be able to share with Michael. It was a vampire thing and my pheromones recognized Asa much more strongly. He and I were now of the same species. At least in part and becoming more so every day.

He laughed quietly in the dark room. "I am certainly smelling lust now, but we can get to that later." He spoke quietly still. In the dim lighting of the room, I could make out that his face no longer held the rage from earlier. It was beginning to look like I might survive another night.

"Tell me about this human?" he demanded, positioning his forearms on either side of my face so I couldn't look away. Even my newfound strength was no match for him yet, despite the fact I was gaining strength every hour.

"A detective. Report came in from a passerby who thought I was nearly strangled in the parking lot of that store we stopped at last night. They wrote down my tags and called it in. That report just happened to coincide with Ms. McElhaney's family finding her murdered. It seems I was a logical place to start." I glared at him now from my position underneath him, hoping he didn't notice I was lying about who called in the report.

"And so what did this detective want?" His voice was still low and controlled, but I could detect a bit of concern.

"He wanted to know who my 'boyfriend' was and where you were now, of course," I explained. "I had to look at photos of poor Ms. McElhaney and see your handiwork. I even had to lie and tell him that you're not a murderer." Staring up into his face when I was done, his face was like a beautiful mask, cold, hard, and emotionless.

"I thought you were more careful. I thought you tried to avoid the police. Of course, they're not looking for a vampire, but they will be looking for someone who fits your description. I have no doubt that the detective will probably stake out my house, making this all the more difficult," I added, sweeping my hands up to take in us and the house. Still not having learned to keep my mouth shut, I had probably said too much as the anger returned to his face.

"I am usually very careful. Maybe consorting with humans is a bad idea after all. You seem to bring out the recklessness in me," he growled back at me.

Sitting up now, he moved to lean back against the headrest leaving me lying beside him in the bed. The embers of lust were dying away, and so rolling over, I moved to join him stretching my legs out in front of me.

"It's not consorting with humans that's the bad idea. It's the killing them that's the problem. Your logic is flawed," I noted into the darkness of the room, since I had not bothered to turn the lights on again.

"My logic tells me to kill this detective after obtaining the name of the passerby who called in this report and then kill them too." His voice became even harder as he said the words.

Throwing my hands up in exasperation, I retorted back, "NO, NO, NO! Killing them will solve nothing. That's insane. The reports have already been filed so killing the detective will only raise more suspicion. Logically, you should just lay low or move on." I was practically shouting, but his logic was flawed so I reiterated again, "Killing more people is not the answer."

I stared at him incredulously as it was hard to imagine anyone, even him, couldn't see the absolute craziness of his plan. He had clearly lost all of his former human perspective.

"Why did you try to protect me? Why not tell the detective that I would be back tonight and let them try to catch me? Or did you not want them to catch me?" His voice was huskier again and I knew his mind was leading in another direction again. He had lost all interest in the detective and whatever potential threat he considered him.

After having my life threatened for several days, I guess I was losing my fear and out of that numbness, I was forgetting my condition. Laughing out loud at the absurdity of his question, I answered back, "Don't flatter yourself. We had an agreement and I protected you only to protect my daughter."

"Your precious daughter. How could I forget?" His voice

was cold, but his eyes were hot. His pupils dilated even wider than I had thought possible and he lowered his lips to mine again, nicking my bottom lip with his fangs. Feeling the blood bead lightly on my lip as he pulled away momentarily, I watched as he lowered his head and kissed me slowly, pulling my lip into his mouth and sucking lightly.

I wondered to myself if it tasted different, as he lifted his head from mine. I could see my blood as it stood out against his bright lips. The color was good, I noticed.

Rolling over onto my back, I welcomed him to me, pulling his mouth to me. Sucking in my breath as I felt his fangs glide through the skin of my neck, I marveled at the fact there was no pain whatsoever. Instead, it felt as if the pain receptors in my skin had been replaced by those for pleasure, or perhaps simply my pain tolerance was increasing.

Feeling him drink deeply, I responded by arching my hips up and grinding them into him. Within seconds, my clothes were off along with his before he stretched himself out beside me again and kissed me one more time before reaching down to pull my legs up to where they were bent. With him stroking my thigh, I couldn't help but let them fall apart.

One strong hand began tracing small patterns around my inner thighs. Nearly dying from anticipation, I gasped when he inserted two fingers into me while continuing to stroke me with his thumb. My changing skin was so much more sensitive and I came quickly with his touch, but he didn't stop. He continued until I had come several more times. I was like jello in his hands and I didn't resist when he lowered his head between my thighs.

Biting through my femoral vein while he continued to stroke me, I could feel my mind beginning to grow hazy as his chemicals moved through my bloodstream, slower than before because of my lower heartbeat, but still effective.

Moving his head lower, I caught my breath as his fangs grazed my most sensitive area. I had to remind myself to breathe as his tongue replaced the stroking his fingers had begun. Coming again and again, I remained awake through it all. Giddy and hazy, but awake.

I lost track of how many times I had come, but he finally stopped and came to lie beside me again. I'm not sure why he was so eager to satisfy me, but whatever the reason, I wasn't going to complain. If I did die, I would die sexually satisfied at last. But the question remained, why was he doing this to me?

His voice broke into my reverie. "I wonder about you, Annalice, if you and I..." Stopping in mid-sentence, his expression became softer and somewhat conflicted but soon hardened. Smiling provocatively at me, he whispered, "Please me, Annalice."

With him still lying on his side next to me, I reached down and took him in my hands. Cool to the touch but swollen with desire, I was hesitant. It had been quite a while since I had done anything like this, but I knew exactly what I had to do and why, so I didn't hesitate for long. Stroking him until he was firmer, I leaned down and took him in my mouth, causing him to take a deep breath of air whether he needed it or not.

Lying back, I continued to orally assault him until, without warning, he flung me down and shoved inside me with great force. It was incredible and I wrapped my legs around him to get as much fluid as possible. Luckily, he still didn't realize what I was doing and so didn't try to stop me.

Finally relaxing my legs from around him, he rolled away and I lay in the afterglow of good sex, thinking about the future. He lay there as well, but I'm not sure if he had an afterglow or not. After a few minutes of rest, I turned towards him. He appeared to be absentmindedly twisting the ring he wore on his right hand. Now I could clearly see the faint remnants of an old vine design as it twined its way around the band. With my human eyes, I probably wouldn't have seen it, as it was so deeply worn. I was curious where he had gotten it. Had it belonged to one of his victims? I'm sure he plundered whatever they had.

The question quietly burned its way through my mind as I realized for the first time that Asa would probably take whatever he wanted from my house as well, including my mother's wedding ring, which I had always intended to give to Ellie. Mom had given it to me after Dad had died.

"Who's ring?" I asked trying to keep the tone in my voice nonchalant. "Who did you take it from?"

Watching him for his response, his right hand paused in its twisting motion and slowly he turned his head in my direction. A single solitary muscle flexed in his jaw, his deep green eyes became slits as he stared at me with well controlled rage again. My track record for not provoking him was suffering tonight.

"Foolish girl, I could snap your neck in the span of one of your heartbeats and yet you still provoke me." His voice was calm and as he spoke, he reached out placing his left hand behind my neck and applying enough pressure that I couldn't help but cringe.

I should have been terrified as he held my cervical spine in his hand and I was, but my heart rate never budged and I knew immediately that he realized it when his eyes moved momentarily down to my chest. His hand relaxed its hold as his eyebrows raised in a look of perplexity.

"What is wrong with you? Your heartbeat is abnormally low for a frightened human female." His tone was questioning but still angry.

The fact that he had noticed did finally get a slight rise out of my pulse, but only minimally. Was he finally realizing what was happening to me? That would prove fatal, I was certain.

"I'm dying. What did you think was going to happen to me, Asa? Humans aren't built for this kind of stress. I probably won't last the week." I wasn't lying. If I didn't complete the conversion, I would die either from cardiovascular collapse or at his hands.

"I am not done with you yet." The words were clipped and, unexpectedly, I realized they were slightly tinged with what I thought was regret.

Laughing out loud at the absurdity of his response, I answered back, "I would have thought a man who was murdered and turned into a vampire would understand that fate is fickle. She doesn't care if you're done with me or not. You may not have a choice."

Laughing some more, I rolled away from him to hide the slightly smug look on my face. Managing so far to keep my secret from him, I didn't need to give it away by gloating.

"Fate dealt me a very cruel hand once but she has no control over me now. I am a vampire and now I AM fate. You will die or will not die when I decide," he answered behind me; his voice resolute.

Laying there beside him, thinking about his words, it took a few moments for them to sink in. What was he trying to say? Was he having second thoughts about killing me? Was there any chance that he would let me go?

Turning over to look at his face, I searched for a clue or sign of the true intent of his words, but could find none on his stony face. He wasn't looking at me, instead he was twisting his ring again, staring at it as if it held some deep secret.

Searching it again with my eyes, I could find nothing in its vague pattern that gave it such great interest to him. Lifting my eyes from the ring when he suddenly stopped, I found his eyes on me.

"It was my mother's." His voice held the remnant of some great emotion.

Tempted to ask more about her, I was brought up short by the sound of a car slowly pulling up into the most distant part of my drive. Listening intently, but trying to conceal the fact, I searched Asa's face to see if he had paid attention to the sounds of the car and the implications. But he had gone back to twisting his ring and seemed to be lost in his thoughts again so I returned to listening.

Realizing then that it was a truck and not a car, I heard it pull off the drive and through the gap of cleared land that ran between my fence and the edge of the national forest.

Cutting its wheels hard, I could hear the whine of the axles as the truck backed into the forest, pushing over a few small fledgling trees and underbrush, before the engine was cut off. They were clearly trying to remain concealed and although I didn't recognize the sound of the truck, I was pretty certain who would be sitting in it.

The sounds of the vehicle had finally caught Asa's attention as well and he was on alert. Stock still at my side, his ring forgotten, he now sprung lightly to a crouched position, balanced on the balls of his feet and looking like a statue.

Trying to cover up my knowledge of what he was listening to, I raised my voice loudly and asked, "What is it?"

"Sssssh," was his only reply as he shot me an irritated look. Now that I looked like a stupid human, I let myself go still as well and listened intently, trying to catch any sound the occupant of the truck was making.

Struggling for the first couple of minutes, I was finally able to suppress the hundreds of other sounds that were emanating from the space between myself and the vehicle and listen for the uneasy breathing of a human.

I was certain he was sitting on leather seats that I could

hear rub beneath him as he adjusted his position, probably trying to get a better look at the house. No sounds of a phone or the radio made their way back to me; he just seemed to be sitting. And watching, I was sure he was watching.

Feeling Asa's eyes on me, I turned to look at him. "A human male, likely the same one that was here today, is hiding in the woods in a vehicle." He gestured with his head to the north of the house as he spoke. "If you have betrayed me, you and he will die and so will the lovely Ellie, especially Ellie, and I will take my time with her." His voice was low and held nothing but hate and mistrust.

"I told you that he would be back. He didn't believe my story. You should never have killed that old lady." Anger laced my voice. Waiting in the dark for his equally angry answer, there was only silence.

"You are right, of course. I almost never kill when I am going to court a human for a few days. It is too dangerous to stay in the area. But I couldn't have her coming down here to check on you during the day when I was away, so I had to dispose of her. I did the logical thing," he responded; his words clipped and short.

"Well you could have at least made it look more natural." The words were out of my mouth without thinking about them and they startled me and ashamed me at the same time. Was I becoming more like him than I realized? Physically changing, of course, but mentally morphing as well into the creature beside me. No, that couldn't be it. Common sense simply said that the way he had killed Ms.

McElhaney was illogical.

"I got irate with her, which tends to make me more violent than normal. I do not make a habit of wasting blood, but when I drank, she tasted putrid and I tore her apart without thinking. She was dying anyhow." He didn't sound the least bit contrite.

Unable to get the picture out of my mind, I could see poor Ms. McElhaney's death playing out. Seeing her awakened in the home where she had spent sixty safe and happy years and opening her old eyes to the monster beside me as he ripped her to shreds.

"She's with her family now, so she's at peace. You didn't take that from her. You can't take that from anyone no matter how you kill them," I noted, shoving my finger towards him while I spoke.

His laugh, sarcastic and cold, filled the room before he retorted, "You are so naïve and unlearned in my ways. I can take anyone's peace and I have been considering doing exactly that to you. You should not tempt me to teach you a lesson just for spite."

"We had an agreement! You promised to leave her alone," I hissed at him, my voice shaking with fear for my daughter.

"Do you never cease to quit thinking about your daughter?" he sounded exasperated. "She will be safe. I have given my word so long as you do not betray me. I am talking about you, solely about you. I can destroy your peace in ways you have never even considered."

"What are you talking about?" The words were barely out of my mouth when we both heard a door squeak open and then very quietly was pushed shut, the way you do when you're late for a funeral.

I pretended not to notice and after what I had been through in the last few days, I was becoming a much better actor. But the noise had definitely brought Asa up short.

Still crouched in the defensive stance he had adopted earlier, I marveled at his ability to keep that pose for so long as he pivoted in one quick motion in the direction of the car. My reflexes were certainly not that precise yet.

Pretending to follow his lead, I turned my gaze in the direction he had indicated. Standing as still as I could, I listened to the sound of Michael climbing the fence surrounding the horse pasture. He was fairly nimble and was soon walking through the knee-high grass in an apparent move to come up on the back of the house.

Hearing each step he took, I followed his progress and expected he would make it to the back yard in about ten minutes, since he would have to walk all the way around the pond in order to approach the house from the back.

Wondering if he even knew that the large pond was there, I got my answer when I heard one of his boots get sucked down in the muck of the pond bank. Swearing lightly under his breath, he struggled for a moment before continuing on. I knew the feeling having lost a boot there myself once.

Casting a glance at Asa, I was caught off-guard as he swung me up in his arms and dashed up the stairs in the span of a second. Setting me down quietly, he gently opened a window without making a sound. *Probably the same one he used to break into my house*, I thought irritably to myself.

Grabbing me up again, he lightly stepped out onto the roof of the house and then climbed up to the highest peak of the house, holding me in his arms during the ascent.

Settling against the scratchy tiles of the roof, he settled me down into his lap and pointed to where Michael was making his way slowly into my new view across the pasture. Now skirting the back edge of the pond, he was turning north and heading back towards the house.

Wondering briefly if he would see us perched up on the roof, I glanced up to make sure no shaft of moonlight would bring attention to our position, but the night sky was black with the clouds of a February night. It probably wouldn't have mattered anyway, Asa could move faster than the human eye could track.

Twisting around slightly to see Asa, I noted he was watching Michael's progress closely, eyes dilated with perverse pleasure at the sight of the unsuspecting human.

"Don't hurt him, Asa. He's just doing his job. Besides, it'll just bring unwanted visitors if you do." My voice was pleading and that was probably not a good thing when dealing with a deadly vampire.

"I am not planning on killing him. I am only up here to observe him. Maybe play a game or two with him." He smiled down at me, fangs wet and exposed with anticipation. Hearing Michael swear quietly again, I turned my head back in his direction as he began to scrape his boot on the grass. So much for those polished boots. Horse pastures are so unforgiving.

Finally giving up on getting his boots any cleaner, he continued on, making it to the more recently mowed grass. From there, his progress sped up as the walking became easier. Stopping as he stepped out into the back yard, it was there I finally caught his scent.

Inhaling quietly so as not to bring attention to myself, I realized I liked the way he smelled of horses and leather. And blood. Yes I could smell that too, and I liked the aroma.

Feeling Asa inhaling behind me, I didn't have to wonder if Michael smelled as good to him. It was obvious in the slight sigh he let out between his red lips. And I realized then that I might be a threat to Michael too as I matured in my conversion.

Climbing the steps to my back deck cautiously, I watched Michael look around, clearly expecting the unexpected. But his idea and my idea of what constituted unexpected were probably as different as night and day at this point.

Watching warily from my position high above him, I saw him approach the windows. Cupping his hands around his eyes, he peered into a couple of different windows before walking over to the door and rapping sharply on the glass. Waiting a couple of minutes for me to answer, relief washed across his face when no one answered. Then with a look over his shoulder, he pulled what looked like a brush out of his pocket and then started sticking pieces of tape around the doorknob.

Realizing what he was doing, I laughed inwardly to myself at the thought of him being able to trace Asa with fingerprints. But you had to give him credit where credit was due, he was really giving this case extra effort. Although I did wonder absentmindedly if what he was doing was legal. Shouldn't he have done that today when he had the search warrant?

Making his way around the house, he took a few more samples before starting back to his truck, keeping close to the tree line after he made it out of the backyard. It was then I felt Asa suddenly move beneath me and at the same time clamp a hand over my mouth.

Despite landing without as much as a quiver of unbalance, the force of his landing caught Michael's attention and he jerked his head back in our direction only to find nothing there. By this time, Asa had moved ahead into the shadows of the trees that lined my driveway, keeping us well hidden.

Turning his head slowly from side to side to scan the area, Michael pulled his gun from his holster, holding it up in front of him. One hand on the grip of the gun, and the other hand holding the butt, I could see the weapon was shaking slightly. From where we stood, I could smell a scent that was fairly new to me. Testing it a little more with my new sense of smell, it didn't take me long to name it. Fear. Michael was afraid and his respirations had picked up, along with his racing heart .

As the detective continued to grow more and more nervous, I finally recognized it as the overwhelming sense of fear that I had experienced the first time I had felt Asa's presence. It would get stronger and, eventually, I knew, it would overwhelm him and he would lose control of himself if Asa didn't end it.

Continuing to back up with the gun held close to his body in front of him, he side-stepped his left foot first and then his right foot, making slow progress back to his truck. I could sense the confusion in him; the knowledge a predator was close by was apparent to his subconscious, but not to the logical part of his mind.

Seeing nothing on which his unease could be blamed, he finally turned and started to run wildly back to his truck, gun still in hand. Setting me down behind him, Asa sprinted away so quickly that I had no time to implore him to stop.

As a human, I had only been able to see a blur of movement but not what was creating it. I could now follow Asa completely with my eyes. I watched as he overtook the detective in a quick second and with what looked like barely a touch, Michael was thrown to the ground, making a complete revolution and landing on his side.

Digging his fingers into the ground to get traction, Michael pushed up, regaining his footing, only to be thrown down again, this time hitting his head when he went down, a small rivulet of blood snaking its way down his forehead where it had made contact with a rock. Appearing slightly confused and glancing furtively around to see his attacker, Michael didn't try to get up immediately but reached for the gun that had been thrown from his grasp.

From my position against the trees, I could see the beads of sweat that had formed on his forehead. A couple had made their way down to his temple and were about to drop onto the ground below. I tried to focus on one of the beads of sweat, but it was impossible to look away from the blood. Sweet but not too sweet, I knew he wasn't a diabetic, and the fear added a nice spice. I now understood what Asa had been talking about and as I watched, I saw Asa slide by him and run his finger through the trickle of blood on his way to a nearby tree.

And I saw red. The red on Asa's finger as he turned towards me and, smiling, licked the lovely liquid off of his finger, swirling his tongue around it for emphasis. But I was jealous and angry at Asa because he had gotten the blood and I hadn't and I wanted it.

Smiling at me from his position high in one of the old oak trees, I could only watch him, trying to keep my expression bland and not let on how much I wanted to run my finger through Michael's blood too.

Asa's touch on his forehead had pushed the poor detective over the edge and I turned back to him just as he fired his gun wildly overhead. Dropping down face first onto the ground, I hadn't come this far just to get shot accidentally, I covered my ears as the noise of the shot was deafening. So deafening that it brought on a wave of nausea followed by a rush of anger so intense, images of killing the detective raced through my mind.

Luckily for us both, Michael had scrambled to his feet and had made it back to his truck. I listened as he jerked the door open and pulled himself into the seat, closing it quickly behind him and jamming his finger down on the lock button. Not wasting any time, he was revving the motor up before he had even gotten it in gear and I could hear the gears grinding as he pulled out of the woods on to the dirt road, clipping the edge of my fence as he went.

Laying there in the dirt, I tried in vain to bring my emotions under control before Asa noticed. Conversion was not a pretty process and the emotional instability alone was pure hell.

It's a known fact that more violent crimes are committed when humans are more irritable, such as in heat waves or overcrowding, and right now I was the one who was irritated. The noise had been deafening and even after the sound waves of the gunshot had dissipated, every nerve in my body was still vibrating with anger and pain.

It was in that moment that Michael's smell in combination with my own rage brought images to my mind that were appalling in every way. I could see my teeth cutting down to Michael's pulsating arteries. His hot blood spurting up to run between my teeth and course down my throat.

I could see my hands holding him down, the blood running between my fingers, staining my fingernails as I forced him to lay still, drinking the life right out of him. I could see his eyes beginning to glaze over, and even knowing I was killing him in my night dream, I didn't stop the images running through my mind. And I knew that if he had really been lying beside me in the dirt, I wouldn't have stopped until I had killed him.

My body started to rise of its own accord. I could catch Michael, I was sure of it. I would have him tonight. His scent danced on my tongue and every impulse begged me to pursue him.

Starting to get up, I could see Asa in my line of vision. I knew I would have to share Michael. That image finally broke my violent train of thought. Michael's smell was just beginning to dissipate on the breeze, which helped to clear my mind, bringing me back to a more normal state of mind.

Disgusted at what I knew I was now capable of, I lay back in the dirt wondering how I had ever come to be in the situation where I would crave another person's blood.

As I lay there considering my fate in this life, Asa nearly flew over to me, laughing as he landed beside me in the dirt. "That was fantastic, Annalice. Conjuring up that kind of terror in your lesser species never gets old. Could you see the look on his face from over here?"

"My lesser species? Your arrogance is impressive. Lesser because we lack your strength and speed, or lesser because we lack your need to kill? I think, Asa," I paused, turning to lie on my belly and look at him, "that you might be the lesser species. Yeah, you're stronger, faster, and prettier, but your self-control is lacking. And how about that death by sunlight thing? Tell me, Asa, does that make you superior to us?"

Flipping over onto his belly in one rapid movement to join me in deep conversation, the smile on his face was wholly sadistic, but still undeniably breathtaking.

"My superiority is unquestionable. The mere fact I will never die is proof enough. Your species can die from most anything and yet the only thing that can touch me is the sun. And as for my lack of self-control, your species has nothing comparable to mine. Humans can barely resist a Twinkie and yet I have managed to keep you alive for nearly an entire week despite my insatiable thirst for blood. And you speak of self-control. It is laughable when I look around at this entire culture. Let me just say that America has not improved over the last one hundred and fifty years."

Lying together on the ground as the wind picked up ever so slightly causing the leaves of the old oak trees to rattle above us, we stared at each other. The full-blooded cruel vampire and the fledgling half-vampire struggling to hold on to life and humanity at the same time. The scent of blood swirled around in the air. That of Michael and Asa mingled together. My mouth watered and I licked my lips. His lips, only inches away from mine, opened in quiet laughter.

"See, perfect case in point. I am planning on killing you and knowing that, you still want me. Your self-control is pitiful."

Rolling my eyes, I looked away to break the intensity of his eyes. "You think too highly of yourself, Asa. I'm just hungry. This pitiful lesser human is hungry. So if you're through playing games with us humans, could we go eat?" I demanded, trying to put some sarcasm in my voice.

"What are you hungry for?" he asked, his voice low and seductive. Having a moment of fear that he knew I wanted his blood, I was relieved when I picked up on the lustful tone in his voice.

"Food. You know, like steak, fries, pork and beans, bread." I was partially lying. The steak sounded OK but the rest of it nearly made me gag just at the thought. "I'm not hungry for you, Asa," I retorted, sneering at him slightly as I got up.

"Then by all means, let us go and find you, the lesser species, something to eat." He was on his feet already and grinning broadly at me. It occurred to me that he seemed unnaturally happy for him tonight.

"You seem almost happy tonight? Not your usual grim self. Has something happened?" I asked, as he swung me up in his arms. Streaking away towards the house, he didn't answer until we were back on the porch.

"Change is in the air I think," he noted when we landed gracefully on the front steps. Looking up at him, he took a deep breath inhaling deeply and so I nonchalantly did the same thing, but the air held only the sweet smell of his blood.

Of course, I could smell the horses and the cow and I noticed for the first time how wonderful the new shoots of green grass smelled, but in comparison to him, those smells were weak. I certainly didn't smell any change.

Looking at him inquisitively, he raised his eyebrows at me and flashed me another smile. Shrugging my shoulders at him, I turned and walked into the house. This was very strange behavior, even for him.

Normally I would have grabbed a coat to go out this time of year and even though I no longer needed one, I wanted to appear normal to Asa, so I grabbed one of my lighter jackets as I walked by the coat rack on my way out to my car.

Feeling Asa trailing behind me, he was in the car by the time I opened my door and slipped into the driver's seat.

TWELVE

Trying my hardest to drive at the speed limit, I struggled to keep my foot from slamming on the gas pedal. Hunger gnawed at me. I could feel it wrapping around my stomach, clawing through my skin to get out.

I headed to the steakhouse that we had skipped out on the other night, knowing it would only partially satisfy me. Not normally a steak lover, it was the only food that sounded even remotely good to me.

Trying to focus on something, anything to keep my mind off my insatiable hunger, I thought about the detective, being careful not to think about his smell. Pretty sure that I had him pegged correctly, I was now even more certain he would be back. He would be spooked but not so much that it would shake his gut feeling about this case. After the events of tonight, I could probably expect a visit from him tomorrow, although nothing that had happened tonight would have any substance in the light of the day.

Pulling into the parking lot, I glanced surreptitiously around but didn't see any cars I recognized so I nodded to Asa and we both got out of the car. Meeting him on the other side of the vehicle, we walked towards the short staircase leading to the front door. I could smell the beef, from outside and I was glad I had chosen the steakhouse. It would at least help a little with some of the cravings.

Just off to my right, a middle-aged couple had parked and were walking towards the door. Clear to me that we were going to intersect, I veered off to the left not wanting to come into contact with them at all. But Asa had other ideas and he reached out and pulled me up against his side, whispering into my ear, "Let us take them together. They have a nice enough smell. It could be fun, you know, if you would just let it."

I'm embarrassed to say that it took a few seconds for my mind to react with a definite no. In that short amount of time, I could picture what their fear would do to the beating of their hearts and to their smell. The desire must have shown in my face because I heard a wicked-sounding low laugh in my ear.

"See, I am growing on you, Annalice," he whispered again, "You could become a killer so easy."

"Go to hell," I whispered back into the air, certain he would hear me.

"I will, Annalice. I cannot escape it. Someday when this hell I live every day is over. The problem for you is that I may take you with me." Not sure what he meant, I questioned him with my eyes, but he said nothing more.

We waited in silence for a table and our waiter arrived a few minutes later to seat us. The restaurant was a pretty popular place even on weeknights and there were very few open tables. I spotted one at the very back and asked the waiter if we could sit there. He smiled and nodded a yes and led the way as Asa and I followed.

We had just arrived at the table and a young brunette

waitress had already dropped off a mini-loaf of rye bread and some warmed honey butter. Taking a knife, I cut off a sizeable hunk and spread it generously with the butter. Asa, of course, being uninterested in food didn't mind I had nearly taken the entire loaf. The bread wasn't very appealing to me, but I was determined to avoid any suspicion from him.

"So you don't eat or drink anything besides blood?" I asked as I bit into the bread. Looking at me as if I were stupid, he didn't answer the question. "Well how am I supposed to know? Maybe vampires eat, maybe they don't. I've seen it both ways on the movies. Why don't you let me in on the secrets?" Taking another bite of the bread, I waited for his answer.

"Are you interested in another deal?" His quiet voice startled me as I had convinced myself he wasn't going to answer.

"What's the deal?" I asked suspiciously.

He smiled at me somewhat menacingly before he spoke. "You spend tomorrow night with me as I truly am, a vampire au natural, and tonight you can ask me any and as many questions as you want. And I will answer them all, with the exception of one, truthfully and completely."

I thought this over for a moment staring at the loaf of bread, the reality of what he was suggesting sinking in slowly. He wanted me to help him kill a human. No, I couldn't do that. Not even to save my own life, much less to get a few answers to my questions.

Looking up at him, I found him watching me closely with

211

that less-than-human look on his face and I expected the worst. "What is it you really want?" I asked between gritted teeth. "You know that I won't help you kill anyone."

Leaning forward on the table with his arms, he looked at me for a long moment before he spoke. "If I take a life tomorrow night, it will be regardless of whether you are there or not. You will not change me one way or the other. I am starting to get accustomed to your company. I have even had second thoughts on whether it will be necessary to kill you. I want the experience of being my true self before I take a companion. Something I have never even contemplated before this week."

I should have been upset by what he was telling me but intellectually I knew this was my one and only option for the information I so desperately needed. I had only one more night after tonight

It suddenly hit me then for the first time that if I did happen to survive the vampire, how would I survive being a vampire? I didn't know how to keep myself from getting killed. Or was it undead? How much sun could I tolerate? Could I be around my family at all? How much blood would I need?

I began to feel myself giving into the panic that was hovering on the edge of my conscious. My entire plan started to unravel in my mind. His offer was a life preserver to a drowning victim.

"Why me?" Frightened at what the answer would be, however, I couldn't help but ask. Did he have some sixth sense that I would become a killer and fit right in with him?

Could he smell something in me? Did I smell evil? I waited expectantly for the bad news that would cause me to have to end my own life. I couldn't become a killer. Ellie would be better off if I simply vanished and died than for my transformation to leave me like him.

"As I have told you, I have only formed this relationship with a very small number of humans. As you would expect, most of my victims could not deal with the scenario they found themselves in and they did not survive. You are the only one of five to not die. Not that five is a great number, mind you, but you are the first to survive me so far. It must mean something is not right about you. I have never had more than a fleeting thought about creating a companion and I only do it now out of sheer boredom. After living over a century and a half, boredom has become my sole companion. It is refreshing to not have to pretend around you. I cannot promise that I will turn you, and you will probably curse me for creating you. But I am willing to trade the information that you seek, for whatever the reason, in exchange for your company as I really am."

Stunned at his words, I sat there dumbly. Speechless for once, I had never considered this possibility. Could I do this? Be with him as he truly was? Did I have much of a choice? I needed the information and he was the only source. Maybe I was justifying my actions, but he would do his foul acts whether I was there or not, right? So having made the decision that I couldn't bring myself to say, I nodded my affirmation.

The waiter had brought my dinner by now and it had

213

been sitting in front of me getting cold while we talked. I wasn't in the mood to talk any further for a while so, picking up my steak knife, I proceeded to eat in silence. The sirloin steak, cooked rare like I had ordered, did seem to quell some portion of the hunger I was experiencing and I ate every last bite. I followed it with three glasses of tea as I still couldn't seem to stay hydrated.

After I finished eating, I anxiously awaited the ticket and tried to use the time to figure out what questions I should ask him and in what order I should ask them. Should I tell him about my viral theories? No, I decided quickly, the less he knew, the better for me.

Our waiter was busy so it took a few minutes for him to make it to our table. Usually, I would have tried to hurry him up by staring at him until he came, but tonight I kept my eyes down, not wanting any extra attention. It was safer for the young man that way.

Despite the fact I was anxious to begin the litany of questions I had for him, I dreaded returning to the prison of my home. Isolation was taking its toll on me. Even being out in public at a restaurant surrounded by a couple hundred people, it was an illusion. I knew I was still totally alone.

Finally the waiter whisked by, and as I had planned, didn't spare me another glance, smartly slapping the ticket on the wooden table top. Getting up, I tossed a couple of twenties on the table and walked out to the car. I didn't look back to see if Asa was following me. I could still tell he was by the constant need to look over my shoulder.

Not speaking again until we walked back into my house,

the silent drive home gave me some time to arrange my thoughts. It was getting close to midnight, leaving me only about five and a half hours.

There was a lot of ground to cover. I needed to know how he was turned and by whom? What was the process? Sure that I knew at least one method of conversion, I was confident there was more than one way, and quite possibly some variability in the timeline. There must be a way to speed the process up and that knowledge was a priority. Next on my list of priorities was how to actually survive as a vampire. Supposing I were able to kill him, I would be alone, helpless like a child.

A sudden thought flashed in my mind causing me to pause in mid thought. If he willingly turned me, would I even have to worry about this? Could I really go on and kill him since he hadn't technically killed me? I mean, sure, I would be a vampire, but I would still be in some part of the world of the living. At least, I was trying to convince myself I would. My mind raced through twenty different algorithms at this new thought, but as interesting as the idea was, I knew in my heart the end result would be the same. I could never be his companion as long as Ellie needed me. He would hardly create a companion just to share her with a child. But did that mean that he necessarily had to die? Maybe we could part on good terms when we were equal. Yeah, it was a pipe dream.

Going on into my bedroom, I changed into some cotton pajamas before returning to the living room. I found him sitting on the couch, flipping through the cable channels. It was very disarming as he looked so human even to me, who had probably known him better than any other human since his death and rebirth.

I was accustomed to him now so my observations might not be as trustworthy and I wondered if he looked human to other humans as well. Would I be able to convince my family of my feigned humanity? Could I go back to work?

"First question?" he asked, catching me staring at him.

"Are you able to pass as a human? I can no longer tell." My voice sounded urgent as I sat down beside him on the couch. It was a small couch so our knees were touching.

"Most humans in casual passing cannot discern my physical differences. When alone with me, or while I am hunting them, they are always aware I am different. They recognize me as a predator, but not as a vampire. The vampiric legends no longer conjure up great fear among humans. But essentially every human can recognize a true predator when they come face to face with one. It is much easier to go unnoticed in crowds as the more alone a human is, the more tuned in to their environment they are." He paused now, waiting for my next question. I watched him for any reaction to his own answer, which was no reaction at all.

"How did you become what you are?" I automatically lowered my voice when I asked, half-expecting the rage I had seen on his face when I had previously asked this same question. But his face remained expressionless, although he did take a deep breath before he spoke.

"I was turned as an experiment in the late 1850s by a

vampire that I met only hours before on business. He was posing as a human and I did not realize something was different about him. I suspect that is because he was not hunting me, for prey that is. Also, he was quite old and over time he had perfected his skills at playing human. We did not know each other and he had no affection for me. He simply wanted to watch the process."

Ta king a moment to consider my next question, I continued on. "How did he turn you?"

Crossing his arms and staring off into the past, he looked almost forlorn. After taking a deep breath, he told me of the last hours of his life.

"I had been sent by my mentor to discuss business with him; I was studying law at the time. As was customary in that time period, we spent a while making friendly conversation. He offered me several glasses of what I thought at the time was wine. It was tainted by his blood, but it was good.

" Our discussion wa s quite interesting a rd before I realized what had happened, I had drunk many glasses of the wine and became incapacitated. His blood converted me and the alcohol left me in a stupor until it was too late. He observed the process until it was very nearly complete and then left me to die on the floor of his home and be reborn as this creature, alone with no direction and no guidance!" He said that with more emotion than I had ever heard in his voice.

I felt for him, despite everything he had done to me. "Where is he now?" I asked quietly.

217

Turning now to look at me, he murmured, "I hope he is in hell." He paused a moment before he continued. "But I have no idea. I never looked for him."

Shocked that he had never sought out his maker, I blurted out, "You've never looked for him? Never heard from him? Didn't you want to kill him for what he did to you? He's probably out killing more people even as we speak."

His laughter at my outburst was low and quiet yet still filled the room with its coldness. "I do not care how many humans he kills. You need to grasp that concept, Annalice. I am not like you. I have not seen the world through human eyes in over a century. The taking of a small insignificant human no longer bothers me. Oh, I remember WHEN I thought like you." He was laughing that awful laugh again. "But I am no longer capable of thinking like you.

"When I remember back to being human, I spent quite a bit of my time worrying over the most ridiculous things that now I wished I had not wasted my time on. Who would become President? Politics, right, wrong, injustices, the thought of going to war, Americans fighting Americans. These trivial matters filled my mind day and night. Money, family, honor. I could go on and on. But after I was changed, I realized the nothingness of it all. The world just keeps going and going. Humans keep living and dying. They all die. The timing is of little consequence," he concluded, leaning back into the comfort of the couch cushions.

"As for killing him," he continued, "I would relish the opportunity if it were to present itself." His voice fell silent now, awaiting my next question.

"You hate yourself, don't you?" I knew I shouldn't have said it as soon as it was out of my mouth, but it was too late. In the blink of an eye, I found my shoulders being crushed between his too-powerful hands. His eyes were dilated and his fangs were fully out. Anger practically danced on his skin.

"I hate myself and I hate you as I hate every human. You have everything I deserved when he took it all from me. What makes you more deserving than me? What! Tell me!" His voice was little more than a hiss.

He was shaking me so roughly by the shoulders, I thought my neck would snap, but my durability had increased slightly. I answered him as quietly and calmly as I could. "I don't know, Asa. I don't have the answers."

I was sure for a moment he was going to rip me apart with those fully extended fangs, but he finally loosened his grip and shoved me away hard.

Nodding his head as if he was answering some question in his own mind, he retracted his fangs. "But he gave me a few things, Annalice. Hate, blood lust, and an appointment with the devil, and now I am seriously thinking about giving them to you."

It was starting to make more sense. He had been turned not just against his will, but also left to fend for himself. Similar to a neglected child who never matures emotionally and becomes a serial killer. Eerily similar. Never releasing his rage on his creator, he had unleashed it instead on himself and every other human with whom he came into contact.

Putting my hands down to steady myself before I spoke again, I asked, "Why didn't you hunt him down?"

He shook his head in the negative while a slight sigh escaped his lips. "Where would I have hunted? You make it sound so easy, but I was new to this life. I had no idea where to look or even how to look. I was just trying to survive and yet hoping to die. Truly die. The peaceful kind that humans find at the end of their short existences. But by the time I had learned to do more than just survive, I no longer cared enough to bother with the search for my blood relative. It is unlikely I could have defeated him in any event. He was incredibly old, nearly four hundred, and many of those years had been spent in combat. Wars were different back then. Very up close and personal."

Twisting his hands in his lap, his voice had a broken quality as he continued. "While I lay on the floor of his house suffering and dying, he told me of his life's journey, giving me little useful information that would actually help with my survival. I am certain that my success as a vampire was of little importance to him. It took nearly forty-eight hours for my heart to finally cease to beat and there was nothing I could do in those hours except listen."

For a moment, I think he forgot he was talking to me. He was lost in memories that must have tortured him for a century and dragged him down deeper each time he remembered them.

Falling silent now, I realized I could smell the fear and rage these memories evoked in him. I took a deep breath so I might never forget what horror smelled like lest I become immune to it.

Venturing on to what I thought was slightly safer ground, but not by much, I posed my next question. "So how did you survive with no one to help you? Did you ever see your family again?" Quietly waiting for his response, I was still human enough to have a twinge of guilt asking the questions that probably hurt him the most. But my guilt was easily suppressed by how much I needed to know. I watched closely, expecting another breakdown.

But he was much more composed and this time only lifted his hands to run his fingers through his hair. He ran them through slowly, pulling at the locks from his crown to his shoulders. A gesture, I decided, he had developed over time to deal with frustrations. I had seen him do it several times before tonight.

"Instincts are powerful in my kind and that is how we survive. Like the dawn for instance. It cannot surprise you for it is always there at the back of your mind. Like a tether you can never truly escape from, pulling you back into death and reclaiming your soul at the beginning of each day. No matter how strong I feel each night, or how alive I think I am, the sun always delivers you up helpless each morning. Vampires do not crave the sun or the sight of it, and I have never missed it. The instinct to avoid it is extremely powerful and cannot be resisted."

He paused here for a short moment. Just enough for me to know that whether or not he had any true emotions left for his family, he still had some reservations discussing their deaths. "As for my family, I did go to them shortly after I

221

was turned. I did not go immediately afterward, of course. I was frightened, naturally, at my changing and for a few nights did not leave the house in which I experienced my conversion. I was thirsty, quite thirsty actually, by the time I did leave, but I did not stop to feed my new hunger, still thinking there was some way I could resist it.

"Convinced that my family could help me, I traveled at night to reach them. How naïve I was then. My mother was so good. So kind. I can still remember the touch of her hand, her smile, and her smell, and I honestly believed she could fix what had happened to me. I struggled to hold onto everything she had taught me. Praying continually as I traveled, I made better time than I had when I was a human and reached them in three nights. As you have probably surmised, they were dead, lying in state. I won't go into the details of how I got in to see them. It would do nothing to increase your opinion of me.

"My baby sister, her daughter, and my parents were all dead. I could smell the stench of the man that made me in every room of my family home. I could have followed him as the path was made so obvious by his smell. But what really caught my attention was the blood left in my sister's body and I could not stop myself from sinking my fangs into her neck and drinking it, even though it was old and starting to rot. I think my maker did it on purpose. He knew I would go looking for them. In fact, he had said his own creator had once told him that a good maker did not leave survivors to search for the new child. Of course, at the time he told me that, I did not understand what he was really trying to tell me.

"And truthfully, I no longer cared and I cannot even say I was that angry over the death of my family at that point. Actually, I was angry with them as well, certain that my maker had treated them far better and with more kindness than he had treated me. The only kind thing he did for me was to kill my beautiful mother. I was glad she was dead. Glad she would not see what I had become. But for me there would be no pity and no justice, and I knew from that moment on that I would never truly feel anything again.

"I left my family home with my great thirst raging and went looking for blood. I found it in the home of a young lady I had courted as a younger man, just a few blocks away. Our previous courtship did not protect her. I could have taken her in her sleep with a quick snap of the neck, never knowing what evil had befallen her. But I did not allow even her that respite; I woke her and saw the recognition in her face before I drank my fill. In my anger and not yet having perfected my bite, I made quite a mess of her with the force of my thirst. Her blood brought a slight calm and I was able to think rationally for the first time since I had been reborn. The sun would be up in another few hours and I wanted more blood."

Stunned by his story, the words exploded from my mouth, "How could you, even you, be jealous of your family's deaths and then go and kill your girlfriend in cold blood? And drinking your sister's blood! That's got to be the sickest thing I've ever heard." My words were hard, judgmental, and cold. I knew my face showed the revulsion

I felt and I knew he could see it too. I didn't try to hide it.

Smiling back at my disgust, he countered, "Death is nothing compared to what could have happened to them, what happened to me. It is nothing compared to what I may do to you. Their death means nothing. Your death will mean nothing. Your rebirth, if I choose that path, will mean only that I have been more cruel than usual."

"Why do you say that? Surely becoming a vampire is better than death?" I could hear the desperation in my words.

He laughed softly now. "Will you think it better than death when you crave your daughter's blood? If I turn you, I should kill them too. To protect you, of course. But I promised you their safety so I will not. But mainly because I do not think I will have to. Like me, you will try to see them. And likely as not, you will kill them for me, especially if you go too soon after you are made. I hope you like blood, Annalice, because you are going to spill a lot of it. Just. Like. Me." He emphasized his words by leaning closer to me with each word.

"How do you know? How many other vampires have you actually known? Maybe that's just you! Maybe I won't become like you. There's at least a chance." Emotion was threatening to overpower me and I quit talking lest I reveal too much.

Raising one hand into the air in a questioning way, he dropped it nonchalantly and smirked. "Perhaps I will change you just to find out. It would be interesting to watch you drain your own child," he noted, leaning back into the cushions of the couch, laughing at my outburst.

His words made me angry and I retorted back, "I could never hurt her." But his words made me nervous and I looked down to see I was twisting my hands in my lap. I refused to give up my only hope, willed my hands to lay still, and forced myself to not argue with him.

"How do you know it was your maker that killed your family? Could it have been another vampire?" I asked, changing the subject.

He shook his head slightly at my naivety. "We take the scent of our maker. I smell like him and he like his maker before him. Humans have their own individual scents. I can no longer differentiate you like I could when I first arrived here because vampire scents are so much stronger than humans. Your scent is being destroyed just by me being here." That was beneficial, I thought to myself as he continued to speak, as it would mask the fact that I was changing.

He was still talking so I turned my attention back to him. "I could only just make out my mother's lemon balm perfume over his overpowering stench. He made the deaths look like the handiwork of a human, but my much stronger senses told me they had been drained. My eyes could pick up the fang marks that were invisible to human eyes."

Four somber and loud chimes split the quiet of our conversation and I just barely caught myself from clapping my hands over my ears. There was very little of the evening left, I realized; time to move on to a new topic.

"How much sun will kill you? How much blood do you

need? If you do turn me, how will you do it?" I wasn't sure if he would answer the last question but it would do no harm to ask.

"The sun is the weapon of God. In its direct power, we will die very quickly. We cannot stand in its purifying rays," he answered, staring me in the eyes without any hint of humor.

Wow. Talk about superstition! Did he really think God couldn't just as easily kill him at night?

"Who says? Did your maker tell you that?" I asked as I got up off of the couch. Pretending to need to stretch my legs, I got up off the couch and made a big show of doing a few stretches, folding down into a yoga pose here and there. Really, I just didn't want him to see me smiling at his superstition.

"I've already told you. My maker was merely an observer. But what I have said is true, I have heard it preached." My question had exasperated him.

Getting control over my expression, I leaned against a wall facing him once more. "I don't think God judges you for things out of your control. I think you're far more likely to get judged for killing indiscriminately than simply for your existence." I knew my words were falling on deaf ears, but I still couldn't help say them.

"Do not forget how easily I seduced you, Annalice. I do not think you know God. But very few in this century do. Your God is friendly and caring. Not at all the God I was raised on. You new Americans have tried to make him more like you instead of making yourselves more like him. Please understand that I do not mind that. It makes for much easier targets. Women and adolescents walking alone at all hours of the night. Secret rendezvous anywhere out of sight. Morals at an all-time low. A vampire's dream!"

I had no plans to argue religion with him, but it was far more likely that the virus didn't have the necessary genes in its genome to reverse the damage that occurs from ultraviolet rays the way the human genome does. It gets less effective with age, of course. I had proof of that on my own face, and I was pretty sure that didn't make me evil.

"Are you listening to what I am trying to tell you?" He was staring at me intently now.

"I'm just thinking things through about what I might be getting into," I lied.

Squinting at me in disbelief, he replied, "I doubt that. More likely trying to think of some way to make an end of me. It is not going to happen," he intoned as he walked slowly over to me.

Rolling gracefully from one foot to another, he stopped directly in front of me and pressed me flat against the wall I had been leaning on. Out of the corner of my eye, I could see the tip of an old wooden cross I kept hanging on the north wall of my living room. Hung just a few feet away was another piece of Old Mexico, a large bronze sun with long wavy arms reaching out in all directions on the wall. This pairing always brought a smile to my face whenever my gaze fell on it.

Purchased on a trip to Mexico with my mother, Mom and I had bickered with the thin Latino store-owner for at least a half hour over the price. I was pretty sure who had won out but each time I walked through this room, it always caught my attention and never failed to take me back to happier times before my dad had died and my husband had left.

How ironic that I now stood beneath the auspices of the outstretched wooden arms and the golden rays while in the grasp of a vampire who was convinced that both were his damnation. Wanting very much to look at them for assurance, I couldn't as his eyes held mine, his lips arched up in a sneer; his face arrogant and beautiful.

Every night I was with him, my desire for him grew despite the fact that my hatred for him grew as well. There was no logic in this at all since his every act was evil and cold-hearted. Yet, I still wanted him.

His gaze never leaving my face, he reached up, knocked the cross from the wall, and grasped the iron sun. The cross ricocheted to the floor, arcing off the crown molding of the nearby kitchen doorway.

With one hand, he bent the iron sculpture in half with complete ease before snapping it in his grasp. His voice whispered low yet silkily in my ear, "If your plan is to bring me to the sun, you are more foolish than I realized." He dropped the twisted sculpture onto the floor at my feet.

If he was making a statement, the theatrics were good, I thought, as I stared down at the bronze remains of the sun. "Oh, not to worry. I'll get another one. They're as common as tequila in Mexico," I noted laughingly into his face. "But if the sun represents purity, were you sending a message to God?"

Sometimes my mouth gets me in trouble. This was one of those times, I realized, just as his lips were at my throat, his hands crushing my throat. What a temper.

Feeling the nick of his fangs as they brushed my skin, my desire for him at that moment grew exponentially and I could smell my own pheromones as they permeated my skin. And as suddenly as the situation had turned dangerous, it now turned into desire.

Turning my head to give him better access to my veins, I could feel him tracing a path with his mouth up my carotid, but I had more questions so I couldn't give into this. "So where do you spend your days?" I asked as innocently as I could.

Laughter rumbled low in his chest. "Remember I said that there was one question that I would not answer. Well, that is the one. Do you actually think I would tell you where I spend my days so you could come and stake me in my death sleep? But it was a nice try. My instincts about you are correct. You are going to be ruthless." He continued to laugh to himself, which brought me to my next question.

"So I guess you breathe?" He had to push air across his vocal cords to laugh, but that didn't mean he actually needed to breathe.

"I breathe only when I want to taste the air or take in a scent more strongly, but I do not need the oxygen. Occasionally strong emotions reminiscent of our human existence will cause us to breathe out of habit."

His mouth continued his assault on my neck and I wanted to give in to it, but I had to hang on to my senses. There were so many questions and not enough answers.

"So, not answering specifically, of course, but where would you typically spend your days? And you didn't answer my question about how you would turn me and how much blood you need?" My breath was coming in short bursts because I still needed to breathe and he was taking my breath away every time he landed a cool kiss on my neck.

"We can go anywhere so long as there is no sunlight. Old crypts are a favorite. That is why vampires love Louisiana, by the way. Great hunting grounds among the alcoholics and safe sleeping places. But old houses and basements will do. If they are not light tight, they are still an excellent place to dig into the ground, which is an acceptable, but messy place to hide. Any sunlight will weaken you, not necessarily destroy you but it can weaken you to the point you can easily be overcome by humans. As for your next question, turning you will require you to drink my blood, which will be erotic, I think, and we require the entire blood supply of a human every six or seven days. I usually drink every day, which means I do not have to drain my source if I choose not to."

Now with my questions answered, I felt his fangs pierce my neck. Inhaling deeply, the scent of his blood was nearly overwhelming at this proximity. It struck a nerve deep within me and I wanted him, or at least his blood in such an overpowering way that almost by instinct, I bit him. I didn't draw blood, but I wanted to as its scent was intoxicating in its sweetness.

He jerked back ever so slightly and took an even slighter intake of breath before he caught himself. Surprise flashed across his face followed by what looked like suspicion and anger. He hesitated for what seemed like an eternity, but I kept my expression as innocent as possible and finally his suspicion seemed to pass.

As he leaned back into me and let his head drop back slightly, I continued to nip lightly at his neck. His breath came quicker as I continued to bite harder until I was leaving marks on his skin. I tried not to think about what I was reminding him of with my bite.

Eventually, his breathing slowed and whatever anger or hesitation he had experienced when I first bit him, he seemed to be over it now and for once, taking his cue from me, I felt his fangs pierce my skin.

I formed my next question while he drank, "If you turn me, I assume we will have to leave here?" Knowing what his answer would be didn't keep me from asking it.

Withdrawing his fangs, he continued to muzzle my neck while he answered, "Of course, Annalice. Secrecy is the one hard and fast rule of vampirism. Even without a teacher, I recognized the need to remain unknown. We live in secrecy not only to protect ourselves from extinction, but also to protect ourselves from becoming too plentiful. In my painfully long existence, I have never met even one human who did not want to live forever. Not realizing of course that immortality among the mortals is its own form of hell, they crave it without fully understanding it. We would be hostage to the desires of humans. It would be us who needed protecting from their cravings."

He was right. How many patients had I diagnosed over the years with terminal illnesses? How many patients had I pronounced? And not one of them had wanted to die. Not a single one had let go of life without a fight. Struggling for just one more breath, one more hour, one more day. Age, race, gender, even religion; none of it changed the fact that nobody wanted to die. Oh sure, some people are ready. But no one is eager. At least not from where I had been standing. And I wasn't any different.

"We have very little time left tonight, Annalice. Surely you tire of these questions. A more entertaining activity awaits us, surely you agree?" The nerve endings were starting to implode under his hands as he caressed my back and shoulders. In a quick movement, my cotton pajama top was gone and his fangs bit into my left breast, setting off another entire plexus of nerves. Gasping as I arched off of the wall and into his mouth, I knitted my fingers deeply into the thick wave of his hair.

I had more questions, but it was difficult to put words into full sentences and I only managed to produce two and three-word phrases. "Stakes...how." I spoke the words into his hair as I leaned down, trying to get closer to him as he continued to suck small amounts of blood from my breast.

"Unknown," was his one-word response when he lifted his head for the briefest of seconds to answer.

His fangs, completely extended, showed pearly white against the curve of his full red lips, which were accentuated more by his fair skin. His scent burned in my nostrils and I was unable to keep myself from inhaling deeply. I wanted to fill myself with it, be covered with it, and become part of it. It was so heavy, I was sure I could lick it off his skin.

With dilated pupils as dark as a moonless cloudy night, his gaze bore into mine and my heart did a little flip flop. Not from love, but from such powerful lust that I felt limp in its grasp. Tons of questions remained, but I couldn't convince myself to care.

I wanted to consume him. My thirst for him was unquenchable and I literally wanted to take him, all of him, internally. The urge to do that was mind-controlling. With my lack of control raging through my body, I pulled his face to mine and plunged my tongue into his mouth.

Tasting my own blood didn't stop me and I let myself melt into his body, wrapping my legs around his waist. Turning, he walked slowly to the bedroom and within seconds, our now bare skin was pressed tightly against each other as we fell onto the bed.

If I had been able to tear my lips from his, I would have been screaming with pain and pleasure as the friction between our bodies wreaked havoc on my nervous system. But I couldn't pull my face from his except to bite him. My hands grasped him, my nails tore at him, my thighs clenched him as I settled onto his full length. And my last greedy conscious thought was of trying to get even closer to him as his orgasm exploded within me.

THIRTEEN

Our evening together left me dazed as usual. I think whatever hormones he released into my bloodstream, which likely strengthened as he became more excited, are simply too strong for the human mind. Honestly, when sex is that good, who cares if you lose consciousness or not.

I'm not sure what woke me up. I had expected to sleep till around noon like every other night when he left. But I had woken up at 5.30 a.m. My period of sleep was shorter than usual. His pheromones obviously didn't have the same effect on my neurological system as earlier in the week.

The sun wasn't even up yet. It wouldn't be long though and getting up out of bed, I padded into the sunroom to watch it come up over the horizon of the mountains in the distance. Not sure of exactly what had woken me up, I didn't want to waste my last opportunity to see the sun rise over the glorious vista to the southeast of my house.

Whatever happened tonight, I would never see the beauty of the sun again. Never warm my skin in its rays again. One more night until I would either live the life of the undead or join the ranks of the truly dead. Knowing my eyes would sear in its brightness, I was determined to see it one last time.

I still hadn't called Ellie. Maybe that was for the best. I wasn't sure I could keep the sadness or the finality out of my voice. My mom would recognize that something was terribly wrong immediately. We had always been close and my death would kill her. Ellie would probably be the only thing to keep her going. That was good, at least they would have each other.

Plopping down into the oversized sofa facing the floor to ceiling walls of glass, I watched the blue-gray mountains expectantly for the first rays of the morning light. Since the room faced into the rising sun, there was no place to hide from the brightness as it illuminated every nook of the room. Sometimes the sunlight was the only thing that could wake up an overtired doc like myself after a week-long stretch of night shifts.

Glancing up at the clock, I knew the sun would soon rise up to fill the valley that ran between the two shortest peaks. The sky was lightening and taking on the pink and purple hues that would eventually give way to the cool blue skies of a late winter morning.

While I waited for the first rays of the sun, my mind returned to the question of what had woken me up. Hovering on the edge of consciousness, some as yet unrecognized idea or question burned at the back of my mind.

As I pondered this mystery, the first golden rays poured through the crevice between two dark blue mountains and, as it had at the beginning of every sunny day since being added on to the house, illuminated the entire sunroom from floor to ceiling. The sun rays, catching the edges of the glass, were cast every direction and there was no place to hide from its brilliance. And although that had been the point of the room's design, I was unprepared for its new effect on me.

As the rays spread across my bare skin, the sensation of a raging fire burned out any previous joy the sun had ever brought to me. As my skin seared in the sunlight, explosions of light burst behind my eyes, despite both being squeezed tightly shut leaving my eyelids to suffer the fire of the sun.

The effect was not unlike staring into the sparklers I had lit for Ellie and myself last Fourth of July. We had danced and twirled around in the dark, sticky July night, little sparks flying from the sparklers to land on our hands and arms, warm but no longer hot enough to burn us. For a few moments, my eyes had only been able to make out silvery streaks of light.

So much more brilliant, the sun had filled my entire visual field with shimmering flashes of light, leaving my head aching and my stomach rolling. Vomiting seemed inevitable.

Certain I would burn to death in the sun's brightness, I buried my head in my hands and struggled to walk into the part of my house that faced north and wasn't illuminated by the sun. Now understanding firsthand what Asa meant, I never wanted to see the sun again.

It was a difficult passage marked by torchlight shafts of sunlight streaming through the numerous windows so common in old houses. Unable to walk any further, I fell to my knees, crawling the rest of the way to my bedroom.

Suddenly, the nausea became overwhelming and lurching

to my feet, I sprinted for the bathroom just in time to heave into the toilet. I retched for at least a half hour until there was nothing more than just yellow foam, and then dry heaved for at least another thirty minutes until it finally subsided and nothing remained of my last meal. I was only able to produce clear spit.

Wiping my mouth with the sleeve of my t-shirt, I collapsed back against the hard wall of the bathroom, not even bothering to get very far from the commode. The tile floor was cool against my legs and although leaning against the wall wasn't very comfortable, I didn't have the strength at that point to go any farther. I simply sat and tried to catch my breath. My head was spinning too fast to think very clearly and I wished I was still in bed asleep.

Pulling my legs in and wrapping my arms around them, I rested my forehead on my knees. Feeling drained and exhausted from my exposure to the sun, it took a lot of energy just to pull oxygen in and out of my lungs.

With my overactive hearing, I could now hear fluid accumulating in the base of my lungs, the human part of me was still actively dying. The sun had worn me out considerably and I was lucky the height of my oversensitivity to the sun had not occurred when I was outside and unable to make it back indoors. I'd be willing to bet that not all vampire converts had been so lucky.

Sitting still to conserve my energy, I was content to do nothing for a while and I tried to not even think, but something was tugging at the back of my mind. Knowing it was important, I struggled to drag it out of the recesses of my memory. Despite my efforts, complete exhaustion set in and I must have fallen asleep for a little while.

I'm not sure what woke me up again but I think it may have been the sunlight. Crystals of silver and white were once again exploding behind my closed eyes when I came back to awareness. The rising sun had reached the level of the skylight built into the bathroom ceiling. Lucky for me, it was only a small window but knowing that I couldn't stay here, I crawled out of the bathroom with my eyes still closed. My skin tingled and burned as I passed through the rectangular panel of light that was thrown across the floor by the skylight.

Stopping when I reached the shadows again, I lay on the carpeted floor of the hallway, trying to decide what to do next. All I could think of was darkness, in fact, I craved it. So getting back up on my hands and knees, I crawled, too afraid to stand up where the light from the windows could touch me, towards the safest room I could think of: the walk-in closet.

Once in the dark coolness of the closet, I felt immediately better. Collapsing on the carpet, I lay there doing nothing but trying not to puke again. That would be very unpleasant in the close quarters of the closet. I kept my eyes closed and my head resting on the cool, thick carpet of the floor. There were no windows and it was only about eight square feet. Resting there on the floor, I waited for the remaining nausea to pass. It must have taken about forty five minutes for my head to quit spinning and my stomach to quit twisting on itself.

239

While I lay there, my memory finally jogged and it occurred to me for the first time that I could have been looking for Asa's hiding place these last few days. I felt so stupid, but then again, he could be hiding anywhere and any number of miles away. Now I had the eyesight and speed to do it, but I was as locked away from the sun as he was.

Slowly sitting up, I opened my eyes for the first time since making my way into the closet. When the lights were off, this room was as dark as the grave even in the middle of the day, but I realized that I could make out the shadows even in the darkness

In the corner to my right, I could see the sharp edges of the safe, and to my left, I could see the uneven line of the hems of my clothes hanging up. It was still black in the room, but I could roughly make out the shape of every major object sitting against the walls.

Able to see in the dark and unable to exist in the sun, I realized the virus had reached critical mass. I was now more vampire than human. My theories were proving correct. It was the first bite that introduced the virus, but if the victim was healthy, their immune system would be able to successfully fight the virus and prevent conversion.

That probably explained the old legend that after the third bite, the victim would turn into a vampire. Not that the third bite was a magic number, it was only a rough estimate. It was most likely dependent on many things including the number of bites, viral concentration in each vampire's saliva, and the timing.

Numerous bites close together was probably much worse than bites spaced farther apart. In my case, I had tried to be exposed as much and as often as possible. The more cells that were infected, the quicker it would spread. I was turning even quicker now than I had been before. Last night pushed me over the edge, I had finally reached the exponential phase of viral transmission. Asa didn't recognize what was happening to me, but why not?

The vampire that turned Asa fed him his own blood from a glass. I had never drank Asa's blood and I was still turning, but Asa said he would feed me his blood to turn me. So did I need to drink his blood? Was his blood required to complete the conversion, or did that just speed it up?

Thinking back through what he had told me about his last night of life, I knew he had not been exposed multiple times like I had been. He only received his maker's blood. Vampiric blood must contain higher numbers of the virus compared to other body fluids so he needed very little time to be converted.

Certain that I would convert without his blood, the only questions were when it would be finished and if I could face him as an equal tonight? With only a few hours left until his return, my time was running out.

Sitting in the dark, I wished I had my computer so I could do some research on the Internet, but it was out in the den and I was unwilling to risk facing the sun. Reaching up, I flipped on the light switch in the closet. Even though I could see the shapes of most everything, I was still sitting in the dark. The closet only had a sixty-watt bulb, but I gasped slightly when I hit the switch. The light seemed brilliant and hurt my eyes, which I squeezed shut as tightly as I could against the light, but at least it didn't burn my skin.

Giving my eyes a few seconds to adjust, I was able to look around the closet and I realized how unorganized this space was. Everything that had ever meant anything to me over the span of my life was tucked away somewhere in the confines of this room, along with all of my clothes and shoes.

The closet also served as the safe room of the house, so it was built of cement blocks wrapped together with rebar and then that was wrapped with quarter-inch steel sheets on the outside. The door was a heavy steel door that bolted from the inside. I had it added to the house shortly after I moved in.

This area was known for tornadoes and that was the only reason I had hired a contractor to build it. It was July, prime tornado season, when I had interviewed the contractors and tornadoes were my only safety concern at the time.

But the contractor had been just as concerned about personal security and home invasion when he showed me the plans. He had looked at me the same way my parents had when I showed him the house. Like I was crazy! I had overheard him telling his employees several times that a single mother had no business living in the middle of nowhere.

Looking around the room, I realized just how safe this room really was. Certain that the contractor wasn't thinking about vampires when he built it, I wondered if it was impervious to them? Or maybe even better yet, would a vampire be safe in this room during the daytime? It was essentially a crypt. Could I use it to hide in until I was fully changed? That was a thought I hadn't considered until I found myself now hiding in here from the sun.

Confident that my only hope was to be changed before Asa decided my fate, the closet was looking like my best option. Eventually I had to come out, but if I could wait until I was fully converted, at least I had a chance. But if I gambled wrong and he could tear this door down before I was changed, I didn't stand a snowball's chance in hell. I eyed the door speculatively, I had never been much of a gambler. I decided not to chance it.

I continued to sit in the closet just staring ahead of me, pondering vampires and my theories when it occurred to me that the safe room had a computer tied into the security system. The contractor had thought it essential to be able to email from the confines of the closet in the event the phone lines were cut or had been knocked down. Now in retrospect, I decided the man was a genius. I wasn't planning on sending out in any emails, but I could certainly spend some time doing research.

Pulling open the security box, the keyboard was a small fold up variety. It looked tiny even after I got it opened up, but at least it was usable and I had access to the web.

Pulling up the search engine, I typed in vampire. I rolled my eyes when nearly three million hits popped up. It would take me weeks to scroll through these, let alone even read many of them. I needed to narrow this down. Choosing "becoming a vampire" as my next search, I got almost seven million hits! Disgusted, I went ahead and scrolled through several pages of these sites.

Disturbing was the only word I had to describe what I saw. Apparently, lots of people want to become vampires and even more claim to know how to become one, although I found very little information that seemed to be useful at all. It definitely didn't seem relevant to what I knew about them. Well, I only knew one vampire, but the information didn't seem to fit with what I knew about him.

I was pretty sure he hadn't become a vampire by falling off of the left side of a wagon, or being the seventh son of a seventh son. Apparently, both were once thought to be common ways of becoming the undead. Had a chicken crossed his grave? Had he been excommunicated? Had his parents put a curse on him? Was he born with red hair? This was ridiculous and I was wasting my time.

I kept flipping through the pages but I was getting desperate, nothing I found seemed even remotely possible. Had I actually sunk to perusing the Internet for vampire tales, hoping to find something helpful? Well, yes I had. All I needed was a grain of truth, I reminded myself. Surely there had to be some small tidbit of useful information so I patiently continued to flip through the sites.

I was about two hundred sites in when something caught my attention. It was a link to a newspaper article dating back to the mid-twenties, printed close to Valentine's day.

Located in the style section of the paper, a drawing of a

middle-aged man was shown above the title that read "Man Claims to be 500-year-old vampire. There in black and white was a sketch of a man who appeared to be about fifty years old. His face was angular and he appeared quite tired. I read the article quickly. Short and sarcastic, the author was clearly condescending and was openly discounting the man's story.

Not that I could blame him, of course, I wouldn't have believed it either a week ago. It probably only made the paper because it was a love story and the author was desperately looking for a Valentine's story with flair. He must have been really desperate to print this. How ironic that he had printed what would have been Earth-shattering news if he had only realized it.

Skeptical at first, I became pretty convinced it was legit about a paragraph into the brief account given by the man.

According to him, he had become a vampire after falling in love with a woman in the early 1500s. Having spent every night with her for about a month, he had died one night in her arms after she convinced him to drink from a small gash she had made with a knife on her left wrist. Thinking this was a poetic manifestation of their love, he had done exactly as she said, not realizing the consequences.

When asked if he blamed her, the man had told the author that looking back on the event, he now knew she had trusted him implicitly because direct feeding would have made her vulnerable. One of the few times that this was true.

According to the vampire, the process of conversion

caused uncontrollable cravings in the one being converted, to the point they could drain their creator without realizing it or caring. Also, the blood provided extreme power in the last few minutes of life. Enough that they would be stronger than their maker, but only briefly. She had loved him completely, enough to put her life in his hands.

"Why was he revealing himself?" the author asked. "Tiresome, so awfully tiresome after the hunters came for her. So let them come for me now. I'm longing for her company," the vampire had answered. That was the last line of the story. Underneath the article was an advertisement for a tonic that could cure any ailment. Talk about a hoax.

The article seemed to be the most legitimate documentation I had come across while searching the web. It explained why Asa's maker had fed him distantly from a glass. Asa could have overpowered him if he had been able to get his hands on him. The alcohol had probably helped to subdue him as well.

Certain that Asa didn't realize the reason for how he was turned, I was grateful he had never bothered to find out more about himself. His lack of knowledge of his own kind was my greatest advantage.

But why? Why would his blood make me stronger than him? There had to be a scientific explanation. There always was. This wasn't very different than the mating of black widow spiders where the male is rendered helpless and eaten by the female. Evolution's way of making sure that the weaker one has a chance to survive. In this case, the human's chances of being turned go way up, ensuring procreation of the species since they don't give birth. At least, I didn't think they gave birth.

My eyes were burning from staring at the computer screen so I turned it off for a while and leaned back against a small portion of wall space that wasn't cluttered up. If he did decide to turn me, I was now certain I could kill him.

Basing my future on an article from the twenties may not have been the most logical thing to do, but the story had a sense of realism to me that was probably missed on its original audience. I was sure the man in the picture was telling the truth. *I hope he got his wish*, I thought to myself.

He had said, "Let the hunters come." Who were the hunters and were there any still around today? Guessing you'd find them on the Internet, I tossed around the idea of using the search engine to find a vampire hunter but gave that idea up pretty quickly.

From what I had seen on the web, it would take weeks to find the real thing, and chances were they would be psycho when they did show up. Plus if they were real, they would want to kill me too. No, I decided I would take my chances alone with Asa.

It was really hard to explain how I felt physically. I didn't feel like myself. Kind of like there was something inside me that needed to get out. Almost like I was wearing skin that was too tight, yet I felt strong, like I could run a race or bench press a few hundred pounds. And I was thirsty. Every other thought was of Asa.

Lifting my arms to my face, I inhaled deeply up the length of my limbs and I could smell him on me. My insides twisted and burned for him.

Feeling itchy and dry, I raised my arms up only to find layers of skin were beginning to lift off of me, reminding me of a snake shedding its skin. I lightly grasped an edge that had lifted near my wrist, gently tugging off a piece that stretched to my elbow. Expecting to find young pink skin like in a second-degree burn, I was surprised to find my new skin was pale and supple. I looked sort of like zebra with my old skin lying against the stripe of my new skin. Asa would surely notice this. Great, how would I cover this up?

Getting to my feet, I lifted up my shirt and saw it was doing the same on my abdomen and flank. Rubbing at the layers, I watched as flakes dropped to the floor. I needed to scrub myself as soon as possible. Maybe I would get lucky and could get into the shower before he came. For the last couple of nights, he hadn't come right at dusk. Of course, tonight he was planning on showing me his true colors. Maybe I would be okay in the hour before dusk since the sun would be coming from the other direction and very few of the rays would make their way into the bathroom.

What else was going to happen to me before I was completely converted? When would my heart stop? I knew it would because I had surreptitiously listened for the beat of Asa's the other night when I was getting exposed. I had not heard it. When I had held his wrists in my hands, I didn't feel a pulse. A vampire's physiology didn't rely on the heart to pump blood. No longer needed, it would eventually cease to beat.

Asa had told me that vampires could be killed by a stake to the heart, but the why remained unknown. That didn't make any sense and I sat there confused for a few minutes. I decided not to worry about it, science didn't understand everything about human physiology, I certainly didn't need to understand everything about the physiology of vampires. If all went well, I would have plenty of time to figure it out.

The clock on the security system beeped that it was 12 p.m. I still had a lot of time to spend in the closet. Strange but true, I didn't have to fight an urge to leave the closet. It felt really natural to be in the tightly enclosed space. That must be an instinctual effect of the virus, craving closed in dark spaces during the day hours. So did that explain the common coffin theme in vampire movies? Probably. And the idea of a coffin didn't really seem that bad to me.

The more I considered it, the more comfy the idea felt. If I survived this, maybe I would look into getting one. No, scratch that idea. No matter what, I wouldn't get so dramatic as to sleep in a coffin. I laughed out loud at the thought. It felt good to laugh so I laughed out loud until my laughter began to take on a slightly psychotic sound and I stopped abruptly.

Tears, light at first, started to trace down the contours of my cheekbones. Reaching up to wipe away the first few that fell, I looked down at them on my fingertips. They were red tinged but otherwise they glistened like normal teardrops. It appeared that now my tears were mingled with blood. They continued to fall so I gave up wiping them away and let them fall where they would, staining my light blue t-shirt.

I simply sat in the closet and mourned my lost life. This was what was left to me if I survived, which despite my newly found advantages was still a big if.

Despite my previous feelings of ambiguity towards Asa, I realized I was happy to be his companion in only one way, to escort him to the grave. He deserved it for everything he had done to me.

Hatred for him surged through me along with my overpowering lust for him. No not him. For his blood. Recognizing the importance of separating the two, I tried to focus on my hatred of him. I would need that hatred to keep me going tonight if I was to survive.

He had taken everything. My life, my family, my career, and my future. What did I or what would I have left? The night? Which meant I had nothing. Could I really raise my Ellie and hold down a career in the dark? And even if I could, my precious daughter would age before my eyes and finally die, leaving me alone in the world. I would never enjoy a sunny summer day again. Never soak up the sunshine with my little girl along the beach. Never watch her play softball or ride her horse again.

Worst of all, she would never understand why and I couldn't burden her with the knowledge. My heart ached and I could feel the crush of sadness on my chest. Maybe my heart would break and I would die of this sorrow.

Humans can die of a broken heart. It's not just a myth. The Japanese call it Tako Tsubo. An emotional cardiomyopathy, and for a few minutes despair overwhelmed me and I wished I could die of it. At least Ellie would have a body to mourn

But I could feel my heart beating slowly in my chest. How much longer would it beat? Letting my hearing take over, I listened to its slow but still rhythmic beat. Right now, for the moment, its sound still connected me to Ellie and to her human world. I was still a part of her life. So despite its progressively worsening sounds of failure, I relished in the fact it was still functioning.

As many dying people do, I think, I had a lot of regrets. Things that I hadn't done with her or for her and now that the end was near, I wished I had. Like all of the scrapbook supplies that were sitting in the corner of the closet. I had been meaning to make her a scrapbook pretty much since the day she was born, but I had never gotten around to it. Why not do it now? I decided.

Pulling out the supplies, I reached into a box about ten inches square, it contained all of the pictures, haphazardly arranged, I had taken over the years. I had always berated myself for not taking my pictures on digital cameras, but now I was glad I was technologically challenged when it came to pictures. Because now I had photos I could actually hold in my hands.

Flipping through them slowly, I divided them up into the different phases of her childhood. Starting with the pictures from her birth, I started to make the first page. I couldn't help but stare at the first picture ever taken of her. Laying across my chest, she was beautiful and I looked so naïve. At least that's the way it appeared to me now.

The second picture was of Ellie in my ex-husband's arms.

Normally, my vision would go red when I saw him or thought back to him leaving us. But I could no longer feel any anger at him. There were many more important things to worry about, I now realized.

If he had been here, he would be dead and for once I was glad for his sake that he had left. Ellie would still have a father and that was good. I stared at his face a moment longer and wished him the best.

Laying those pictures aside, a photo of Ellie on her first horse caught my attention. Auburn hair streaking out behind her in the wind, she sat as tall and proud as could be on that little horse. Tracing her outline, I was grinning as proudly as the day I had bought that horse. He was still grazing out in the pasture.

There were pictures of rodeos, T-ball games, school programs and holidays. Each picture brought blood-tinged tears or laughter and sometimes both. God bless her. I would miss her. I missed what she would become. I mourned for her first date, her prom, her graduation, her wedding. I even mourned for my grandchildren.

Three hours later, however, I had a very presentable scrapbook. Why had I not done this sooner? I had dreaded this for years and now in a matter of a few short hours, I had done it. I would put it on her bookshelf in her room tonight, and someday she would find it. If I didn't survive this, it would be my goodbye to her. An idea hit me and at first I hesitated, but then deciding I had nothing to lose, I wrote a letter to her.

I told her about the day she was born, how I had held her

in my arms and marveled at her perfection. I described her inquisitiveness and her raw energy. I recounted some of our best days together. I told her that I loved her, I told her that I knew I was dying, and that I made this for her to remember me.

I reminded her to take care of her grandmother, to work hard, go to college, and to be picky when it came to boys. She was worth the best, I told her, and lastly, I told her again that I loved her.

Folding the note up, I slipped it down behind one of the pictures in her scrapbook. I prayed she would find it someday. Not immediately, but in a few years when she might understand all the sentiment that I had tried to cram into those few sheets of paper.

A couple of blood-tinged tears landed on the papers and I didn't bother to wipe them off. They were representative of how I felt.

The clock gave a short bleep. It was 3 p.m. The sun would now be coming from the west. There were several rooms in the house I could probably go into now. The bathroom being one of them since it faced east. Since I wasn't a full vampire yet, I could probably venture out in the rooms that didn't have direct sunlight. It was a gamble but one that had reasonable odds I thought

Opening the door slightly, I stayed hidden behind the door and stretched my right arm out into the hallway. Nothing happened. So I stepped out cautiously and headed slowly into the living room, the scrapbook tucked under my left arm. So far, so good. I stopped at the entrance to the living room and peered around the doorframe into the dimly lit room.

Luckily, all the blinds were closed and the doors into the kitchen and hallway leading to the sunroom were closed. I was safe and had not burst into flames.

Placing the scrapbook down on an end table, I turned to go take a shower when my eyes landed on the wooden cross lying on the floor where it had been knocked during the previous night's encounter.

Having only been made to look old, the wood was actually quite strong and the end was beveled. It would take very little to turn this into a nice stake. Oh my gosh. Had I really just thought that?

Thinking again of the scrapbook, I reached for it and placed it inside the magazine rack just in case I forgot about it and Asa happened to notice it was out of place. He would be able to smell me or him on it and probably recognize it for what it was.

Pushing it down deeply between two older fitness magazines, I placed the stack of magazines that had been sitting there for at least a month back on the top. Satisfied that nothing looked out of place, I turned my attention back to the cross.

Grabbing it up off the floor in a quick movement, I realized I could do nothing without a knife. Too afraid to venture into the sunny kitchen, I headed back to the closet where I kept my dad's old pocketknife. That was kind of fitting. My dad would want to rip Asa's heart out if he could see me now.

Kneeling down in the closet, I made short work of the stake. I left it intact thinking that the T would give more leverage, but decided to make it shorter and shorten the arms as well. It didn't need to be nearly as long to go all the way through Asa.

Holding it with my hands, I was able to break the hardwood with my foot, so the length of the stake was no more than twenty inches and the arms no more than about four each. Just enough to allow for a good grip. Using the knife and my increased strength, I shaved away shards of wood until I had a very sharp stake indeed.

Judging it in the light of the closet, I decided it could be a little sharper so I spent another ten minutes before forcing myself to move on. Tucking my new stake in behind a stack of jeans, I turned my attention to the next important item on my agenda, a shower.

In an older house, it always takes a couple of minutes for hot water to reach the nozzle and I spent that time looking at myself in the mirror after I had taken my clothes off.

Looking like a strange albino zebra, I freely acknowledged that I looked like crap. My human skin was slightly darker than my new vampire skin, but the main difference was not so much the coloring but the texture.

The developed vampire skin was supple, like a child's. There were no wrinkles, no moles, and no cellulite. No plastic surgeon could create skin like this. My only hope was to get as much of my old skin off. With a long-sleeved shirt on, maybe Asa wouldn't notice.

Stepping into the shower, I grabbed a loofah sponge and

some sea salts and went to work. The old, dying skin came off pretty easily with the loofah. Starting first on my hands as they would be the most visible part of me besides my neck and face, I scrubbed both hands and arms until my skin was mostly the same color. Still a little darker in the creases, but it would have to do.

Going next to my face and neck, I scrubbed harshly and then started on my chest and abdomen. Grabbing another loofah specifically designed for the back and shoulders, I was about halfway down my back when I noticed I was up to my ankles in water, which is a very strange feeling when you're standing in a shower. Looking down, a large clump of soggy brown oatmeal-like material could be seen covering the shower drain.

I almost gagged when I realized what it was. Dead skin. I had pulled off enough dead skin to actually clog the drain. I stood there for a moment, dreading what I had to do but knowing it had to be done. Besides, I still hadn't done my legs.

Disgusted, I reached down and grasped the slimy mess. Very large, it took both hands to scoop it up. Heavier than I expected, it overflowed through my fingers as I squeezed the excess water out and used my toes to pull open the shower door. Stepping out of the shower, I flung it into the commode as quickly as possible and flushed it, all the while trying not to look at it.

More of the slime awaited me, but hearing the dreaded but not unexpected sounds from the toilet, I turned back around to face the swirling brown discolored water rising in the blocked toilet.

The breath rushed out of my lungs as I huffed my outrage at my newest dilemma, but reaching for the plunger I was happy to find it only took a couple of strokes with the plunger to send the mess on its way. This was good considering I had precious little time left.

Stepping back into the shower, I grabbed the loofah and resumed my scrubbing by finishing my back and moving on to my legs. I had to repeat the unclogging process twice more before I was finally finished, but I took care to flush it in small increments each time. Almost by habit, I grabbed the moisturizing body wash and was about to slather it on when I realized that I probably wouldn't need it any more.

Leaning out of the spray of warm water, I glanced cautiously up at the skylight. I could still see filtered light coming in and decided to go ahead and wash my hair.

Reaching for the shampoo, I poured a good-sized amount of lightly scented shampoo on my hands and scrubbed at my scalp viciously. It probably had skin cells that needed to come off as well. After I finished assaulting my scalp, I leaned over to let the soap run through the rest of my hair.

To my disgust but not surprise, more of the oatmeal-like tissue ran out into the bottom of the shower along with a few long black locks. Seeing it was much more than could be attributed to usual hair loss, I pulled my hair through my hands.

Holding my hands up in front of me, I gasped at what I saw. Hair hung from my nails and twisted around my fingers, trailing down onto my forearms. Shocked by what

257

had happened, I stood up quickly, spattering the back of the shower with more oatmeal and at least a thousand long hairs that clung to the shower wall.

Studying the hair closely, the white tips could be seen quite plainly with my new vision. It had come out by the roots. Not being able to help myself, I reached up again with both hands and began to pull out more and more of my normally thick hair. The more hair I pulled out, the more hair that followed. It didn't take very long until I had no hair left except a few stragglers. The shower floor was covered in it.

Red-stained tears came uncontrollably at this point. Not only because I had lost my hair, which was one of my best features, but also because I wondered how I would keep this from Asa. He would definitely notice that I was bald. Well not completely bald, I still had those few stragglers.

Getting my razor while I continued to cry red-tinged rivers down my body, I made short work of the few strands that were left. Now I was truly bald.

Not wanting to stain the white grout of the bathroom tile, I stood dripping in the shower until my red tears had stopped. Grabbing a towel from the linen cabinet, I dried off and threw the towel in the dirty clothes.

Putting my robe on, I walked over to the sink counter and got a trash bag out of the cabinet. Getting down on my knees, I started scooping up large handfuls of my hair out of the shower, not wanting my family to have to clean this up when I was declared missing and/or dead.

I had decided that my chances of survival were now slim

as Asa would quickly realize what was happening to me. Hair loss is pretty dramatic and he had been through this all before when he was turned. I could cover up the skin changes for the most part, but the hair?

Sitting there on my knees desperately wishing for a wig, I had a flash of what was either pure genius or complete desperation, or possibly even both. Probably more desperation if I'm honest. Hair extensions! Every girl that has ever ridden in the rodeos has them and I had worn them a couple of years back when I had shorter hair. They had been matched both to the color and texture of my hair. Surely there was something I could do with them.

Walking back into the closet, I found them buried half way down in a trunk where I kept evening gowns and other similar items. Grabbing them and an old sewing kit that I kept in the closet, I sewed the weaving of the extensions onto the rim of a university hat I had stored in the chest. I sewed as quickly as I could, but tried to make sure the hair was even all the way around the ball cap. When I was finished, I walked back into the bathroom and tried it on.

"Not bad," I murmured to myself as I turned slowly in front of the mirror. "As long as the hat doesn't come off, I might pull this off."

Going back into the closet, I yanked two long-sleeved layering t-shirts off the hangers and put them on over some jeans. Next I grabbed my hiking boots and the cap. Reaching up out of habit to brush back my hair that was no longer there before I put the hat on, I felt stubble all over my head. It was already growing.

259

I pulled the cap down tightly over my head and grabbed a coat to pull on over the t-shirts. Although I wasn't the least bit cold, I wanted Asa to think I was preparing for the chill when we went out tonight. It would help explain the hat. Lastly, I picked up the stake and tucked it into the waistband of my pants. The jeans were snug and kept it tightly against my body. The layers of clothes along with the coat completely obscured its outline and I could only hope Asa wouldn't try to feel me up tonight. That would certainly be my doom.

Now with nothing to do but wait, I stood in the hallway, trapped and anxious. There was really nothing else I could do to prepare and nowhere I could go. The sun still hadn't completely set and the apprehension that it created had never subsided, although it had been relieved by the confines of the closet.

The anxiety had been building all day but I had so far been able to ignore it as I had something to occupy my mind. But now there was nothing left to do except wait. Wait for Asa to return and for me to meet whatever future lay ahead. Needing to find some way to keep it controllable, I walked into the living room. Glancing around the room, my eyes fell on the scrapbook I had made for Ellie. Grabbing it from where it was hidden, I dashed into her bedroom.

Kneeling down in front of her bookshelf, I ran my hand across the bindings of her favorite books. We had read them together so many times that the spines were beginning to give way and even though I would buy her new books, she insisted on reading these on a weekly basis. Pushing my fingers between her two favorites, I slid the scrapbook between them.

Standing up, I walked over to her bed and lay down, hugging her pillow to my face. I breathed in her smell as deeply as I could. Her scent was like heaven and realizing that this might be as close as I would ever get to her or heaven, which were one and the same really, I sucked in my breath several more times. But knowing I couldn't stay here forever, I put her pillow down giving it one last final pat and walked back into the living room.

Even though I was not completely vampire yet, I could tell the day was drawing to a close and the night would be here soon. I could feel it coming and I wanted it to come because I felt like I was suffocating in this house.

I checked my pulse. I'm not sure why since I had listened to my heart all day, but its slow rise and fall against the pads of my fingertips was still reassuring and I left my fingers there over my radial artery. Would I realize it the moment it stopped? Would I feel that along with the rest of my enhanced sensations?

My heart seemed to beat in unison to the ticking of the clock. Slow and steady, marking the time until the sun was completely set. Would it be this way every evening? Would I feel as though my skin was crawling right off my body, waiting for the sun to go down?

You could have spun me around in the house blindfolded, and I could have stopped and pointed in the direction of the setting sun without uncovering my eyes. Its power sent tingles down my spine even from within the house.

Slowly, it seemed like an eternity, I felt it dip down behind the peaks of the not-so-distant mountains. The night had finally returned and the only way I can explain how I felt is to say I felt alive again.

Breathing a sigh of relief. I couldn't wait for Asa to arrive, I wanted to… I wanted to… I'm not sure what it was that I wanted to do. But there was something I needed to do.

Hunger. That's what it was. I hadn't eaten or drank anything all day and I was hungry and thirsty. Both of which had suddenly become overwhelming but I couldn't decide which was stronger. The hunger or the thirst. They were both too powerful to ignore. I had to have something now.

Walking into the kitchen, I jerked open the refrigerator door. Grabbing the turkey and cheese only because they were the first food that my eyes fell on, I began ripping the wrappings off of both, shoving each piece into my mouth as quickly as possible.

Chewing only enough to be able to swallow, I ate every last piece of both packages. But I still wasn't full. And the thirst was even greater. My throat felt like it had crevices from how dry it was. I drank almost half a gallon of orange juice, all that was left in the refrigerator, and I was thirstier than I had ever been.

Throwing the carton onto the floor out of anger, I pulled out a barstool and sat down, not knowing what else to do. I had to wait for Asa. Not that I could explain any of this to him, but at least maybe he would be able to distract me by his presence alone. But the more I thought about it, the more sure I was that I was wrong.

It seemed I had been listening for an eternity now as I sat there waiting for Asa to arrive. The clarity of my new hearing had been a constant reminder of my ever approaching death as I could not even escape the sounds of my life running out. Even the oppressive silence of Asa's dead heart weighed heavy on my ears.

I had listened as the mundane world around me had morphed into something I would have never acknowledged only a week ago. Sitting here waiting for certain death, one way or another, I struggled to keep from clamping my hands against my ears to drown out the noises of a world that in a few short hours might no longer be recognizable to me.

Despite my anger at my ever constant listening, I could not keep from straining my ears, hoping that I would catch some sound that the Detective had returned. Even during my seclusion in the saferoom, I had studied the occasional noise that made it through the thick walls, hoping for the doorbell or even police sirens. But Michael had never came or at least, I hadn't heard him.

What had I expected? He had no real reason to return other than a gut feelings and night terrors that could not be substantiated away from Asa's terrifying presence. But still I had been sure that I had not seen the last of him.

Alone all day, I couldn't help but wish for some living companionship, to see a face that didn't want me dead. I reminded myself to be glad that he hadn't came. I was in no condition to see him. More likely than not, I was as dangerous to him as Asa and so I forced myself to listen for my reality and not my fantasy.

Almost on cue, I heard footsteps and I recognized them. Asa moved almost without sound and I would've never heard them as a human. Still unaccustomed to my recently acquired hearing, his footsteps sounded close enough that I thought he must be in the entryway.

Standing up suddenly enough that I knocked the barstool over, I walked as lightly as possible towards the front door, expecting to see him at every turn. I felt territorial and it angered me that he was even here. This was my home, my territory, and he shouldn't be here.

After making my way into the entryway, I realized the footsteps I had heard weren't coming from the entryway. I had heard him coming across the yard and he was now walking in through the front door.

Instincts told me to rip him apart, piece by piece, but luckily my will was stronger than my instincts and I knew I had to hold this together until the right moment. Doubting that I was strong enough to challenge him now, I needed to buy as much time as I could so I would have as much strength as possible.

I had been feeling my strength increasing throughout the day, but not knowing when it would peak, I was afraid to attack him too soon. Urges that I couldn't explain or even put a name to were rippling through me. I wanted to kill him now more than ever.

I had wanted him dead before but now my desire to kill him seemed to have territorial overtones. I needed his knowledge almost as much as I needed time, and so I needed to keep my emotions and instincts under control. And to do that, I needed to get out of this house.

Taking a deep breath and putting on my most placid face, I turned towards him just as he turned the corner into the room. We were facing each other now and I recognized the predator in him as well. Not that I had been immune to it before tonight, but now I recognized it in his every movement.

There was something missing though. I wasn't quite sure what it was, however, since I had never spent a great deal of time around true predators. I took a deep breath as he walked over to me. He didn't smell of fear. He smelled of lust. I could smell my own fear, which I'm sure had been present since his arrival so he didn't recognize it as different or new. But he wasn't afraid of me, which was good; it gave me an advantage over him.

"Let's go." I nodded towards the front door. I turned and walked out the door without waiting for his reply. I could hear his near silent footsteps behind me, but I turned around to appear that I needed to see him following me, walking backwards for a moment.

"In a hurry?" he asked, quickly closing the gap behind me.

Nodding my head slightly to indicate my agreement but not so much as to tip my hat, the words flowed freely. "I'm ready to see you for what you truly can be tonight. What I may become."

Turning back around to not give away my significantly

improved balance, I walked to the garage.

Just as I was about to punch in the code to open the overhead door, Asa grabbed a hold of my hand saying, "We are going on foot tonight. You need to see how I live."

Smirking at him, I replied, "There's no way I can keep up with you." Of course I would make sure that I didn't. Actually I felt like I could run a marathon.

"The night belongs to us and we have only one goal to accomplish. I will move slowly, just for you." His voice held the touch of sarcasm.

Stepping together away from the light of the house out into the night, I glanced up at the night sky. It was dark but a hunter's moon shone brightly overhead, obscuring the stars with its illumination. The dark sky was broken up by an occasional thick and heavy bunch of clouds.

Glad to get away from the lights of the house, I followed Asa as he walked off in the direction of the forests that cut across the back fields of my property. Even though the inner house lights were fairly minimal, the contrast between their brightness and the dark caused some degree of discomfort in my eyes. I wondered fleetingly if that would improve with time.

Coming up on the wooden fence separating the lawn from the pasture, Asa cleared it in one leap as easily as the deer lured in by the garden.

Longing to jump it as well, I climbed through it instead, opting to pretend to be human to camouflage my burgeoning strength and agility. Asa hadn't stopped but continued on towards the woods surrounding my pastures.

I followed several paces behind taking in the smells of the night. The sweet smells of the horses wafted across the slight breeze and I turned to look at them standing under an oak tree about a hundred feet away. I could see my favorite gelding watching us.

Normally he would have whinnied a greeting and started towards me in the hopes of finding some goodies in my hands, but tonight he watched me warily as I passed. He no longer recognized me. His sense of smell was probably as strong as mine and we would have to become reacquainted. At least, I hoped a horse could tolerate a vampire.

So many smells made up the night. Having never noticed them before, I marveled at their intensity and their numbers. Each tree smelled differently as did the different types of grasses starting to shoot up from the ground. I could smell the cows and the chickens, even the onions I had planted in the garden only a few short days ago. The hay in the barn had its own distinctive smell as well as several more flavors that I didn't recognize as we got closer and closer to the woods.

Walking on through the pasture, my eyes fell on a subtle change in the outline of a small slope off to my left. I was sure it was man-made and I had never even noticed it before. I caught a waft of Asa's scent, and then mine, coming from that direction. Is that where he had been each day? Was this his hiding place? If I survived tonight, I would have to remember to check it out better. It could come in handy in the future.

We were in the woods now and its darkness enveloped us

even further. It felt good walking through the canopy. Almost like the trees provided some layer of protection. It was still cold out and an occasional snowflake fell slowly in front of my eyes. Reaching up, I caught one in my hand and stared at it intently. Interestingly, it didn't melt right away as it normally would after landing on my bare skin.

Catching Asa's eyes on me, I realized I had forgotten to put gloves on and quickly shoved my pale hands deep down in the pockets of my jacket, feigning cold. Not taking my eyes from his, I saw his cold smile.

"Just think, Annalice. You will never feel cold again after tonight." Not sure of what he was hinting at, I smiled back slightly.

"I guess there's perks to everything, Asa. I've never really liked being cold." Watching another flake zigzag slowly down and land on my jacket, for the first time in my life I could see the different facets of the snowflake without the aid of a microscope.

Glorious in its complexity, I watched for a full minute before it finally melted, becoming only a tiny drop of water on the cool leather. Licking another off of my hand, I continued to follow Asa deeper into the woods, hoping I would survive to study more flakes another night.

We were on an old four-wheeler path now and it made for easy walking since it was kept pretty clear from the amount of use it got. Four-wheeling was quite popular in the area and on any given day if I had been walking in the woods, I would probably have come across a few people out riding. It was nearly eight o'clock in the evening so I didn't think we would come across any riders this time of night. But hunters were another story.

The path was smooth and I didn't even have to pretend it was an easy walk, which was good because I wasn't completely sure of my acting skills. So far, he didn't seem to have any suspicions and so far he was keeping his pace slow, true to his word. Without warning, he stopped in his position about twenty feet ahead of me and, lifting his head like a pointer dog, he took in a deep breath. He wasn't paying attention to me and so I did the same.

I caught the smell easily enough. Humans, at least three different ones. One older and two younger gauging by the difference in the strengths of their smells. The scent wasn't faint, but not overwhelmingly strong either. Guessing only since I had no experience at this, I estimated they were a couple of miles away. The wind was blowing slightly, carrying the scent towards us.

Testing the air again, anticipation rippled through my muscles and I was immediately disgusted at myself. The hunger and thirst that I had experienced back at the house had been pushed to the back of my thoughts for a little while. But in a split-second, a devastating thirst rose in me, tenfold stronger than I was prepared for. My mouth watered and shivers ran down my spine in response to my anticipation.

In that split-second, I was questioning my ability to retain some portion of my human self. Pushing the questions to the back of my consciousness, I reminded myself that I didn't have any other alternative. Surely I would be less of a threat than the vampire in front of me. As he turned towards me, I dropped my head down a bit so he couldn't tell I was testing the air like him.

"Three humans up ahead. One of them will likely suffice for tonight. I warn you now and one time only. Do not try to alert them in any way or they will all three die unnecessarily and you as well." Turning back to the trail, he began to follow the delectable smell beckoning through the trees.

The scent was easy to follow and became stronger with each step into the woods. Closing my eyes, the aroma seemed strong enough that it should have been visible in the dark, like a ribbon intertwining through the thickly wooded forest that anyone could have seen.

No longer following the four-wheeler trail, we went as the crow flies, or as the vampire walked, I supposed. Winding through the trees and easily climbing over the occasional fallen log that blocked the most direct route to our prey; I let Asa help me over a few, being careful to keep my hands balled up in my jacket when he helped me so that he couldn't detect the drop in my core temperature that must have occurred, given the snowflake hadn't melted on my skin.

A few fallen trees we came across he didn't deem worthy of his help and I grasped the trunks, pulling myself up and over like the clumsy human I was pretending to be. I felt a couple of my fingernails give away, ripping from my nail beds.

Expecting pain, I clenched my mouth shut to keep from yelling out. But none came. Looking down, I could see why.

New nails had grown underneath my old nails. Soon they would have pushed my old nails off anyways. Grasping hold of the rest of my human nails, I pulled them all out as we continued to walk deeper into the woods. A couple of my fingers bled slightly as they were not quite ready to give way, but the flow stopped very quickly.

Testing my new nails in a passing tree, I found that I could scrape marks into the bark. Pulling my nail through the nearest tree, I looked at it closely. Not even a crack or chip. I was definitely going to save money on manicures. Staring at my nails so intently, I hadn't noticed Asa stop ahead of me. He hadn't yet turned in my direction but was still facing in the direction of the humans.

With what appeared to be some difficulty in taking his mind off the scent, he pivoted to face me. "What is that sound you are making?"

Shrugging my shoulders at him, I gave him my best look of complete cluelessness and watched for his response. He kept turning slightly to face the scent while trying to keep his attention on me. How could I have been so stupid as to scrape my nails in the trees? Like I could possibly explain that away. Waiting anxiously, I was relieved when he turned back towards the scents.

"I have let myself get too hungry by staying too long with you each evening," he noted, turning narrowed eyes on me before continuing up the path.

It was mid-February. Prime time for coon hunting in this part of the country. I was betting the men we were hunting were out here on a hunting trip themselves, it would never occur to them that they were about to become the prey.

We continued to move in the general direction of the men but Asa had stopped moving directly towards them. He seemed to be crisscrossing his trail some. I wasn't sure why and I couldn't ask him since that would give away my ability to track their scent as well. The night was still quite young so time wasn't an issue. Maybe he was just dragging it out for my benefit.

If we hadn't been on our way to kill someone, I would have enjoyed walking through the dark woods. The scents, the breeze, the darkness were all more comforting than I would have ever expected.

Having spent quite a bit of time on horseback here, I had never failed to notice its beauty, but I now saw it with a whole new set of eyes, quite literally. The snow continued to drift lightly not enough to even dust the ground. If I were completely human, I wouldn't have been able to see the glaze the snowflakes created on the trees.

I could hear the crunch of every leaf and stick that my feet trampled on. It sounded deafening to me as I was still not used to the overwhelming sense of hearing I had developed.

Noticing new sounds in the general direction of the human smell, it was only a second before I recognized the baying of dogs. Probably coon dogs that had been let loose to run the game. The men would give the dogs time to catch the scent of their prey and would then follow their baying until they came to where the animal was cornered. Each of the humans would most likely have their own dog and they would split up when the hunt started.

Asa had stopped in front of me again, listening intently, turning his head in the direction of the hounds. Sure that he was formulating a plan by the look on his face, I felt for the men up ahead, knowing there was nothing I could do for them.

There were three, all men, I was now certain of their scents. One was quite young, one was middle-aged but very healthy, and the third was elderly but still smelled vibrant.

Probably a three-generation hunting party with wives, children, and grandchildren at home. Out for a good time, they never considered that these woods held any real threats. Would Asa stop at one like he had said, or would he go after all three?

We were getting very close to their base camp now. I could make out the flicker of their campfire through the densely packed pine trees. The camp had been made in a small clearing located in the midst of the largest of the pines. Judging from the size of the trees I could see up ahead, it was likely scheduled for clear-cutting soon, but for now it made a great camp area.

Stepping into the camp, Asa stopped to look around for a moment. Three small and weathered campers were arranged into a semi-circle pattern at the far edge of the small clearing. The fire ring sat in the middle, a neat circle of smoke-blackened rocks surrounded by several different types of old lawn chairs. A dented coffee pot, its bottom beginning to show signs of rust, sat on the corner of one rock.

Still warm coals glowed brightly against the dark of the

night. Had I still been completely human they probably would have appeared more grayish in color, but with my new eyesight any light looked bright. A thin curl of smoke rose from the small fire that burned in the remains of the logs that had been heaped into the center of the ring. The smell of the smoke along with the occasional pop of the fire gave the camp a cozy feel and made this all the more awful.

Walking over to the camper nearest to us, Asa pulled the unlocked door open. Stepping inside with a single step, I heard him rummaging through the cabinets. A moment later he walked out with a small wad of cash and then followed suit with the next two campers.

"First lesson for you." He looked at me as he spoke. "Do not forget to take what you can from your victims. Money will come in handy even for vampires from time to time. Humans also carry other items of value. Shoes, clothes, credit cards, identification. You never know what you will find. They carry the most unusual things." He sounded like some sort of bizarre commentator you might hear describing the steals you could find at a yard sale rather than at a soon-to-be murder scene.

Shoving the small amount of money deep into his jeans pocket, he stopped in the middle of the camp and took in a deep breath. I did the same behind his back, letting the delicious scents of the three men fill my lungs.

He had obviously chosen the youngest of the three because he moved in the direction the youngest had gone. I couldn't really blame him, the younger man smelled divine, like gourmet chocolate compared to the dollar-store variety.

If I were drinking for sport, I would have chosen him too.

But I wasn't drinking for sport. I was only here because I had to be. An agreement. In exchange for the information I needed. Asa was going to kill this young man and I would have to watch, unable to help him. He had also said that he didn't have to kill and that many times, he didn't. But a dread in the pit of my belly told me he would tonight. If for no other reason than to show me how cruel he really was. But I needed no proof, I had seen enough already.

We trailed slowly through the woods, following the scent of the man, letting his wonderful aroma pull us further into the younger pines that had begun a couple hundred feet west of the campsite. As a human, I could have followed him just by the howling of the hounds and now I could hear them as if they were standing right next to me. The dogs didn't take a direct path, but followed the exact trail of the prey.

The human was trailing the dogs as quickly as he could. His trail was more as the crow flies and ours was even more direct than his. We would have overtaken him very quickly but Asa slowed his pace; I was sure it was to let the man get deeper into the woods before we intercepted him. But why? The other two humans certainly stood no chance where Asa was concerned.

"Why are you letting him get so far into the woods? Why the games?" I lashed out at him with my tongue as I continued to follow him.

Stopping, he turned to me, a smug look on his face. "Do you not enjoy the hunt? That is part of the sport, Annalice.

Besides, I do not want the other two humans close by when his end is near. Trying to drink while batting off his would-be protectors would ruin my meal and I like to savor the taste." He grinned at me, but I saw no humor in his joke.

"Will you kill all… all of them?" Studying his face closely, I was relieved to see that his mind wasn't on me but on the prey ahead of us in the woods. Hunger was gnawing at him, I could sense it in his body language.

"I have not decided. I usually do not kill more than one at a time. As I said before, I try to avoid undue suspicion if I can. But sometimes I simply cannot help myself and I am quite hungry tonight. A mistake brought on by my obsession for you," he added, his voice tinted lightly by anger. Was he blaming this on me?

"How often?" I asked point blank, not bothering to specify as I was sure he knew what I was asking.

"About once a month do I take the liberty to drain a human. I usually reserve that delicacy for the lucky days I find a drifter or someone foolish enough to be alone. The more I drink at once, the less often I need it, but I am like most Americans, I often eat for the fun of it, not out of necessity." He flashed me a mocking grin.

He turned back to the scent trail and we resumed our hunt, the thick underbrush that is so common in clear-cut forests pulling at my legs and clothes. Vines and bushes covered in thorns that reached to my thighs tore at us both as we walked through them, making our own path. Asa didn't appear to notice the thickness of the thorns but I, playing my human role, moved slowly pretending to be slowed down.

Looking down as a thorn tore sharply into the skin on the back of my hand, I watched in amazement as first one drop beaded up on my pale white skin and dripped down my wrist, only to see the next drop bead up and coagulate in a second in front of my eyes. In the next few seconds, the puncture wound was no longer visible. I hardly felt any pain, my new skin being much thicker and more impervious to the sharp points of the thorns.

My clothes didn't hold up so well and I noticed several small pieces of my t-shirt hanging on some of the taller bushes.

The vampire ahead of me, stopping to wait for me, pinned me with a look of contempt. "I am growing tired of your human speed. You are keeping me from my meal." Reaching over as I caught up to him, he knocked me backwards and caught me in his waiting arm. Not fighting him, I let him scoop me up as he resumed the path towards his meal.

"I can barely make out the disgusting smell of your anemia over my own scent," he noted, aiming his piercing eyes down at me.

Looking up at him as innocently as I could, I countered, "You have only yourself to blame, Asa. I would still smell delicious if you had just kept on walking when you passed my house."

Smiling down at me, he acted as if we were talking about the weather tonight before replying, "You have such a sense of humor about all of this, Annalice. It would have been such a waste to pass you up. Not to worry. In a few hours, you will have a new smell. Whether of rot or of vampire, I have not yet decided. But either one will be better than this sickly anemic smell that clings to you now."

"I guess that depends on who's doing the smelling," I replied quickly. "I think I would take the aroma of anemia over decay any night." I didn't believe for a second that he didn't already know what his decision was going to be, but telling me now would no doubt spoil part of his perverse fun.

"It is my professional opinion that you could become a first-rate vampire. All you really have to do is hold it together tonight, enjoy the kill, and then we will wake up together tomorrow night," he intoned into the night air as he dropped me down roughly onto the ground, the worst of the thickets behind us.

Before he turned away, our gazes locked again for a brief second and I looked for my future in his eyes. But they were blank. Unreadable. Was he trying to show some mercy by not telling me outright that he was going to kill me at the end of the night, or did he really plan to turn me? Was it possible that I had changed him just slightly enough that he felt something, even if only pity, for me? Would he kill me so quickly that I would never know the outcome? Finally breaking his gaze from mine, he turned back to the scent trail.

The human pressed on and soon the horizon changed as we broke into the native woods as the new growth pines gave way to the oak trees that made up the native forests of this area. Shortly thereafter, the ground started to slant upwards as we climbed into the lower elevations of the foothills that slowly transformed into the mountains.

Although I could tell the human was slowing somewhat because of the increasing elevation, Asa kept the same pace. The scent of the other two humans had become quite faint and I knew that they were no longer in the vicinity. We had the young man all to ourselves and despite my best intentions, I felt a small wave of anticipation as we began to close in on our prey.

Continuing up into the foothills, neither Asa nor myself was winded at all. With his attention fully focused on the man ahead, he didn't notice that I climbed just as easily as him. We had reached a small cliff of rocks, about ten feet tall, that stretched on for one hundred feet in both directions. We could have skirted it easily enough but Asa didn't deviate away from it.

Leaping flat-footed with no effort, his attention stayed riveted towards the scent ahead of us. It took all of his focus to pay any attention to me at all. Blood lust was shockingly clear on his face. During my many nights with him, I had never seen him this hungry.

Pretending that I couldn't get a handhold to pull myself up, I stood looking up at him hoping he would go on ahead. "I'll go around," I whispered up at him, but he lay down on his belly, reaching for my hand. Stepping up onto the tallest foothold that I would normally have been able to reach, I stretched my hand out to bridge the gap between us. By rising up on my tip-toes, he was able to grasp hold of my hand and hoist me very easily onto the top of the small cliff.

For the split-second that I was poised on the foothold, I considered using the momentum of his strength to bring my stashed stake into his chest, but my courage failed me in the last millisecond.

Regret nagged at me momentarily as I landed beside him with his heart intact and my stake still hidden. That might have been the perfect moment and I had just missed it. I could have kicked myself, but something had held me back.

As I looked into the face of my possible maker, I asked myself whether or not I could really do this. My mind flipped through random memories of the last week. I couldn't deny that he had loved his mother and still did. He had even shown me an occasional tenderness and even now was considering keeping me.

Didn't that mean that there was something salvageable inside him? Could he ever become more than what he was now? Had he not been changing, at least a little, over the last few days? Could it become more? And did it matter if he couldn't change because in the end, I might not have it in me to kill him anyhow?

"I've never seen you like this, Asa. You're, I'm not sure how to describe it. But you're more dangerous than I've ever seen you." My voice trailed off leaving the answers hanging in the air.

Letting go of my hand, he nodded his agreement and lifted his head to take in a deep breath. A broad smile spread across his face. "I am ravenous and the hunt carries with it a certain thrill. It fulfills a need that is more than just blood. It satisfies the predator within us. I wanted to be really thirsty tonight although even I did not realize how hungry I was getting by spending so much time with you. I have drank from you for the last week but your blood has not touched me for the last two nights. Very strange. The smell and color were right up until last night, but it has lost its zing. Never spending this much time with one human, I had no experience with how weak your blood would get. But this will work out even better. I will be at my best for you tonight."

Feeling my heart miss a few beats at his words, I froze in place thinking he had finally put it all together. Hoping I could distract him, I whispered in my lowest, most seductive voice, "Let's go then and not waste my opportunity to see you at your finest."

Taking him by the hand, I turned back towards the direction we had been heading; the direction of the human I was helping doom to a gruesome death. I had never had such a low opinion of myself.

As we continued to walk deeper into the woods, the clouds began to dissipate, putting to an end the lovely display of snowflakes that had drifted down slowly while we trailed the human. I could feel the temperature had dropped since we left the house, but it didn't bother me, it was merely an observation to me now.

With each step we took deeper into the forest, the human's scent became stronger and soon I could make out a low earthy sound that I recognized immediately.

Rhythmic and strong, the beat of his heart struck a chord

deep within me, reaching down into my bones and marrow. His strong pulse seemed to be pulsating within me, making me want him and I could taste him on my tongue.

Beating at a rate well over normal, his pulse was elevated because of the climb up the mountain that we had begun about a half a mile back. And its speed only made its resonation within me that much more intense.

An ache, so deep and so severe that it bordered on painful, flamed up deep in my pelvis. I tried to suppress it, but I found I couldn't because the more I concentrated on not noticing the desire, the less I could keep my mind off it. It was a lust, not just for blood, but for him in his entirety. Individually, each lust was strong, but together they were inescapable and it was paradoxical that I didn't want to hurt him yet my skin tingled with the thought of Asa bringing him down.

Looking ahead and to my right, Asa had taken on more of a stalking stance and I shifted automatically into the same stance in response to him. We were close enough now that I could see the focus of our attention between the barren trees of the woods. Asa paid me no attention whatsoever, so deep was he in the lust of his hunt.

Dressed in camouflage that did nothing to hide him from us, he was tall and heavily muscled. His hair was blond, streaked through with brown, and cut short. His smell was strong, musky, of the earth and the woods where he obviously spent a good amount of time. In his right hand he carried a shotgun with a well-polished but well-worn stock, and in his left hand an LED flashlight. Its penetrating beam danced off the trees up ahead as he followed his hounds.

Comfortable in the woods, he paid little attention to his surroundings, as equally intent on his prey as we were on him. Continuing to catch up with him silently for another hundred yards or so, we quickly closed the gap between us.

Sensing a terrifying and unnatural sensation behind him, I saw the fine blond hairs on his neck rise in response as simultaneously an intense contraction of the muscles that ran the length of his spine overtook him in a cold chill.

For a moment, fear paralyzed him as it had me the first time I became aware of Asa's presence. Stopping in mid-stride, he cautiously turned towards us in the dark.

Glancing around to identify the source of his unease, his eyes found nothing amiss. "Dad?" he called out into the quiet of the woods, his voice shaking slightly. The silence of the woods was his only answer.

Calling out again, he lifted his flashlight up, his arm shaking just enough that I could tell he found it a bit difficult to focus on what the light fell on. Moving it defensively in front of him like a weapon, I saw the relief wash across his face when the bright LED beam landed on Asa. Standing diagonal and a bit back from Asa, I was out of the range of the arc of light and he didn't see me.

But the relief he had momentarily experienced was short-lived as he took a closer look at Asa. In the LED light, his skin was paler and more alien looking and the young man jumped back in surprise. Trying without success to regain his composure, he was spooked and it showed on his face.

Recognition of the danger that he was in was clearly

evident in his expression, along with the fight for reason and logic. "Man, you scared me," he called in Asa's direction. His voice shook slightly and I could smell the fear that colored his words.

Asa, silent, stared intently at the young man, locking the young man's gaze in his. The man stood uncomfortably, his hands no longer just trembling, but shaking uncontrollably. He waited for a moment before saying anything else.

From where I stood, I could see logic warring with his instincts, expecting Asa to smile and wave, explaining that he had heard something and came to check it out. And then ask a few friendly questions about how the hunt was going tonight. But instinctively, he knew the entire time that he was in great danger.

Taking a couple of steps forward unintentionally, I found myself in the glare of the beam. My pupils constricted only a little in the glare of the light and I found myself staring into the dilated pupils of the young man.

Assuming that my presence would make us appear less threatening, I found I was wrong. Hearing his heart rate speed up and smelling the surge of fear that saturated the air around us, I could see in his eyes that I was no less frightening to him than Asa was. Looking down at my skin as the LED light landed on me, I looked alien even to myself.

"You guys out hunting?" He tried to diffuse the situation he found himself in as Asa began to walk slowly towards him, still saying nothing. Backing up, the young man lifted his right arm up, leveling the gun at Asa's chest. Not flinching at the sight of the gun, Asa continued his painfully slow stalking of the young man. I supposed the gun was of no consequence to him, but I dropped back and to the right as I could likely still be killed.

"This gun's loaded, man. I'll use it. Stay back! I mean it. I'll shoot. Son of a bitch! Are you listening?" He was yelling now while he continued to ease back rather clumsily.

Changing his tactics, the man began yelling for his dad, for help. What was left of my heart ached for him. Ached for his father and for the son he was going to lose.

I could imagine, one parent to another, what this was going to be like for him, because there was only one reason I was standing here watching his son die, and she was as important to me as this boy was to his dad. But there were no humans close enough to hear him.

Seeing that Asa wasn't going to stop, the man buried the gunstock in his right shoulder. I could see his left hand, knuckles squeezed white trying to steady the shaking weapon. It made little difference, the gun still danced around in his hands.

Asa continued his advance and the human sucked in a deep breath, gathering his nerve before firing off a shot. Watching the bullet erupt out of the barrel, I followed its course, watching it arc through the air and implode in a tree, bark exploding into the air, about twenty yards behind us. The space where Asa had stood was now empty. Even with his shaking hands, the human was a good shot, but he never stood a chance. Asa could simply move too fast.

I watched as true horror spread across his face when his

eyes found Asa again. I could see the fetters of logic break in his mind by his facial expression. He stood slack-jawed, unable to think clearly.

His arms and hands went limp. The gun dropped quietly to the ground, muffled by the thick layers of rotting fall leaves. The forgotten flashlight hung loosely by a strap around his wrist and it swung out in an arc as he turned and began to run deeper into the woods and into the foothills

Laughing his quiet and sadistic laugh, Asa began to walk quickly to keep up. It wouldn't have taken a vampire to follow the man as his flashlight created a bobbing light trail through the woods, along with the noise as he crashed through the underbrush.

Continuing to walk at my earlier pace, I trailed after them, again not wanting Asa to see the ease with which I moved.

Asa could have taken him in no more than a couple of seconds, but he was letting the man run wildly in front of him. His speed despite the fact that he was moving uphill was getting faster.

Asa sped up only slightly, however. Why was he running the human? Was it to cause more terror for the young man? Did he want to prove something to me? I wasn't sure and as much as I hated it, I had a morbid curiosity so I sped up to catch him.

Stepping out of the woods into a small clearing, I saw Asa's right hand reach out and with a flick of his wrist, he knocked the young man to the ground. As he fell, his right ankle twisted in a depression in the frozen ground and he went down hard.

I suspected that Asa had chosen to make his move in the clearing so he would have more room. It appeared to be a natural break in the trees and not man-made. About thirty feet in diameter, it was more ovoid than circular and was situated in a less steep area of the mountainside.

Turning my eyes back to our victim, I watched as he tried pulling himself along the ground, his hands grasping at the knotty roots of the oak trees, partially exposed through the leaves. His nails cracked with every grasp as he inched along on the floor of the forest. Bleeding from hundreds of scratches and lacerations, I realized how much sweeter he smelled now. The run had simply made him tastier.

Crying now, his words were essentially incoherent as he struggled to pull himself along, trying desperately to find some escape from this hell.

Asa walked purposefully behind him until finally the human had inadvertently worked his way backwards down the length of the clearing and had pinned himself up against a large oak tree. His strength had given out at this point and he lay on his belly waiting for the end, crying and praying quietly to himself, his soft sobs releasing breaths of fog into the night air.

Asa stood over him and pushed him with one foot, rolling him over. Reaching down with his right hand, Asa caught the man behind his neck and pulled him to his feet, his ankle making a sickly pop as his weight was forced onto it. The human cried out louder for a second before continuing his mumbling prayers. I could barely make out what he was saying.

Asa, supporting the man's weight, pulled his head up and stared him deeply in the eyes. The man's frantic breathing blew small puffs of fog into the space between them. Meeting Asa's gaze, the young man's forehead rose slightly and his eyes went wider. "You're not breathing." His voice suddenly calm, reconciled.

Asa, arching his eyebrows up in response, countered, "Well, I have to say you are the first to have noticed with me this close."

"Why…" His question cut off as the force of Asa's bite crushed his larynx.

This bite was meant to kill; it was completely different than what I had experienced. I was shocked at the viciousness of the attack. Rooted in place, I could do nothing but stand and watch. I couldn't tear my eyes away from the horror that was occurring in front of my eyes, nor from the blood that leaked out of the corners of Asa mouth as he leaned over the young man.

My mouth watered at the sight of the blood and although I was disgusted by myself, I longed to feel the human's blood on my tongue, to taste its combination of sweet and salt. Wanting to join Asa, I reached out to my side, digging fingernails into a nearby tree to help hold me in place.

But before I could get my nails deeply embedded, an intense pain emanated from deep within my maxilla and mandible. It felt as if the bones in my face were exploding from the inside out. The pain burned its way downward into my gums. Reaching up, I cupped my right hand over my mouth and immediately brought it back down again to see it was full of bright red blood mixed with an inordinate amount of saliva.

Bringing both hands back up to my mouth as my teeth begin to give way, I caught several of them in each hand. Staring at them, I recognized a couple of them as my upper canines. Bleeding freely for a minute, it stopped spontaneously, leaving long strings of coagulated blood hanging from my lips. It took several swipes with my cupped hands to wipe the blood away from my face before I was able to spit three large mouthfuls of clotted blood onto the ground.

Asa had turned from his victim to look at me with a disgusted look. He probably thought I was vomiting at the sight of what he was doing. He hadn't drained him yet as I could still hear the heartbeat pounding in my ears. It was slowing, but for the moment it still beat if not for much longer.

Asa had turned his attention back to the man and was drinking again. The human was draped backwards over Asa's legs as he knelt on the floor of the forest. Asa's mouth was at his neck, the young man's arms thrown back above his head. It might have appeared quite intimate if a stranger had passed by, but it was pure deceit.

I struggled to remember this was a person. A person that I couldn't protect, but a person just the same. Probably someone I had seen once around town. A friend of a friend. A person with family, friends, and hobbies. A family would be searching for him tomorrow. He deserved better than this and I tried to focus on his mother, who like me with my child, probably remembered his birth as the greatest day of her life.

But I wanted his blood. I craved it with a growing intensity. My right foot moved forward in my first step towards giving in to my cravings. My left foot followed and before I knew it, I had taken a couple of steps to what I wanted so badly.

Managing to stop, I resolved that I wouldn't do this. I needed blood. I wanted it. But not like this. I wouldn't be part of this.

Leaning over at the waist, I grasped the backs of my legs and willed myself to stay where I was. To not take another step into the hell that Asa lived every day, knowing in my heart I might never come back if I stepped off into that darkness.

I held on as tightly as I could, both internally and externally, in the hope that I could keep myself rooted to the spot where I stood until this was over. It would take every shred of resolve and willpower that I had developed in my thirty years of life to fight off my desire.

Not looking up, I forced myself to focus on the details of the ground beneath me. Staring intently at the smallest of pebbles and the minute cracks in the yellowed leaves, it was all I could do to not lift my eyes to watch Asa drink what I knew must be the richest blood I would ever smell.

"Momma."

That one word, the cry of a desperate man, jerked my head up. The human was incoherent now and like most of the dying, he craved his mother. And with that one word, he brought me back to my senses.

I could feel the hate build up to a new level inside me. Rage at everything he had done to me, to my family, and to this man boiled inside of me. "Stop," I screamed at him. My fists were still balled up at my side. My voice was inhumanly loud and it reverberated among the trees causing Asa to pause in his drink. Taking one last swallow, he tilted his head back slightly, running his arm across his mouth. Turning to look at me, I could see the rage and the questions in his eyes as well.

Finally, after what felt like hours but in reality was probably less than a minute, I heard the human's body slip from Asa's arms to land very quietly on the ground beside him.

Turning away from the dying man and towards me, the vampire took a deep breath and released it slowly into the cold February night. It looked like a cloud of smoke as it slowly dissipated on the cold night breeze. Proof of another kill.

The man's blood had warmed him up enough that it gave him the appearance of breathing. But it was an illusion. He was dead and I'm not talking physically. Spiritually and emotionally, he was dead.

But did I have any right to stand in judgment over him? I, who had stood by for so long before saying anything, without even trying to save him. I probably would have lost, but I should have made an effort. Was his life not worth the same as mine or Ellie's? It was a regret I would live with for the rest of my life or die with tonight.

The human still lived but barely. He was dying. I could hear his heart attempting to circulate the small amount of blood he had left, his heart beginning to fail and infarct from the lack of flow. Red tears, one at a time, began to run down my face and I looked down so Asa wouldn't see them and know what I was.

"I prefer to let them run for a while when the situation allows before I feed. It gets their blood warmer, but you have to be careful. If they run too hard or too fast, it ruins the flavor. It is important to pace them individually, they are all so different. Human men can go farther and longer, but women tend to taste better to me. I suppose every vampire is different." He stopped now. I guess he was waiting for me to say something.

Not knowing what to say, I blurted out the first thing that came to mind. "Lactic acid. That's probably what ruins the flavor. It builds up while they are running."

We stood there in silence and I could feel his eyes on me and I wondered what he was thinking.

"There is something different about you, Annalice. Have you finally had enough?" Asa was looking at me strangely now. "Yes, I think you are done for. Your heart is giving out. You are running out of time, my dear." He had that look on his face again, that sarcastic smile, cold and unfeeling.

"I've seen enough, Asa. I'm done here and I'm going home. Let's leave this man here. His family can find him and maybe save him. But I won't stand here while you kill him." Keeping my head down while I talked, I took a few moments to wipe the blood-tinged tears away before I looked up at him.

"I agree, Annalice. You have seen too much, but I do not see the point in going back to the house."

Jerking my head up sharply at his words, a cold chill ran through me and I realized my moment of reckoning had come.

"I have decided I really do not desire a companion, Annalice. Although you made it farther than I would have ever expected. So you can take some pride in the strength of mind to have made it this far. Do not worry. You have nothing to be afraid of. It will be very quick and I will even allow you the dignity of a true burial if that is want you want, of course. I can take your body back to your home so your family can find it, or I can bury you here. Whichever you prefer. And more importantly for you, your daughter will live."

He thought he was being gallant and I should be happy that he thought so highly of me. "I think I'd rather my family find me. It'll give them some closure." But I had no plans on going peacefully, despite my calm words.

"Always thinking of your family. That is very noble of you. It is interesting actually how you view your daughter. Arrogant in the extreme really. You actually thought I would stick around here for her to return home just so I could kill her. Like I would waste my time. Humans are a dime a dozen, I can take my pick of whom to kill. I certainly would not wait around for the life of an inconsequential human girl," he concluded, laughing at me, mocking my love for Ellie. "But it served its purpose; you did as I told you. If there had been any evidence that you had called the police that first day or even if you had just simply disappeared, I would never have considered following you. No one would have believed your stories of vampires, but I avoid controversy whenever possible. It is not worth the risk with so many other humans at my disposal."

At his words, I began to see red again. Crimson overtook my visual field as the rage traced its way through my veins again, only now more strongly. My fingernails pushed farther forward from their nail beds and my fangs, that had partially receded once I had become accustomed to the blood scent, pushed out of my gums once again.

"You talk too much," I noted as I launched myself at him, reaching up underneath my coat and pulling out the stake I had concealed there.

Not expecting my attack or my conversion, he was unprepared for the suddenness of my movements. Where I had been standing a good fifteen feet from him, I now flew through the air, knocking him backwards in less than a second.

With exact precision, I aimed for his xiphoid process at the tip of his sternum. Directing the stake towards his left shoulder, I used all my strength to pass the wooden dagger through his heart and then out.

As I felt the give of the stake passing through his intercostal muscles and out of his body, I gave another thrust, forcing the stake through the tree behind him, driving it a good six inches into the interior of the tree, splinters erupting out in all directions. I had chosen my stake well.

Surprise had overtaken his expression as the stake penetrated first his skin and then his heart. Blood erupted out his mouth, running in ribbon-like streams down either side of his lips. His arms flailing uselessly at his sides, he was unable to grab for me as he had been rendered impotent by the stake.

Despite my knowledge that he was helpless now, I had flown backwards as soon as I had buried the stake in him, putting some distance between us for fear that the myths weren't correct. Now unable to completely hold his head up in his weakness, he watched me out of the corner of his eyes, his chin resting on his chest.

I could see betrayal in his eyes and rage washed through me again. How dare he feel betrayed? With my anger came the need that had been rising in me as I had watched him drink from the human dying a few feet away.

Hunger spreading from my chest downward into my belly, it coursed through each of my blood vessels. I could feel the fire rip through every one individually. Asa's blood called to me and, unable to stop myself and not wanting to, I sprinted the short distance between us.

Lifting his head in both of my hands, I stared at him intently for a moment. Then leaning my head back and pulling my lips back, I buried my fangs in the large carotid in his right neck. Thick blood, warmed by that of the human, sprang into my mouth and I swallowed down mouthful after mouthful until I could get no more.

Angry that he had produced so little of what I so greatly

desired, I wra pped my a ms a ound him. Using my fingernails, I pushed first through his skin and next through muscles and facial planes until my hands hit bones. Wrapping my fingers around his ribs, I squeezed with every ounce of my strength, forcing more blood up and into my mouth. Swallowing each mouthful gratefully, I wrapped my legs around his waist and coaxed out every last drop that I could.

Knowing that I had gotten his every last ounce, I pulled away, hearing the air suck through the holes in his body that I had created with my hands.

Lifting his head up again with one hand, I looked at his ashen and sunken face. Despite everything he had done to me, I was disturbed I had this in me. That I could do this to anything was repugnant, although logically I knew he deserved this and more.

Dropping his head back down and with every instinct warring inside me, I grasped the stake and pulled it out. He was too weak to do anything, but with the stake out he wouldn't die immediately. Why was I doing this, I questioned myself? But I knew why. I wasn't yet ready to be a killer, to have intentionally taken another life no matter how horrendous a creature sat before me. It was a line that I wasn't sure I was ready to cross.

With another sickening gush and the passage of air, the stake pulled out and Asa, empty and broken, slid down the trunk of the tree. I didn't ease him down, staying a safe distance from him in the event he found a reserve of strength. He had just enough energy left to pull his knees up as he landed on the ground, his back still against the tree.

The decay that I had smelled a few minutes ago wafted gently on the breeze, but didn't get any stronger. His lips were gray and his skin sallow. With the suppleness gone out of his skin, his face was flaccid and sunken. I didn't let that fool me as I knew he could regenerate if given enough time and a little bit of blood.

"How long?" he questioned. His voice was barely above a whisper, but I could still hear him.

"Since the first time you bit me. I've been changing every day, Asa. I was amazed you never noticed but I guess you didn't know the signs," I answered with a level voice.

"You did not have any of my blood. I was careful." He had dropped his eyes now and was no longer looking at me.

"It's not the blood that's special. I think it's a virus, you know, similar to a cold, only the effects are different. Get enough of it and the results are the same, regardless of the source. I exposed myself as much as I could and I knew that all I had going for me was the element of surprise. It was a race against time," I answered, never taking my eyes off of him.

Beginning to laugh quietly to himself, he looked up at me with his sunken cloudy eyes. "What do you plan to do now, Annalice? Are you going to try to play Mommy?"

Not answering his question directly, I shouted at him, "I'm not like you. I could never be you. I will never hurt her." But inside, I quaked with fear.

"How naïve you are. You think you are so different than me. But you are a killer too. I could smell it in you that first night. That is why you have done so well with me. It was in your blood. Just like mine." He continued to laugh, mocking my attempt to save Ellie.

"Wrong again, Asa. You became a killer out of self-pity. Out of jealously. You reveled in your bad luck, letting it consume you. Never bothering to grow, evolve, or change. I won't let that happen to me." Shouting at him, I shook my head back and forth, refusing to allow his words to sink into me, to become a part of me.

"You knew so little about your own kind that you didn't even realize I was becoming like you. Did it ever cross your mind to look for help? To learn to cope with what had happened? Did you? No. You have no excuse, Asa. You deserve to go to hell. But I'll be different. I swear it. You may have changed my body, but you haven't changed my soul. Or my heart. You can't change that. You. Can't. Take. That." I was so angry that my nails cut into my hands as I balled my fists up, streams of blood dripping down onto the ground.

Asa's eyes were on my blood now. It could probably save him and he knew it. "The best part of this, Annalice, is that you will kill her yourself. I will get my revenge through you as your new fangs slice through her ivory throat. It will be a fitting tribute presented to me by the new self-righteous vampire you have become." Looking up at me, he smiled his usual condescending grin and I hated him even more than I had thought possible.

"I'm no killer, Asa," I screamed at him, my eyes going awash with red, but no sooner were the words out of my mouth, than I lost control. Overwhelming doubt and fear washed over me now as I closed the distance between us. Baring my fangs at him, I lifted him off the ground with one hand, shaking him like a rag doll.

"Tell me how to keep from killing her. Tell me. You dying piece of shit. I am not like you." I was rabid with rage.

Dangling above me in my rage, he only smiled at me and whispered, "Drink some for me."

Closing my fingers around the stake that had never left my hand, I shoved it upwards through his body with all of my force. At the same time, I brought him down to meet his end. It was easier this time as his body no longer contained the strength it once had and my rage had never been stronger.

Eye to eye now as he was limp in my hand, I whispered my lie, "I'm no killer." Looking up, I could see the truth in his eyes.

"Told you so," he muttered. He was right. Part of me was a killer and I dropped him to the ground.

Taking a few deep breaths while looking up at the now cloudless night sky, I finally turned to stare down at him from my position of strength. His eyes were open, but appearing dull and fixed on me. His once beautiful skin now had the appearance of a true corpse, mottled and bluish in color.

Although he was dying and he didn't have much time left, he was still alive for the moment and he stared at me with dim eyes. His face held dread and fear as he realized it was time to pay the piper. I stared back with no guilt or sympathy.

"Thank you," he mouthed at me, and despite everything he had put me through, I still wished there had been another way, another ending. I wished he hadn't stamped out every piece of his humanity over the years—that he would have let me teach him how to care again.

Reaching out to grasp his hand, he was gone before I could reach it. The expression on his face would never leave me and I committed it to memory to remind me of the danger of losing my own consciousness and human spirit.

Standing up, I backed a few feet away, never taking my eyes off him. I guess I was expecting him to just turn to dust before my eyes, but that didn't happen. I could see decay starting, but it would take hours to occur in the dark at the rate it was preceding. Most likely the rising sun would finish it fairly quickly.

The sluggish beating of the human's heart brought me back to the reality of his situation. I had forgotten the human who lay dying just a few feet away. Going quickly to him to see if there was anything that could be done, I found him on his back on the cold ground. After all he had been through, it was astonishing that the man still lived.

As I took his head gently into my lap, he tried to say something to me, a small stream of red blood running out of a corner of his mouth. Luckily, I was so full of Asa's blood that I could focus on him. His airway had partially collapsed and was lacerated. With each breath that he took, the air could be heard moving over his exposed vocal cords. His eyes open, he looked up into my face as he continued to mumble unintelligible words.

Shaking my head at him to indicate he shouldn't try to talk, I placed one hand over his lacerated neck and gently tried to apply some pressure, but the effort was fruitless. At least it made me feel better to try something. Having an idea, I used my fangs to lacerate my own skin. Blood, darker than the normal human blood, beaded up on the surface. Swiping two fingers through it, I rubbed it onto his lacerated neck, but nothing happened.

Trying the same thing with my spit, I noticed some coagulation, but it was too little, too late. His pulse and respirations were getting more erratic as the seconds passed and with no cell phone on me, I didn't even have a way to call for help.

In the aftermath of the struggle, I had completely forgotten about the completion of my conversion, but it was quickly brought back to my mind by the sudden and excruciating pain that began in the center of my chest and spread like a wave outward to the left, following the contour of my heart. It was so intense that it threw me onto my back, the dying human getting tossed mercilessly to the ground again.

It was a myocardial infarction, a heart attack, the final stage of my human death, I realized. The pain began to radiate from my chest through to my back and down into both arms until it reached the tips of all my fingers. The pain was so intense that I lost my breath and couldn't get it back. Squeezing my eyes shut against its intensity, the severity of the pain caused me to twitch uncontrollably.

Muscle spasms tore through my body from head to toe, affecting all my organs. There's so much to being alive that just had to end. Uterine contractions along with colonic contractions pulled my knees to my belly and emptied out the last of my human remains and I vomited up the leftovers of Asa's blood, spraying the coagulated mess across the rotting leaves of the forest floor.

Lying in the dirt, I willed my diaphragm to work between the wracking spasms, and gratefully accepted the short bursts of air I could get in. Opening my eyes, I found myself face to face with the human. Our eyes locked and we both knew I was dying too.

Using the last bit of his energy to enunciate, he parted his dry lips, whispering. But what, I would never know. Did he wish me good luck, tell me to go to hell, or something altogether different?

It was my turn to pay the piper, I knew, as my heart began to fibrillate. I could feel it squirming in my chest from the arrhythmia and I closed my eyes from the human's gaze, not wanting it to be my last vision if I didn't survive.

Instead, I pictured Ellie the last time I had seen her. Her honey hair swaying as she walked to my mom's car, blowing me goodbye kisses.

The fibrillation lasted longer than I would have thought possible as my dying heart struggled to maintain its hold on humanity, but I finally felt the ventricular fibrillation give way to small little jerks until it finally lay silent in my chest.

A moment of panic engulfed me when the organ I had always counted on didn't restart. Within a couple of seconds of flat-lining, I felt the forward flow of blood throughout my body just stop and settle.

The intense pain I had experienced previously ebbed with the final silencing of my heart and yet I remained conscious. I had died as a human, but I had survived. I had survived Asa.

Laying there on the ground, I began to laugh and cry blood-tinged tears, out of happiness instead of sadness. Jumping to my feet in one movement, I threw my arms wide, roaring my triumph to the world. It reverberated in the night, echoing out for miles, stopping all the sounds of the forest with its alien sound.

Feeling alive and immensely strong, I was about to celebrate my survival with another roar of delight when my eyes landed on the now-dead human.

There had been a price to my survival. I stared at him for a couple of minutes, burning the image into my mind in case I ever forgot that price. In case I ever tried to forget him or Ms. McElhaney and anyone else who had fed Asa while I struggled to live.

Glancing down at the two bodies lying in the clearing, I knew I had work to do. I decided to leave the human where he lay so he would be found. I did try to arrange him in a respectful position, smoothing his clothes down and his disheveled hair back into place. There was nothing I could do about his neck, it gaped open into the night.

Open and mangled, it would be easy for anyone to see the viciousness of the attack. But at least his family would be able to bury him, although they would never know what happened to him.

After I finished, I stood looking down at him, wishing there was something else I could do, but I had converted too late to save him.

Pulling the stake out of Asa, I went to toss it aside before I realized I should probably take it home. It would look very conspicuous lying out here in the woods next to the human. Pulling it up and down my pant legs, I removed as much of the blood as possible. Then I stood there not quite knowing what to do with it.

To be honest, the stake scared me. Like the way a gun had made my hands tingle when I was still human. Starting to stick it down my pants, I changed my mind several times before deciding to just carry it in my free hand. I certainly didn't want to accidentally stake myself.

Leaning down, I swung Asa's remains up over my shoulder and loped off towards my house. Looking for a good burial place along the way, I settled on a low lying spot in an area of the forest covered by pine trees, off the beaten four-wheeler trails.

Laying the stake aside and using both hands to clear the old pine needles out of the way, I dug through the cold dirt, making pretty good time until I had a fair-sized hole about four feet deep. His dead eyes stared up at me with his mouth slightly agape, and I desperately wanted to get him into the grave.

Closing his eyes with my free hand, I gently placed him into the wet of the grave and began to fold the dirt in, wishing I had something to place between him and the earth that covered his face.

It was more than he deserved, I decided. I could have let him rot in the sun, but I buried him for the human he had once been. For his mother, father, and the sister that had lost him so long ago. I tried to mask the disturbance in the landscape as best I could, but I was sure that if someone looked for it, they would find it. I didn't think there would be a body left to discover when they did.

Glancing up at the sky out of habit, the movement was wasted as I knew there was little time left. I could feel the sun although it wasn't up yet. My skin crawled with the knowledge of the coming sunrise and wasting no more time for Asa, I raced home through the trees and to the security of my safe room.

I did slow down and stop just once as I passed by close to the human camp. I could hear them on their cell phones talking about their missing family member, presumably to the police. Grief and guilt ripped through me and I struggled to remember I hadn't caused his death. I was merely a witness. I could do nothing more for him and so I began to run towards home again.

Our trip during the night had taken us several miles into the forest, but since I was not tracking a human this time, I made the trip in less than five minutes with time to spare. Stepping out of the woods that bordered my property, I sprinted across the pastures. Without even stopping, I slipped into the pond and out of my clothes, letting them sink into the murky depths of the old pond, taking with them the excrement of my conversion.

Taking two more strokes, I was at the edge of the pond and in mid-stroke I came up out of the water and ran the rest of the way across the pasture. Up onto the deck at the back of my house, I landed gracefully, the water dripping down my cool skin.

Out of habit, I exhaled a sigh of relief. I was home. Alive. Well something like that. Turning to give the night one last glance, my gaze landed on the trail I had taken home. It was as visible and clear through the dewed grass as if I had marked it purposefully from the woods to where I now stood.

Panic hit me as I realized that human eyes could probably see it just as easily. Then I remembered the stake. Having placed it down beside the grave while I dug, I had left it there.

I would have to worry about this later as I could not only see the earliest glow of the sun just beginning to clear the horizon, I could feel it tingling on my skin. Jerking open the door, I raced through the house and flung myself into the safe room. My last truly coherent thought was to slide the lock into place and then I collapsed onto the floor.

Feeling myself slip into nothingness, I grasped at lucid thoughts, but I was too heavy and my surroundings too thick. Like trying to pull your fingers through marshmallow cream. Tunnel vision set in and I could see the world getting farther and farther away. Using both hands, I clawed at the empty air in front of me, inhaling and exhaling large volumes of air as I tried desperately to hold on to the day and reality. It was like dying all over again, and just as suddenly as it started, I was waking up.

FOURTEEN

A doorbell. I was pretty sure that was what I was hearing. Very annoying, but I followed its incessant high-pitched yet hollow chime back to reality. I clawed my way through the blackness, following its sound. My eyelids flying open, I awoke to find myself lying on my back in the darkness of the safe room. Had I dreamed the doorbell? I could no longer hear it, but it had been real enough that I knew it wasn't imagined.

Memories of the preceding night caused me to sit up abruptly. I was a vampire. My life as I knew it was over, but Ellie would be here tonight. The sole reason for my survival would finally be back safe in my arms.

Anxiety overtook me at the thought. Asa had said I would want her, want to kill her, and I felt myself tremble with fear. What if he was right?

Letting my senses expand out from the small room where I was sitting, I listened intently, forcing myself to ignore all of the background noise that existed in the old house.

Finally able to calm myself, I could hear the beat of two hearts at the front door. One high-pitched and fast. The other slower and deeper. And something deep inside me knew it was her. She was here with my mother.

I considered just sitting there in the dark until my mom gave up and took Ellie to a hotel in town. She wouldn't stand in the dark of my front yard for very long, but despite my fears, I longed to see her. So with trepidation and anxiety, I left the safety of my room, grabbing a robe on the way, and walked towards the front door.

The doorbell was ringing again, followed by my mother's sharp rap on the old oak door. She called my name in that tone that said, "I'm annoyed but worried at the same time." Using all of my restraint to walk calmly to the door when I really wanted to rip the door off of its hinges, I managed to not go to such extremes, but just barely.

Swinging the door open with only a fraction of my strength, I tried to look casual and not as though I had been dying to see her.

"Hey Momma!" she called as she bounced up into my arms. Burying my face in the scent of her hair, all of my fears simply melted away. I would never as long as I lived, smell anything so good, and I could never hurt her.

Asa had been wrong. Nothing in the world could make me want to hurt her. Wrapping my now powerful arms around her, I gave her an easy squeeze.

"Hey, baby girl. I'm so happy to see you." She would never know how much, and I tried not to let my emotion color my words too much. I needed to sound normal.

"What did you do to your hair?" My mom was looking at me like I had sprouted a tail. A typical reaction from Mom that would have needled me a week ago, now it just caused me to laugh.

"I got the bug to change it," I replied, making quotation marks in the air, laughing at my own medical humor.

Mom just frowned. "Well if change was what you were looking for, you hit the nail on the head. Next time, don't go so drastic. OK, help us get the suitcases. We thought you were never going to let us in. We've been standing out here for thirty minutes. Where have you been? I told Ellie I wasn't standing here in this creepy yard in the dark for much longer. Are you listening to me?" Her voice died out now and I realized I was standing there smiling so much, I probably looked intoxicated.

"Of course I'm listening. I was just thinking how good it is to see you both," I answered, trying to tone down the smile. "I was sleeping and I guess I didn't hear the doorbell." I shrugged my shoulders at her. It was the best excuse I could come up with on such short notice.

"Well, you didn't hear your phone either. I went against my good judgment driving out here without talking to you first but I'm trying to be more rational about this place." Mom declared as she walked from the entryway into the living room, pulling one of Ellie's suitcases. Stopping abruptly, she cried out. "Oh my gosh!" The handle of the bag slipped out of her hands, banging against the floor. "What happened in here?" Her face was white as she turned towards me.

Honestly, housekeeping was the last thing on my mind and I hadn't realized just how bad the house looked, but now as I looked around the living room and saw it was an abysmal mess. "I had a break in." Again it was the best I could come up with at the moment.

"Have you called the police?" she demanded, her voice

still a little tremulousness.

"Of course," I replied, matter-of-factly. "They came but said there wasn't much they could do."

Walking into the kitchen still surveying the damage, I could see the shock on her face. "Did he eat you out of house and home too?" she asked, gesturing to the counters piled high with empty boxes and wrappers and the open and barren cabinets.

"No, Mother. I just… Well you know. I stayed at home after the break in, mostly. The police said not to clean up till they gave the go ahead. So, I, um. You know, just hung out here. It's ridiculous, I agree I made such a mess. I know. I guess I was a little overwhelmed." I gave her my best pitiful me look.

"I'll say it again although it always makes you mad. You and Ellie should come live with me. This place just gives me the creeps. It's no place for a single woman. Anything could happen out here."

How right she was. The anything had happened. If she only knew, I mused silently to myself. "You know, Mom, I may take you up on that. You were right. Right about this place the whole time. Don't ever change." Smiling to myself, I realized for the first time in too long how much I had missed her. "I'm glad you're here, Mom. Let's go into town and get something to eat. There's some things we need to talk about. I'm considering some career changes that I need to talk to you about."

Mom was looking at me incredulously now. "What has gotten into you? Two weeks ago, you would have never thought of living with me," she noted, as she walked closer to me. I watched as a slight shudder worked its way down her spine and she stopped in her tracks. Taking a step back, her hand came up over her heart, and she whispered, "Annalice, there's something different about you." Her voice shook slightly.

Well, I guess you just can't keep anything from your mother.

Printed in Great Britain
by Amazon.co.uk, Ltd.,
Marston Gate.